For the first time in three years, Cassidy was having a few hopes.

At least, she thought that was what the quivery, anticipatory, apprehensive feelings in her gut were. She'd been without hope for so long, though, she couldn't be sure.

It would be foolish to start hoping again, she chastised herself. So what if she'd been safe and happy at Buffalo Lake? So what if she'd let other people into her life, even on the most superficial basis, for the first time in three years? So what if some of those people seemed to genuinely like her—like Jace? She couldn't stay. Sooner or later, something would happen. Jace would get tired of asking questions and start snooping into the stories she'd told him. And sooner or later, he'd want to know why Cassidy McRae didn't really exist.

Dear Reader,

As always, Silhouette Intimate Moments is coming your way with six fabulously exciting romances this month, starting with bestselling Merline Lovelace, who always has *The Right Stuff*. This month she concludes her latest miniseries, TO PROTECT AND DEFEND, and you'll definitely want to be there for what promises to be a slam-bang finale.

Next, pay another visit to HEARTBREAK CANYON, where award winner Marilyn Pappano knows *One True Thing*: that the love between Cassidy McRae and Jace Barnett is meant to be, despite the lies she's forced to tell. Lyn Stone begins a wonderful new miniseries with *Down to the Wire*. Follow DEA agent Joe Corda to South America, where he falls in love—and so will you, with all the SPECIAL OPS. Brenda Harlen proves that sometimes *Extreme Measures* are the only way to convince your once-and-only love— and the child you never knew!—that this time you're home to stay. When *Darkness Calls*, Caridad Piñeiro's hero comes out to...slay? Not exactly, but he *is* a vampire, and just the kind of bad boy to win the heart of an FBI agent with a taste for danger. Finally, let new author Diana Duncan introduce you to a *Bulletproof Bride,* who quickly comes to realize that her kidnapper is not what he seems—and is a far better match than the fiancé she was just about to marry.

Enjoy them all—and come back next month for more of the best and most exciting romance reading around, right here in Silhouette Intimate Moments.

Yours,

Leslie J. Wainger
Executive Editor

Please address questions and book requests to:
Silhouette Reader Service
U.S.: 3010 Walden Ave., P.O. Box 1325, Buffalo, NY 14269
Canadian: P.O. Box 609, Fort Erie, Ont. L2A 5X3

One True Thing

MARILYN PAPPANO

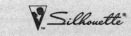

INTIMATE MOMENTS™

Published by Silhouette Books

America's Publisher of Contemporary Romance

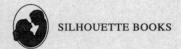 SILHOUETTE BOOKS

ISBN 0-373-27350-9

ONE TRUE THING

Copyright © 2004 by Marilyn Pappano

Visit Silhouette at www.eHarlequin.com

Printed in U.S.A.

MARILYN PAPPANO

brings impeccable credentials to her career—a lifelong habit of gazing out windows, not paying attention in class, daydreaming and spinning tales for her own entertainment. The sale of her first book brought great relief to her family, proving that she wasn't crazy but was, instead, creative. Since then, she's sold more than forty books to various publishers and even a film production company. You can write to her at P.O. Box 643, Sapulpa, OK, 74067-0643.

Prologue

"I wish you would reconsider."

Jace Barnett didn't look up from the desk he was cleaning out. He didn't need to see to know it was Tim Potter who stood on the other side. The captain had tried to stop him when he left the disciplinary hearing, but Jace had gotten away without speaking to him. He'd known his luck wouldn't hold until he left the building, but after the hearing, he just hadn't given a damn.

"You caught a bad break, Jace—"

He shoved the drawer shut and began gathering the few items on the desktop. "A bad break? I didn't do anything wrong, but the department hung me out to dry anyway because it was politically expedient." He loaded the last two words with every bit of the disgust he felt for them, for the higher-ups who'd sat in judgment of him, for the machine that had sacrificed him for the chief's greater good.

"I know," Potter said, his tone as conciliatory as Jace's wasn't. "You got a raw deal, and I swear, we'll make it up to you. But that's going to be hard if you go crawling off with your feelings hurt.''

The only personal item remaining on the desk was a photograph taken two months earlier. The Barnett clan at Thanksgiving—his parents, Ray and Rozena; his uncle Del and aunt Lena; his cousin Reese and his wife, Neely. Jace stood in the middle with Amanda, his arm around her shoulders. She was gone now, part of the fallout of his ''raw deal.'' She'd liked cops in general and him in particular, but not after the suspension. Not once he'd become the target of a very public and negative witch-hunt. Last he'd heard, she was seeing some detective in Vice, and she was *in love*.

He hoped the vice cop had a more realistic understanding of what that meant than he'd had. He'd believed her—had even been planning to ask her to marry him once this mess was over. He'd been a first-class sucker.

He put the photo in his gym bag, then stood and met Potter's gaze. ''I'm not crawling off. I'm getting the hell out.''

''But, Jace— A couple more years and you can retire. You don't want to give that up.''

Jace switched the gym bag to his other hand, scooped his coat off the desk and headed for the door. ''Screw retirement. Screw the job. Screw you all.'' Just like they'd screwed him.

He was almost outside when Potter caught his arm. ''Forget the resignation, Jace. We'll consider this a temporary leave of absence. Take some time to cool off and think about it clearly.''

He'd had nothing to do *but* think since they'd pulled him off the job weeks ago. He'd thought until he was sick of it, and he'd always reached the same conclusion. It was time to get out. If this treatment was the best the Kansas City Police Department could do for one of its wronged veteran detectives, he no longer wanted to be a part of it.

It had begun snowing while he was inside. He stopped, pulled on his coat and gloves, then opened the door. Frigid air along with a few flakes rushed inside as he looked back at Potter. ''I've given this department my best for more than fifteen years—my dedication, my loyalty, my support—and the first time I need some of it back, you tell me to bend over and take it quietly, then get back to the job as if nothing happened. Well, Captain, it ain't gonna happen. I'm outta here.''

He stepped out into the snow and headed for his truck. Potter stepped out after him, but didn't speak. When Jace pulled away from the curb, the captain was still standing there, snow coating his gray hair and shoulders.

His fingers tight around the steering wheel, Jace headed for his apartment. He'd been a damned fool. All along he'd believed today's hearing would exonerate him. The suspension, the investigation, being yanked off his cases—that was all routine whenever allegations of wrongdoing were made against an officer. He'd hated it, but he'd been positive everything would turn out in his favor. Hell, *he'd done nothing wrong.*

Except believe in the department and the people he'd worked with.

Except think that seventeen years of outstanding service counted for something.

Except assume that the truth actually counted for something.

Today he'd learned better. The police chief had a run for the governor's office in mind, and justice for one detective stood little chance against his ambitions.

Seventeen years patrolling the streets, working Homicide and Sex Crimes and Narcotics, seventeen years of dealing with scum, working long hours for too little pay, facing danger more often than he wanted to recall, and this was the thanks he got. Sacrificed for the benefit of the chief's public image.

He was only a few blocks from the apartment when he saw a car at the side of the road. Its right wheels were in a ditch, its headlights pointed up and illuminating the snow that darkened the afternoon. A woman stood near the rear of the car, huddled in her coat and looking helplessly at the vehicle. Automatically he eased his foot off the gas and switched on his blinker to pull onto the shoulder.

Deliberately he shut off the blinker and pressed the gas pedal down instead.

He was out of the help-giving business.

Forever.

Chapter 1

Slow as molasses in winter, the sun crept across the morning sky, bathing the landscape in bright light so harsh it leached the color from the day. Somewhere in the not-too-far distance, an overly excited canine burst into a frenzied fit of barking and...

Oh, jeez, that sucked. Frowning, Cassidy McRae gazed at the scene in front of her and tried again.

Fat clouds stirred overhead, casting lazy shadows over the forest. A hawk circled, its wings outstretched, its fingerlets rippling in the self-generated breeze, its eagle-eyed gaze searching...

An eagle-eyed hawk? Sheesh.

How about... *In the distance, a buck appeared on the verdant lakeshore, its gaze alert and wary as he approached the water for a drink, his impressive antlers casting equally impressive shadows on the smooth glassy surface.*

She snorted in much the same way her imaginary buck might. There were many things she couldn't do in life, and it looked as if turning an evocative phrase was one of them.

Calling herself a writer couldn't make it so, any more than claiming to be a Martian would make that true.

For example, take the scene in front of her. A *real* writer would be able to describe it in such rich detail that her reader would feel the morning air, soft, still bearing the faint memory of the dawn coolness but growing heavy with the promise of heat. She would smell the clean fragrances of the woods, the lake, the wildflowers blooming in profusion in the tall grass, and she would hear the birdsong, the faint hum of insects and the gentle lapping of the water against the shore.

She, not being a real writer by anyone's definition, would say the scene was rustic. Very country. More accurately, very un-citylike.

See? She couldn't even decide for herself what it was.

Besides *safe.*

Buffalo Lake stretched out to the north and west, still and quiet in the morning. Trees lined the shore—blackjack oaks, cedars, an occasional maple and elm. A mimosa grew to one side, its leaves lacy, its blossoms about to burst into bloom.

The centerpieces of the scene were the cabins, one on each side of the narrow inlet and connected by an aging wooden footbridge. One cottage stood front and center, the other a hundred feet to the south and west. She ignored that one. It was empty, the real-estate agent had told her, and virtually identical to the one in front of her—the one that was going to be her home for the next however many days.

It had been used as a hunting cabin, the agent had told her on the drive out from Buffalo Plains the day before. Cassidy might not have the best imagination around, but she'd translated that into *nothing fancy* with her first look. Wide brown planks formed the siding, with a brown shingled roof. The window frames and door had once been painted turquoise, but had mercifully faded to a dull sky-bluish shade. There were two chairs on the deck that fronted the house—metal, with contoured seats and backs. At one time they had been a green as hideous as the turquoise, but years of relentless Oklahoma summers had left them dull and faded, too.

This was it. Home—for as long as she felt safe. In the past three years that feeling of safety had proved elusive at best, but maybe this time it would last a whole month. It would be a first, but if there was one thing she'd learned, there was a first time for everything. Love, loss, betrayal, deception, treachery…

The silence, heavy and complete, made her realize how long she'd been sitting in her car. With a fortifying breath, she pulled the keys from the ignition and climbed out.

In the thirty minutes since she'd left the motel in Buffalo Plains, the June heat had become a palpable thing. It created a sheen of perspiration across her forehead and down her arms, and made her clothes cling uncomfortably. She would pretend not to notice, she decided as she unlocked the trunk. She'd been pretending a long time. She was good at it.

Hands on her hips, she gazed into the trunk. Everything she owned was packed here. Her clothes. A laptop computer and printer. Linens and cookware. A few mementos. Every tiny thing that said Cassidy McRae existed, crammed into a space half the size of a small closet.

It was pitifully little.

She slung the laptop case over her shoulder, then hefted the largest of the suitcases before turning from the car. Immediately she froze and the suitcase slid from her fingers. When it landed on the uneven ground, it fell against her leg and leaned there.

A man stood at the near end of the footbridge, his gaze on her. His feet were bare. Heavens, most of his *body* was bare, except for a pair of faded cutoffs that rode low on his hips.

Mentally she clicked into author mode. *The midday sun overhead gleamed on all that exposed skin, adding depth to the rich, warm brown and found highlights in the hair secured in a ponytail with a leather thong, despite the dull matte hue of the black. He looked hostile, she thought with a shiver of apprehension. Dangerous. Savage.*

A hot blush that could compete with the blazing sun for intensity warmed her face at that last thought. She couldn't

say for certain, but thought it was probably politically incor-
rect to describe a Native American as savage, even if it was
dead-on accurate. Those flinty black orbs devoid of emotion,
that long, hard, lean, muscular body poised to attack, the com-
plete and utter lack of emotion on his ruggedly handsome
face....

She gave her head a shake to clear it. The physical description was accurate, if wordy, but the emotional part was way
off. He didn't look the least bit hostile, dangerous or savage.
Truthfully he wasn't so much standing there as lounging, not
so much poised to attack as loose and relaxed, and his eyes,
brown rather than black, showed a normal amount of friendly
curiosity.

His gaze moved over her, shifted to the car, then back.
Leaning against the railing with a confidence she wouldn't
display around the silvered wood, he folded his arms across
his chest. "It's a sure bet you're not one of Junior's kin," he
said in the accent she was quickly coming to associate with
Oklahoma. There had been a time when she'd thought all
Okies spoke like Reba McEntire, but two hours in the state
had convinced her otherwise. It wasn't really a drawl, not a
twang, not as readily identifiable as a Southern accent or a
New Englander's. It was pleasant, she decided, sounding of
the heartland, of cowboys, ranchers, farmers and good-natured,
small-town folks.

"Who's Junior, and how do you know I'm not related to
him?"

"Junior Davison. He owns that cabin." He nodded toward
the house behind her. "And I know you're not related because
all the Davison kin have an unfortunate tendency toward red
hair, freckles and fat." His gaze skimmed over her again.
"You don't."

No, her hair was blond—this week, at least—her skin was
freckle-free and her metabolism made short work of the cal-
ories she took in. The rest of her life might have been shot to
hell, but at least she had a few things to feel grateful for.

Having a neighbor wasn't one of them.

She stooped to pick up the suitcase again. "No, I'm not related to Junior."

She made it only a few feet before he spoke again, this time with a hint of a challenge. "Then who are you?"

It was a legitimate question, no matter that it made her stiffen. If the situation were reversed and a complete stranger was moving into the house next to hers, she would at least want to know his name. As remote as these cabins were, she would probably want to know a hell of a lot more than that about him.

Still, when she turned back to answer, it was grudgingly. "Cassidy McRae. I'm renting Junior's place." She paused, not wanting to give the impression that she was neighborly, but she *was* moving in next door to a complete stranger in a remote location. The least she needed to know was what to call her only neighbor for three miles. "Who are you?"

"Jace Barnett. I live there." He gave a jerk of his head to the house behind him.

"Really. The real estate agent said that place was empty."

"No matter how often she insists she knows everything, she doesn't."

So he was familiar with Paulette Fox. The woman had spoken with great authority on every subject that came to mind, as if every word had come straight to her ear from God's mouth. Why, she'd lived her entire life in Buffalo Plains and Heartbreak, the wide spot in the road some twenty miles south, and there wasn't a soul in the county or a thing going on that she wasn't intimately familiar with.

Except for the rather major fact that the isolated, neighbor-free cabin she'd promised Cassidy was neither as isolated nor neighbor-free as she'd thought.

"Actually, to be fair to Paulette, I just moved out here a couple of months ago. I haven't seen her since then."

"Lucky me," Cassidy murmured.

He pretended not to have heard. "Not that she wouldn't have lied to you if it meant renting this place. No one's stayed there in years—not since Junior's kids put him in the nursing home.''

"Too bad for Junior."

"Nah, he doesn't know the difference. His mind's gone. He doesn't even know his kids when they come to visit—which isn't necessarily a bad thing."

He was probably right, especially when those same kids had seen fit to put their father in a home the minute he'd become trouble. She couldn't imagine doing such a thing to one of her parents…if she *had* parents. At least, in the real world.

Shoving away the thought—the regret—she glanced at Jace. "I've got to go. I've got work to do." When he showed no intention of returning to his side of the bridge, she deliberately went on. "That's why I'm here. Not to relax or make small talk with the neighbors. To work."

Her first lie of the day. There had been a time when the only lies she'd told were harmless little fibs. *I love the gift… Yes, that dress looks wonderful on you… The cake was to die for… No, you don't look like you've gained five pounds.* Those days were long gone. Now the number of lies she told was limited only by her exposure to people to tell them to. Ask the same question ten times and she would give ten different answers. That was how she lived her life these days.

Correction—that was how she lived, period.

"What kind of work?" Friendly curiosity again.

It shouldn't have annoyed her, but it did. She wasn't the type to become chummy with someone just because they happened to live in the same building or on the same block. It had taken some time, but she'd learned not to become chummy with *anyone.* Leaving wasn't such a big deal if there was no one special to leave behind.

"The kind that requires a great deal of privacy. Nice meeting you," she said in a tone that made it clear she'd found it anything but nice. Then she turned toward the house as if she hadn't just been rude to a friendly stranger. She didn't look back as she let herself in, and didn't peek out the window on her way to deposit the computer on the dining table and the suitcase in the bedroom. She did glance toward the bridge when she returned to the car for another load and saw that he'd gone, but not far. He was sitting on his deck in a metal chair that matched her own, a bottle of water in hand, and watching her. She pretended he wasn't there.

It was harder than it sounded.

Within an hour she'd unloaded and unpacked everything. Cheap aluminum pots and pans, cheaper plastic-handled cutlery, an off-brand boom box with a box of CDs. White sheets and pillowcases, a yellow blanket and a blue print comforter. Clothes that came from Wal-Mart, Kmart and Target, shoes from Payless. Her days of upscale retail experiences were long over. She'd been a world-class shopper, and some days she missed it a lot.

Other days, when she got overwhelmed by the enormity of the life that had been taken from her—twice—she couldn't care less about shopping.

With nothing left to do, she walked through the cottage, out of the bedroom, past the bathroom and into the living room/ dining room/kitchen. "Well, there's three seconds out of my day," she said aloud. Only eighty-some thousand to go.

Finally she let herself wander to the window. There was no sign of Jace Barnett. Good. Life was safer without the complication of people.

And lonelier, her inner voice pointed out.

She turned away from the window and gazed around the room. Her monthly two hundred dollars' rent included furnishings—sofa, chair, coffee and end tables, dining table with three chairs, bed and dresser. All of it was early-impoverished American, all of it ugly enough to make her wonder what in the world the people who'd created it had been thinking. It was a far cry from the leather, stone and luxurious fabrics of her old home, and for one instant it made her want to cry. It was so shabby. Her *life* was so shabby.

This wasn't the future she'd envisioned for herself twelve years ago, or five, or even three. She'd intended to follow in the footsteps of every blessed female in her family for generations. She'd planned to be so middle-class, married-with-kids, minivan-PTA-soccer-church-on-Sunday average that she would bore to death anyone who wasn't just like her.

Odd how easily a little curiosity, greed and bad luck had changed everything.

Her sigh sounded loud and lonesome in the big room, and galvanized her into action. She fixed herself a glass of instant iced tea, then sat at the dining table and opened the laptop. "I am a writer," she announced as the machine booted up. "I *am* a writer."

When she was a yoga instructor, she'd practiced affirmations daily, but it was easier to believe *I can do this* when "this" was nothing more complicated than the Salute to the Sun routine. Writing a book was a whole other business, and one she knew little about.

"Failure is just another chance to get it right," she murmured as she clicked on the icon for her word processing program. She had a million such lines. *Work is 1% inspiration and 99% perspiration... Whether you think you can or you can't, you're right... You can't win if you don't play the game... Today is the first day of the rest of your life... If you can dream it, you can do it.*

Not one of them helped her when faced with a blank screen. She thought maybe a candy bar *would* help, so she got up and rummaged through her purse until she found one. Music might help, too, so she detoured past the boom box and put in her favorite Eric Clapton CD. Finding the screen still blank, she decided a few games of Free Cell might get her creative juices flowing.

Two hours later, the screen bore a heading that read Chapter 1 and nothing else. Oh, she'd typed a few lines, then mercifully deleted them. After the third wipeout, her fingers seemed to pick out keys on their own.

I am a writer. I *AM* a writer. I am a *WRITER*.

"So write, damn it!" she muttered under her breath.

Frustrated, she pushed away from the table and went to stare out the window, refusing to let her gaze stray to the southwest.

The bulk of the lake lay to the north, the rental agent had told her. This section was just God's afterthought, so it had the peace and quiet Cassidy had told her she needed.

Except for Jace.

She wondered why nosy Paulette didn't know he was living next door. Why would he *want* to live all the way out here? Of course, she'd passed houses along the dirt road on her drive out from Buffalo Plains that morning, but mostly they were ranch or farm houses. Naturally someone who earned his living off the land would live here, too.

But the lake was surrounded by thousands of acres of woods. No pasture for livestock, no fields for crops and, as far as she could tell, no other means of support. She would certainly never choose such a place if she had to drive into town to a job every day.

The idea of going to a job every day—the *same* job—made her melancholy. She'd done that for a lot of years and had never really appreciated it until she'd found herself working for a week here, ten days there—if she was lucky, three weeks someplace else. As soon as she'd learned a job and started to fit in, she'd had to move on. Finally she'd quit fitting in. This time she didn't intend to even try. She would pass her time here at Buffalo Lake just as she'd passed it at a hundred other places and, when it was up, she would move on, just as she'd moved on from everywhere else.

Just once, though, she would like to settle down, to call the same place home next week and next month and next year. She would like to think in terms of forever instead of right now, to make friends, to have a life…but that was impossible. Like the shark, if she stopped moving, she would die.

But knowing that didn't ease her longing. It made it a little more bearable, but nothing, she was afraid, would ease it.

Besides death.

Though Jace had gotten his first official job when he was fifteen, he'd been working years longer. His parents had believed that taking care of the house and the livestock was a family responsibility, so he'd started pitching in as soon as he was old enough. He'd worked his way through college, taken three days off after graduation to move to Kansas City, then gone straight to work for the department.

He liked not working for the first time in his life. Not having to get up at five-thirty to run before work, not spending more time at the shooting range each week than he did on dates, not dealing with lowlifes and lawyers, not carrying a gun with him everywhere he went. He liked not being a target for scorn and disdain, or for nutcases with weapons, and not spending more time frustrated than not.

He liked being a bum, sleeping until noon and not seeing a solitary soul unless he wanted. He'd told his parents, Reese and Neely so repeatedly. They didn't believe him, but that didn't make it any less true. They thought he was burned out. Brooding. Bored. In serious need of a badge and a gun.

Burned out? Maybe. Brooding? Nah, he'd gotten over what happened in Kansas City. Now he was just bitter. In need of another cop job? Never.

What about bored?

His gaze shifted to the window and the Davison place. Cassidy McRae had pulled up out front around ten-thirty. It was now six-fifteen, and he'd spent way too many of those hours watching the place, even though he hadn't caught more than a glimpse of her passing a window. It wasn't as if he didn't have other things to do, like...clean house. Take Granddad's old john boat out on the lake and catch some fish for his mother to fry. Drive into town and replenish his supply of frozen dinners. Mow the little patch of grass out front that he hadn't yet managed to kill.

But why be productive when he could kick back on the couch and watch the neighbor's place during commercials on TV? Being curious took little energy and less incentive and, as a bum, he considered the less energy and incentive expended, the better.

Besides, she was the first woman he'd really looked at since Amanda had moved out of his apartment and his life. She was

the first woman he'd noticed as a *woman,* with all the possibilities and risks that entailed—the first who had reminded him
of how long he'd been alone. Granted, he didn't know anything about her—whether she was married, where she was
from, what she did, whether she was aloof because she was
shy or preoccupied or disagreeable by nature.

What he did know was minimal. That she drove a red
Honda with Arizona tags and a heavy coat of dust—a two-
door that blended in easily with thousands of other little red
two-doors on the road. There were no bumper stickers, no
college affiliations or radio station advertising on the windows,
no American flag or novelty toy flying from the antenna, no
air-freshening pine tree hanging from the inside mirror. It was
about as unremarkable as a car could get.

He knew *she* was far from unremarkable. She was pretty,
slender, five-eight, maybe five-nine, with short blond hair and
pale golden skin. He hadn't gotten close enough to identify
the color of her eyes, but hoped they were brown. He'd always
been a sucker for brown-eyed blondes, especially ones with
long legs and full lips and an innocent sensuality about them.

He knew next to nothing, but affairs and relationships and
almost-engagements had been built on nothing more. As long
as she wasn't married, a cop or too needy, he could enjoy
having her next door. He didn't lust after married people, he'd
had enough of cops to last a lifetime and enough of people
who needed something from him to last two lifetimes.

He couldn't help but wonder, though, what had brought her
to Buffalo Plains, and why she was staying all the way out
here. She'd said she was here to work, but people didn't come
to Buffalo Plains to work. They came for reasons like
Neely's—hiding out from an ex-con who'd thought killing her
was fair punishment for his going to prison. Or her sister,
Hallie Marshall, escaping a life that had become unbearable.
Or Hallie's stepdaughter, Lexy, who'd run away from home
to find the father she'd never known.

But to work? When any work she could do over there in

Junior's cabin could just as easily be done someplace else? Someplace better?

Maybe *she* was hiding, escaping or running away, too.

He wouldn't even wonder from what.

He was debating between SpaghettiOs and a sandwich for supper when the sound of an engine drew his gaze to the window. Reese parked his truck under the big oak nearest the cabin, then he and Neely got out, each carrying a grocery bag. By the time they reached the deck, Jace was opening the screen door. He stood there, arms folded over his chest. "Hey, bubba. Don't you know it's rude to drop in on someone without calling first?"

"We tried to call," Reese replied, "and all we got was voice mail. You have your cell phone shut off again, don't you? And you don't check your voice mail, so you leave us no choice but to drive all the way out here."

In spite of his scowl, Jace wasn't really pissed. Reese was his only close cousin, and they'd been raised more like brothers. They'd been buddies and partners in crime since they were in diapers. They'd gone to school together, kindergarten through twelfth grade, and attended the same university. When a shoulder injury had ended Reese's pro baseball career, he'd gone into law enforcement in part because Jace was doing it.

Now Reese was the sheriff hereabouts…and Jace was a disgraced ex-cop.

Though he hadn't invited them in, Neely nudged him aside and crossed the threshold. "We come bearing mail and food, and we're staying for dinner." Retrieving a rubber-banded packet of letters from the bag, she handed them over, then continued to the kitchen.

Stepping back so Reese could enter, too, Jace thumbed through the mail sent in care of his folks. Bills for the necessities of life—electric, gas, cell phone, car insurance. He didn't have to pay rent because he and Reese had inherited this place when their grandfather died. He'd never relied on plastic much even in Kansas City, and had even less use for it holed up out here. His only other expenses were groceries and an occasional tank of gas, plus his one luxury—satellite TV. A man had to do *something* day after day.

Reese left the grocery sack in the kitchen, then helped himself to a beer from the refrigerator—fair enough, since he'd brought them the last time he'd visited. After brushing his hand against Neely's shoulder, he returned to the living room and dropped into a chair. "What have you been up to?"

Jace shrugged. "The usual."

"Exciting life," Reese said, his tone as dry as the Sahara in summer.

"I'm not looking for excitement." Truth was, he wasn't looking for *anything,* and he wasn't sure that would ever change. For as long as he could remember, all he'd ever wanted to be was a cop. Since he couldn't be that anymore, he didn't have a clue what he *could* be.

"You give any thought to coming to work for the sheriff's department?"

"Nope."

"You give any thought to anything?" Now there was an irritated edge to Reese's voice that had appeared somewhere around the tenth or twentieth time they'd had this conversation. Reese thought Jace had had plenty of time to get his life back on track, and he wouldn't accept that Jace's only plans for the future dealt with sleeping, eating and fishing. He didn't believe Jace could walk away from being a cop.

The hell of it was, Jace couldn't even accuse him of not understanding, because Reese had been through it before. All *he'd* ever wanted to do was to play baseball, and he'd lived the dream—made it to the big leagues—then had it taken away from him.

But Reese had found something else he wanted—two other things, Jace amended with a glance at Neely. The only thing Jace wanted was for life to go back to the way it had been a year ago. And since he couldn't turn back the clock...

"You looking for an answer that doesn't suck or just ignoring me?" Reese asked.

"I think about a lot of things." But being a cop again wasn't one of them.

Reese watched him for a moment, his gaze narrowed, then apparently decided to drop the matter for the time being. "Whose red car is that out there?"

"Her name's Cassidy McRae. She's renting Junior's cabin."

"Oh, yeah, I heard about her from Paulette."

"What did you hear?" Jace could find out anything he wanted to know about his neighbor with a little effort. But he knew from experience it was better to keep Reese's mind on something other than *him*, or the conversation would inevitably drift back to old discussions they were both tired of having.

"Not much. She's from Alabama, she's a writer, and she's working on a book. Wanted someplace quiet where she wouldn't be bothered."

Alabama, huh? That wasn't a Southern accent he'd heard this morning. But living someplace at the present time didn't mean she'd been born there. He'd lived nearly half his life in Kansas City even though he'd been born and raised right here in Canyon County. Most of the people he knew had gotten where they were from someplace else.

What kind of book was she writing and why had she come all the way to Oklahoma to do it? Surely she had an office at home where she wouldn't be bothered. And why did she have Arizona tags on her car if she was from Alabama?

He let the aromas from the kitchen distract him for a moment. Tomatoes, onions, beef and cheese…his mother's lasagna. For an Osage married to an Okie, Rozena made damn good lasagna. That for supper, along with leftovers for tomorrow, was worth putting up with Reese's bitching.

"Want to eat inside or out?" Neely asked, standing in the kitchen doorway with plates and silverware. When both men shrugged, she made the decision by heading for the door. She returned for a clean sheet from the linen closet, disappeared again, then came back once more for a bowl of salad. "Why don't you invite your neighbor over for dinner?"

Oh, yeah, that would go over well with Ms. I'm-not-here-to-make-small-talk-with-the-neighbors. Dinner with said neighbor, his cousin the sheriff, and his cousin-by-marriage, who would need only one look at her to start visions of matchmaking dancing through her head.

"She's not particularly neighborly."

"Oh, she's probably just a little shy or busy getting settled in. But she has to eat, and we have plenty of wonderful food. Go on. *You* be neighborly. Show her how it's done." Then Neely gave him a suddenly sly look. "Unless there's some reason you don't want us to meet her. Is she pretty?"

Matchmaking, he reminded himself. She'd tried it a dozen or so times when they'd both lived in Kansas City, with often painful results. She nagged him as much as Reese did, just in a gentler fashion, about giving up the vegetating and getting back to living, and she thought a romance with a pretty woman the perfect solution to his problem.

So he lied. "She's old enough to be our mother. This tall." He held his hand about four feet above the floor. "Round. Wears thick-soled shoes and nerdy glasses. Not my type."

Apparently she thought she'd been more subtle because the look she gave him was reproving and the words she said an outright lie. "I'm not trying to get you a date, Jace. I'm talking about inviting a woman who's new in town to share the dinner your mother so generously made for us. Do you have a problem with that?"

Not trying to get me a date, my ass. She'd tried to set him up with the checker at the grocery store just last week. Two weeks before that, it had been her secretary's visiting niece, and the month before that, it had been the new waitress at Shay Rafferty's café in Heartbreak. Neely wanted to fix his life, whether he was willing or not.

Scowling, he rose from his chair. "Jeez, she bosses me around in my own house. All right, I'll invite her to dinner, but she's gonna say no."

"But you'll feel better for having made the effort," Neely sweetly called after him.

After checking out McRae that morning, he had eventually put on a shirt, but he'd never made it to shoes. He winced as he stepped on a rock on her side of the bridge, then again when he walked onto the deck. Where his was sheltered by the cabin from midafternoon on, hers got full sunlight until dusk. The weathered boards were uncomfortably hot underfoot.

From across the inlet came the sound of his screen door banging—Neely making another delivery to the patio table—so he deliberately stood at an angle that would block her view of the door, then knocked. The *Unplugged* version of "Layla" was playing inside—the only sound at all until suddenly the door opened a few inches. Cassidy McRae looked none too happy to be disturbed.

He wouldn't mind being disturbed a whole lot more.

She had changed from this morning's jeans and T-shirt into shorts and a tank top in shades of blue. Her feet were in flip-flops edged with a row of gaudy blue flowers, and her toenails were painted purplish blue. She would have looked depressingly young if not for the glasses she wore. The blue metal frames added a few years to her baby-owl look and made her eyes look twice their size.

She pushed the glasses up with one fingertip. "Yes?"

Brown eyes, he noticed. Dark, chocolatey brown, staring at him with only a hint of impatience that made him remember his reason for bothering her. "My mother sent dinner—the best lasagna outside of Italy. Want to join us?"

"Who is 'us'?"

"My cousin Reese and his wife Neely. He's the sheriff here, and she's a lawyer over in Buffalo Plains." He wasn't sure why he'd offered the extra info. To assure her that they were respectable, which might make him respectable by association?

She glanced in the direction of the kitchen. Looking over her shoulder, he saw the laptop open on the table, the word processing screen filled with text. Her book? He wondered what it was about, how she sat and pulled coherent thoughts and sentences from her brain and transferred them to the screen. He would rather face a short drunk with a bad attitude than sit at a computer all day trying to be creative.

"I'm working," she said at last when she looked back. "I shouldn't stop."

There—that was easy. He could accept her reply and go home. Reese and Neely wouldn't see her and find out he'd lied in his description. Neely wouldn't get that evil gleam in her eye and, with her none the wiser, he would save himself a lot of future hassle.

But instead of saying goodbye and leaving, he shifted to lean against the jamb. "You have to eat."

"I've got food."

"Already cooked and ready to dish up? The best lasagna in the English-speaking world?"

For a moment her clear gaze remained fixed on him, as if she was wavering. Then she glanced at the computer again and went stiff all over. "I appreciate the invitation, but I can't accept. I have to get back to work."

Definitely no Southern accent. No accent at all, in fact. Had she consciously gotten rid of it, or had she lost it by living in a lot of places?

"Okay. It's your loss. You won't find such good company for…oh, a few miles, at least, the food can't be beat, and there's probably something incredible for dessert."

"Sorry," she murmured.

He was supposed to feel relieved. Neely and Reese would return home, none the wiser about his neighbor. He wouldn't have to spend the evening hiding any hint that he thought she was gorgeous from prying eyes or have to deal with Neely's inevitable attempts to get them together. He wouldn't have to explain why he'd lied when describing her.

But mostly what he felt was disappointment. It was no great loss, no matter what he'd told Cassidy. Sitting across the table from a pretty woman would have been a nice change from the way he'd spent his last one hundred and eighty-plus evenings. Being tempted to spend his night differently would have been damn nice. But not tonight, apparently.

When he reached the bottom of the steps, he turned, walking backward for parting words. "If you change your mind, you know where to find us."

She gave no response—no nod or murmured *thanks* or *sorry*. She simply stood there and watched.

He was on his own side of the bridge before she finally closed the door.

Chapter 2

She watched him leave, unaware of the wistfulness that marred her face. How she would have liked to walk across the bridge with him, to sit down at the small round table and enjoy the cool evening air, the savory aromatic food and the company of strangers. She was tired of being alone, tired of having no friends, tired of having to be on guard all the time. She was tired, tired, tired, tired.

Besides, she hadn't had lasagna in a long time.

Wednesday morning found Cassidy stretched out on the couch, the television turned on but the sound muted. The picture was filled with snow and the static made the audio unbearable—and this was the channel that came in the best. She'd noticed the satellite dish on the neighboring cabin's roof with some envy while washing the breakfast dishes. Too bad she couldn't run a cable over there and tap into his better reception, but that would be illegal. Besides, she had no clue how to do such a thing. Inserting a plug into an outlet was the extent of her electronic abilities.

On the dining table, the laptop made a faint hum as the fan

came on. The screen was dark, but if she walked over and moved the cursor, the WordPerfect screen would pop up with the same lines that had been on it last evening when Jace Barnett had knocked. She'd been lying on the sofa then, too, trying to read a magazine but finding concentration too difficult to come by. She had tiptoed to the door, turned down his dinner invitation, then watched until he'd crossed the bridge. After closing the door she'd peeked through the blinds as he'd joined the man and woman on the deck. They had talked and laughed and eaten…and she had watched. Like the little match girl in the story her mother had read her long ago, on the outside looking in.

Except she was inside looking out. More like a prisoner locked away for her crimes. But the crimes that made her a prisoner weren't her own. She was the victim, but she was getting all the punishment.

Unable to stand the flickering TV any longer, she surged to her feet, shut it off, then went to the window. The other cabin was still and quiet. She'd heard a boat putt past more than an hour ago, sounding as if it were coming from that way. If Jace Barnett was out on the lake, there couldn't be any harm in her spending a little time outside in the sun, could there?

She got a sheet from her bedroom, a pair of sunglasses and a book, and headed outside. After another trip back in for the boom box and a glass of water, she spread the sheet over the grass, settled on her stomach and started reading to the accompaniment of B. B. King.

It was a peaceful, easy way to spend a morning, with the sun warm on her skin, the soft lap of the water against the shore, the buzz of bees among the wildflowers. Trade the sheet on the ground for a rope hammock and the glass of water for lemonade, and she would be as contented as a fat cat drinking cream in a sunbeam. As it was, she was almost contented enough to doze off. If she wasn't careful, she would wake up with the sunburn to end all sunburns, and then what would she do?

Gradually she became aware that the music had stopped.

The sun's pleasant warmth had become uncomfortably hot, and the bees' buzzing had been replaced by slow, steady breathing…and it wasn't her own.

She opened her eyes and tried to focus on the lush embossed floral depiction an inch from the tip of her nose. She *had* dozed off, using the novel for a pillow, knocking her sunglasses askew. All the moisture had been sucked out of her skin that was exposed to the sun and redeposited in places that weren't, dampening her clothes and making her feel icky.

And there was that breathing.

She lifted her head, sliding the glasses back into place, and saw her neighbor sitting a few feet away. He wore cutoffs, a ragged Kansas City Chiefs T-shirt and tennis shoes without socks, and he looked as if he hardly even noticed the heat. His own shades were darker than hers, hiding her eyes completely, but she didn't need to see them to know his gaze was fixed on her. The shiver sliding down her spine told her so.

"Working hard?"

Hoping the embossed cover wasn't outlined on her cheek, Cassidy slowly sat up, rubbed her face, then combed her fingers through her hair. "Doing research," she said, holding up the book, then laying it aside.

"Checking out the competition?"

She shrugged.

"So you write—"

"Watch it," she warned.

"I was just going to say—"

"I know what you were going to say. It was the *way* you were going to say it." She picked up her glass, its contents lukewarm now, and took a sip. "'So you write romance novels.' Or 'So you write trashy books.' Or 'So you write sex books.' Wink, wink, leer." Her gaze narrowed. "I didn't tell you I write anything."

"Reese did—my cousin. He got it from Paulette."

Cassidy was half surprised the real estate agent had remembered long enough to pass the information on. The woman had shown little interest, other than to remark that she was going to write a book someday. Everybody was, Cassidy had learned in her short career.

"Paulette says you're from Alabama."

"California," she lied without hesitation.

"You have Arizona tags."

"It's on the way here from California."

He didn't seem to appreciate her logic. "I can see confusing Alabama and Arizona, both of them starting and ending with A. But Alabama and California?"

"They both have 'al' in them. Besides, when people talk, Paulette listens for the silence that indicates it's her turn to speak, not for content."

"That's true. She does like to share her vast knowledge with everyone."

"Sounds like you know her well."

"She's my cousin, three or four times removed."

It must be nice to have family around. She had relatives, too, but she hadn't seen them in six years. No visits, no phone calls, no letters. It was worse than having no family at all, and so she pretended that was the case. Fate had decreed she should be all alone in the world, and there was no use trying to fight it.

"Then you're from around here," she said, then shrugged when his gaze intensified. "You said yesterday you'd just moved out here a while ago."

"I was staying with my folks outside Buffalo Plains."

"Why move?"

"Because I'm too old to live with my parents any longer than necessary."

Why had it been necessary? she wanted to ask. Had he lost his job? Gone through a lousy divorce that left him with nothing? Been recovering from a serious illness? Offhand, she couldn't think of any other reasons an able-bodied adult male would move in with Mom and Dad.

But instead of asking such a personal question, she asked another that was too personal. "Do you work?"

Again his hidden gaze seemed to sharpen. "Nope. I occasionally help Guthrie Harris with his cattle, or Easy Rafferty with his horses, but that's about it.''

"Easy Rafferty. What a name.''

"You heard of him?''

She shook her head.

"He used to be a world champion roper until he lost a couple fingers in an accident. Now he raises the best paints in this part of the country. He could teach that horse whisperer guy a few things.''

A rodeo cowboy. She knew nothing about them—had never been to a rodeo or gotten closer to any horse than passing a mounted police patrol in the city—but they were popular in the books boxed up inside. So were Indians of all types, including cowboys. Though she had no trouble picturing Jace Barnett in faded Wranglers, a pearl-snapped shirt and a Stetson, something about the image didn't feel quite right. She had no reason to think he was lying to her—other than the fact that she usually lied herself—but the man was more than a part-time cowboy.

"Are you researching this area?''

She was still imagining him in jeans and scuffed boots, with a big championship buckle on his belt. The question caught her off guard, leaving her blinking a couple of times until her brain caught up. Research, the area, her book—remember? Her reason for being here?

"Oh…no…not really. I just wanted someplace quiet to write.''

"And you had to come halfway across the country to find it? Why not just rent a place close to home?''

He obviously didn't believe her, and that made color rise in her face. "Oh…well…I mean, the book is *set* in Oklahoma, but I—I did most of my research from home. On the Internet, you know. But I needed a break from California, and I like to do the actual writing on location.'' She shrugged carelessly. "I know it sounds strange, but there are as many different methods of writing out there as there are writers. A lot of us are strange.''

''Huh.'' He put a wealth of skepticism in that one word, but didn't pursue it. ''Where do you live in California?''

She gave the first answer that came to mind. ''San Diego. Actually, one of the suburbs. A little place called Lemon Grove.'' She'd been to San Diego once—so many years ago that she remembered little about it besides the beach being closed due to a sewage spill down the coast and the fun they'd had at Sea World. If a visit to Lemon Grove had been a part of the trip, she didn't remember it, but it was an easy enough name to recall.

''You live there alone?''

''Yes.''

''What about your house?''

There was a reason she didn't encourage casual conversation when she found herself with neighbors, she thought with a tautly controlled breath. Too many questions, too many chances for missteps. Not that the consequences were likely to be deadly, but she never knew.

''I gave up my apartment and put everything in storage,'' she replied, deliberately injecting a distant tone into her voice. ''Finding a new place to live is easy.'' She'd done it more times in the past few years than any sane person should have to endure.

She stood, slid her feet into her thongs, then carried the book and her glass to the deck. Returning, she shook out the sheet and started to haphazardly fold it. ''I've got to get back to work.''

Jace showed no intention of leaving. Instead he leaned back, his arms supporting him, and stretched his legs out. ''Writing must be hard work.''

''More for some than others.''

''How long have you been doing it?''

''A while.''

''Have you sold anything?''

''A few books.'' After all, a writer who could travel fifteen hundred miles to write a book in a rented lakefront cabin had to have some source of income, right? And it had to be a source that didn't require eight-to-five workdays in an office somewhere, and to pay well enough to justify the expense of a temporary cross-country move.

"How many is that?"

She shrugged.

"Fewer than five? More than ten?"

With a roll of her eyes, she pretended to count mentally, then said, "Seven." It was everyone's lucky number, and though her life had been utterly devoid of luck the past couple of years, she could pretend like everyone else, couldn't she?

"Seven. Lucky number."

She smiled thinly. "Seventy will be luckier...but if I don't get to work, I won't even see eight."

She intended to march into the house then, but he finally moved to get up and she couldn't resist watching. His legs were long and muscular—runner's legs, though she couldn't imagine him summoning up enough energy to jog from her house to his—and he moved with the grace and ease she'd sorely needed for ballet class when she was seven. Instead she'd been the clumsiest student Miss Karla had ever taught and, after falling off the stage during a recital, she had gladly hung up her slippers.

When he was on his feet, he stretched and his T-shirt rode up to display a thin line of smooth brown skin above the narrow waist of his cutoffs. Her fingers tingled to see if it was as warm and soft as it looked. She knotted them into a fist under the cover of the sheet.

"The invitation for lasagna still stands," he remarked.

"No, thanks. I'm not hungry." Her stomach chose that moment to remind her that breakfast had been skimpy and a long time ago.

He grinned. "Are you sure about that? Mom makes it all from scratch—the noodles, the sauce and the garlic bread on the side—and it's even better the second day."

She hadn't had lasagna in ages. She didn't like the frozen stuff, and cooking for just herself was an unnecessary reminder of how alone she was. Granted, a ham sandwich would fill her stomach just as well and had the added benefit of no conversation to stumble through. But she'd had a ham sandwich for lunch the day before, and for supper last night, and would have one for supper tonight. Besides, she could control the conversation. She'd been doing it long enough, giving out only what information she wanted to give, manipulating it to go in the directions she wanted. She'd just gotten clumsy this morning because he'd literally caught her sleeping.

He was rocking back on his heels, waiting for an answer. She eyed him warily. "What's for dessert?"

"Strawberry pie with whipped cream."

Cassidy stifled a groan. She loved strawberries. When she was a kid, every Saturday in strawberry season, the family had driven to a pick-your-own berry farm and filled quart containers by the dozen. They had always managed to eat at least three quarts on the way home, where she'd helped her mother make strawberry shortcake, pie and preserves.

"I suppose it can't hurt this once," she said reluctantly. It wasn't smart, but it wouldn't be the dumbest thing she'd ever done, either. Sure, he was a stranger, but he was a local. He had family here. He didn't know her from Adam. He had some doubts about her stories, but so what? He was a cowboy when he worked at all. What did it matter whether he believed her? Who was he going to tell? The horses and cows?

Or his cousin, the sheriff? the little voice whispered.

So what? she stubbornly repeated. There was no law against lying…well, unless you were doing it under oath. Or profiting from it. Or doing it to stay out of jail. But what she was doing—lying to strangers about things she had a right to keep private…it might not be ethical, but it wasn't illegal.

"I'll put the lasagna in the oven. Dump your stuff inside, then come on over," Jace said.

She watched until he stepped onto the bridge, then went inside with a sigh. The sheet went on a shelf in the tiny linen closet, the glass and the boom box on the kitchen counter. She shut off the computer, then went to the bathroom to wash up. The face reflected back at her in the mirror was pale with pink spots on the cheeks—and the flush came from a source much closer than the sun. Her hair looked as if she'd forgotten to comb it in recent memory, and her eyes…

She'd read an article on age-progression computer programs that said the one single feature that never changed, no matter a person's age, was the eyes. You could change the color with contact lenses—she'd done that a time or two—and enhance them with makeup, but the basic shape stayed the same. Hers seemed terribly different to her, but of course it wasn't the shape. It was the shadows. The wariness. The distrust. The fear. Did Jace the Cowboy recognize any of that, or did he, like most people, simply see a pair of unremarkable brown eyes?

Truthfully, she didn't want to know. If he was perceptive, she would have to keep her distance from him—which she intended to do anyway, of course. But doing it by choice was better than doing it because she had to.

She changed into clothes that weren't damp from sunning—tailored and cuffed shorts in khaki, a cotton shirt in olive drab, sand-colored sandals. The shirt was tucked in, the shorts belted with a matching olive belt. She combed her hair, added a touch of makeup, then frowned at herself. Would he think she'd dressed up for him? Maybe she should switch to denim shorts and a tank top, or jeans and a T-shirt. Maybe…

Still scowling, she shut off the light and left the bathroom. She stopped at the dresser long enough to slide a few things into her pocket—a tube of lip gloss, her keys and a small round canister—then she headed for the door.

The lasagna and bread were heating in the oven, the pie chilling in the refrigerator. The windows and door were open and a box fan set in the lakeside window blew cool air through the room.

Jace leaned against the kitchen counter, sucking down his third bottle of water for the day. He was that rarity among cops, as well as Barnetts—a man who didn't drink. He'd run too many miles to stay in shape, had worked too many years at a job where the concept of being off duty was a joke. Trouble could find a cop at any time, and he'd wanted his senses unimpaired when it happened.

He glanced at the clock while waiting for Cassidy to put in an appearance. He'd been home ten minutes—more than long enough for her to carry a few things inside, then walk across the bridge. He wouldn't be surprised if she'd locked herself inside instead. She'd obviously had misgivings about coming over.

She obviously had something to hide.

Okay, maybe not so obviously. Maybe, even after six months off the job, his instincts were as sharp as ever. He was used to people being less than honest with him. It gave him an itchy feeling down his spine and he'd been wanting to scratch the whole time they'd been talking. He couldn't say she'd flat-out lied to him, but she'd certainly been evasive, and wondering why came as naturally to him as breathing.

But it wasn't his job to find out. In fact, his only job was to do a lot of nothing. To kick back, relax and stay out of trouble. He was free to take advantage of whatever entertainment he could find along the way, but that was the extent of it. No poking around in anyone's background. No ferreting out inconsistencies or solving mysteries. No getting involved in anyone's troubles but his own.

A board in the middle of the deck creaked and he shifted his gaze to the screen door. An instant later Cassidy appeared there, looking lovely and unsure, as if she might bolt back home at anytime.

"Come on in," he called as she raised her hand to knock.

She stepped inside, smiled faintly in greeting, then glanced around. The layout of the cabin was identical to hers—living and dining room stretched across the front, kitchen in back on the left, bedroom and bathroom on the right. He hadn't been inside Junior's place in years, but knowing the Davisons, he would bet the same ratty old furniture was still in residence.

That was the only way his cabin was better than hers. He'd brought some of his own stuff—a leather couch, an oversize armchair, a couple of bookcases—and borrowed the bedroom furniture and dinette from his parents. The table was an oval oak pedestal, with four ladder-back chairs, and the bedroom set was his grandmother's antique mahogany.

He'd added rugs, too, and a television, DVD and stereo system, but he hadn't unpacked a single thing for the walls. Photographs, a couple of meritorious commendations he'd received, gifts, mementos…anything that would personalize the space and reveal anything about the past seventeen years was packed up in his folks' attic. It could all stay there until it rotted.

What would her space reveal about her past? Someday he would have to wangle an invitation into her cabin to find out.

"Lunch will be ready in a few minutes," he said as her gaze finally reached him. "What would you like to drink?"

"Water will be fine."

"That's all? I've got beer and pop, too."

She gave a slight shake of her head, then came to stand at the table, her hands gripping one of the ladder-back chairs. He figured her goal was to look as if she was casually resting her hands, but her fingers were clenched so tightly that the knuckles turned white. Why so nervous? He wasn't likely to throw her to the floor and have his way with her, not when it meant burning the lasagna. Force wasn't his style. Persuasion was way too much fun.

But maybe force had been someone else's style. Maybe that was why she was cautious and evasive.

But it wasn't his business, remember?

He got two bottles of water from the refrigerator, then set the table. As the timer went off, he pulled the lasagna from the oven and stuck the foil-wrapped bread inside, then asked, "What's your book about?"

She'd been looking out the window. Now her gaze jerked back to him. "My…my book?"

"The one you're writing. The one that's set here in Oklahoma. What is it about?"

"Oh…well…" Her fingers tightened even more around the chair back. "It's…it's a love story."

"Most romance novels are, aren't they?" he asked dryly.

"Yeah. Of course."

Using insulated mitts, he carried the lasagna pan to the table, then returned with the bread. After he slid into the nearest seat, she slowly pulled out the chair she'd had a death grip on and sat. He waited until they'd served themselves, then gave her time to take a bite before asking, "So? What's it about?"

"It's about…" When she looked up, her face was warm but her eyes were cool and her full lips had flattened into an aloof line. "I'm really not comfortable discussing it. If I tell people the story in detail, then there's not much purpose in writing it—is there?—because I've already told it."

He wasn't asking for a scene-by-scene description. A general overview would have been fine, something like "a story of a spoiled Southern belle during and after the Civil War" for *Gone With the Wind*. He didn't need names, subplots or even the highlights.

"Do you publish your books under your own name?"

This time she didn't look at him, but kept her gaze focused on the plate in front of her. "No, I don't. You were right— this is excellent lasagna. Is it an old family recipe?"

"Someone's old family, but not ours. Mom came across it years ago, made a few changes and has been fixing it ever since." Just as bluntly as she'd changed the subject, he changed it back. "What's your…aw, hell, I can't think of the word. Your alias?"

For a moment he thought she might laugh, but the twitch at the corners of her mouth faded. "Alias?"

"You know, your fake name. Cassidy McRae aka what? Jeez, don't you ever look at Wanted posters?"

"No, I can't honestly say that I do." She paused. "Do you?"

"I used to. A lot."

"Looking for anyone in particular?"

"Not for pictures of myself, if that's what you're thinking.

Trust me, if I was wanted by the cops, Reese would turn me in so fast I wouldn't know what hit me.''

''Your own cousin?''

''He's a cop first, my cousin second.'' That wasn't entirely true. Reese would never break the law, but he would bend it a little if circumstances warranted it. Sometimes that was the only way to see justice done.

''Then what's your interest in Wanted posters?''

He wasn't sure why, but he didn't particularly want to admit that he'd been a cop himself. With his luck, she would probably have a lot of questions he wouldn't want to answer. The few writers he'd met in the past, mostly reporters, were filled with them. ''Curiosity,'' he said with a shrug. ''I watch *America's Most Wanted*, too.'' Once again he abruptly shifted direction. ''You never told me what your alias—''

''Pen name.''

''—is.''

''Why do you want to know?''

''Maybe I want to pick up a couple of your books and see what they're like.''

''They're very hard to find. Most of them are out of print.''

''Then you could loan me some copies.''

Her smile was quick and uneasy. ''I don't have any. Sorry.''

''Oh, come on…you don't have a single copy of your own books?''

''Well, of course I have some, but not with me. They're back home in my office in San Diego.''

''Lemon Grove,'' he corrected.

She grimaced. ''Hey, it's all one big city.''

''And they're in storage, with the rest of your office.''

Her face turned almost as red as the sweet tomato sauce that oozed between the layers of noodles. ''Yeah,'' she agreed. ''Everything's in storage.''

His back was itching again. He shifted in his chair, rubbing against the spindles. If he checked Directory Assistance for Lemon Grove, California, would he find a listing for Cassidy McRae? Instinct said no, but that wouldn't mean anything.

Most women who lived alone in big cities had unlisted numbers. But if one of his cop buddies checked the utilities and didn't find a recent account in her name...

It would prove she'd lied about where she lived. So what? She was an author, and no doubt had fans. For some people it was a short step from fan to stalker. If some stranger was buying *his* book and thought he was making some sort of connection, he would want personal information such as where he lived kept private, too.

As he pushed his plate away, he slumped back in the chair and fixed his gaze on her. "You're not married."

She shook her head.

"Any kids?"

"No." That was accompanied by a faint regret. It wasn't as if it was too late. She couldn't be more than thirty, thirty-two. She still had time to bring a dozen or more kids into the world before Mother Nature said no more.

"Family?"

Her smile was faint. "Don't have one."

"No parents, brothers or sisters?"

She shook her head again. "No aunts, uncles, cousins or grandparents, either. I'm an only child from a long line of only children."

"No family. Jeez." Then... "Want some of mine?"

She pushed her plate away, too, having cleaned it. "Your parents live outside Buffalo Plains, your cousin is the local sheriff, and your cousin four times removed sells real estate around here. Who else is there?"

"Reese's folks live in town. My mom's parents are about forty miles from here, and her two brothers and three sisters all live within an hour or so. There are a lot of cousins, some great-aunts and -uncles, some in-laws and out-laws. Last time the family got together, there were about seventy of us."

"That's nice."

It was nicer when he lived in another state and didn't see them that often, he was about to retort but stopped himself. There was something wrong with complaining about too much

family to a woman who didn't have any. Instead he agreed—
more or less. "Yeah. It can be."

"Are you married?"

"Nope. Never have been."

"Ever come close?"

He thought of Amanda and the diamond ring he'd been
considering for a Valentine's Day surprise. The few people he
kept in touch with in Kansas City never volunteered any news
about her and he never asked. "Nope." It wasn't a complete
lie. They hadn't been nearly as close to a lifetime commitment
as he'd thought.

"Any kids?"

"Not without being married first, or my mother would tan
my hide."

"That's an old-fashioned outlook."

"She's an old-fashioned mother." He thought about dig-
ging up another question, then stuck to the subject. "She be-
lieves parents should be married before they start having children, that honesty comes first in a relationship, and that
marriage shouldn't be entered into lightly. You don't have to
stay in a bad marriage, but you damn well have to do everything you can to keep it from going bad."

What if he *had* married Amanda? What if politics hadn't
derailed his career or had done so six months after the wedding? Just how bad could that marriage have gotten? Very bad,
he suspected. Bitter-divorce-and-protective-orders bad. His
mother would have been incredibly disappointed in him for
making such a lousy choice.

So one good thing had come out of the mess. Amanda had
saved him the hassle of a divorce down the road and spared
him Rozena's disappointment.

"Your mother's a smart woman." Cassidy slid her chair
back, then held out her hand for his dishes. Stacking them
with her own, she carried them into the kitchen.

He followed with the lasagna pan. "How long does it take
you to write a book?"

"It varies." She turned on the water in the sink, waited for it to heat, then put in the stopper and squirted in dish soap.

"Give me a ballpark figure. A week? A month? A year?"

She shrugged. "Sometimes three months, sometimes six, sometimes longer. Some days I *want* to tell the story. Other days, I can't force myself to get within ten feet of the computer."

"Did you always want to be a writer?"

"Not really."

"How long have you been doing it?"

"A few years."

Just like her earlier answer that she'd sold a *few* books. He'd pinned her down to a number then, and sometime he might pin her down on this, but not now. Instead he put the last square of lasagna in the refrigerator and took out the pie and a tub of whipped cream. "Where do you get your ideas?"

She scowled at him over her shoulder before turning her attention back to the dishes. If she scrubbed that plate any harder, she was going to take the pattern right off of it, he thought, and wondered why she was so tense. "They come to me in my sleep," she said, clearly annoyed.

Another evasion, if not an outright lie. He was beginning to think "evasion" was Cassidy McRae's middle name.

Too bad he was no longer in the business of finding out why.

Chapter 3

*S*he had regrets—a lot of them. More than any ninety year old who'd squandered her life should be burdened by on her deathbed, and she was nowhere near ninety. Looking into his amazingly handsome face, with his sharp black eyes, his straight nose, his stubborn jaw and his full, sensuous, sensitive-looking mouth, and lying through her teeth to him was only the most recent in a long string of regrets.

He believed in honesty between a man and a woman—had said so in no uncertain terms, and yet she had lied to him.

And all the regrets in all the world wouldn't stop her from doing it again.

Cassidy directed her sharpest scowl at herself. She didn't regret lying to Jaçe any more than she regretted lying to anyone. There was nothing special about him, nothing that separated him from the countless people she had deceived in the past.

Except for the fact that he was handsome as sin.

And more tempting than chocolate.

She hadn't looked twice at a man in thirty-five-and-a-half

months— No, that wasn't true. She looked two and three and four times, searching faces, praying she didn't see any particular face. She looked at men as a potential threat to her freedom, her safety, her very life.

Jace was the first one she'd looked at as *just* a man. Someone to be attracted to. Someone to share a meal with. Someone to stir her long-sleeping hormones back to life.

Someone she couldn't even *think* about getting involved with. He had that honesty thing going for him. She had a million lies and counting. He belonged here, with his family all around. She didn't belong anywhere. He was an easygoing, unsophisticated part-time cowboy. She was a woman for whom people would kill.

All those things were among her regrets.

And hopefully, when she left here, Jace Barnett wouldn't be.

Avoiding him would be the best way to prevent that. No matter that he was handsome and friendly and his mother made the best strawberry pie she'd ever had. No matter that she had been—to borrow a line from Hank Williams—so lonesome she could cry. She needed to stay away from him. He asked too many questions and she didn't have the right answers. He was suspicious of her—she had seen it in his eyes yesterday at lunch. Maybe he wouldn't do anything with his suspicions.

Or maybe he would.

The hell of it was, it was her own fault. All she'd wanted was a little time to do nothing. Peace and quiet in a place where she wouldn't have to worry about fitting in, having friends or meeting enemies. She'd wanted to be as alone in her private little world as she was in the world at large.

She shouldn't have lied to Paulette Fox, but the woman had been so damn nosy, wanting to know why Cassidy had chosen Buffalo Plains, refusing to believe that anyone would come to the shores of little Buffalo Lake for a vacation. After all, the lake offered no amenities beyond a few picnic tables. There was no resort, no place to rent a boat or Jet Ski, no charmingly quaint vacation cottages, not even a convenience store for a quick run. The only cabin for rent had no telephone and lousy television reception and depended on a window air conditioner to keep it cool.

You can tell me, honey, the woman had wheedled with a gleam in her eyes and a confidential air. *What are you* really *here for?*

Cassidy had thought of the paperback in her purse and the lie had found its way out before she'd even thought about it. *I'm a writer. I'm looking for a quiet place to finish my book.*

It wasn't the first time she'd lied and wouldn't be the last. Besides, how hard could masquerading as a writer be? It wasn't as if she needed a degree to hang on her wall. She skimmed the author biographies in every book she read—and for the past few years that number was in the hundreds. There were doctors, teachers and lawyers writing, sure, but there were also housewives and mothers and high-school graduates.

And what did a writer do? She sat around dreaming up stories, then put them on paper. Cassidy sat around dreaming up stories—that sounded so much better than *making up lies*—and she could pretend to put them on paper. In fact, she'd decided to actually try her hand at writing. Lord knew, she had a story to tell.

There was just one small problem—at least, it had started out small. It seemed to get bigger with each passing day.

What she didn't know about being a writer would...well, would fill a book.

And Jace was reaching that conclusion, too, if he hadn't already.

Suddenly too antsy to sit still, she exited the Free Cell game, then stood and stretched before grabbing her car keys and purse. She needed a few groceries—she never wanted to eat another ham sandwich as long as she lived—and she could certainly benefit from some fresh air and a change of scenery.

After locking up, she climbed into her blisteringly hot car, backed out, then headed down the narrow dirt lane. The air conditioner was turned to high, all the windows were down, and the wheel was so hot that she steered using only the tips of her fingers, but she felt damn near giddy at the prospect of getting out and seeing people.

She was *not* cut out for a life of isolation.

A few hundred yards from her cabin, another narrow lane forked off to the northwest. She'd paid it little attention the times she'd been by it, but now she knew it led to Jace's house—partly because it was logical, and partly because he was sitting there in a dusty green SUV, half in his driveway, half in the road, watching her approach.

Her car was small enough she could ease around him, give a neighborly wave, then drive on—and let him drive in her dust for the next ten miles—but she politely slowed to a stop.

Instead of driving on, he got out of the truck and leaned in the passenger window. "Where are you off to?"

"The grocery store."

"Me, too. Why don't you park your car and ride with me?"

She wanted to coolly say *no, thanks,* almost as much as she wanted to agree. She needed conversation, to hear other voices, and his was a damn easy voice to listen to.

But he asks questions, her own inner voice reminded her, *and he wants answers.* She could be satisfied talking to the clerk at the grocery store, couldn't she?

Oh, sure, that would be a great conversation. *How are you today? Will that be all? You want paper or plastic?*

Apparently her reluctance was obvious, because he grinned a killer grin. "Aw, come on…I bet you don't even know where the closest grocery store is."

"The *only* grocery store is in Buffalo Plains."

He made a sound like a game-show buzzer. "The Heartbreak store is five miles closer. I'll even treat you to lunch at the Heartbreak Café."

Heartbreak. Sounded like her kind of town, she thought with a touch of irony and rue. And lunch…in a restaurant…with people. Sounded too good to pass up. And it wouldn't hurt, would it? Not just this one time?

"Let me take my car back."

With another grin, he lifted his hand in a wave, then returned to his truck.

It took some effort, but she managed to turn around without getting too far off the road. On the brief drive to the cottage, she tried to talk herself into reneging, but when she got out of the Honda, she didn't blurt out an excuse, rush inside and lock the door. No, she climbed into the cool interior of the SUV, buckled her seat belt and glanced at Jace.

He wore gym shorts in white cotton with a gray T-shirt, worn-out running shoes and no socks, and his black hair was pulled back in a ponytail again. As a general rule, she didn't like to see men with hair longer than her own, and she couldn't help but think he would be a hundred times handsomer with it cut short. Even so, he was still incredibly *hot*. Heavens, *she* was hot just looking at him.

She adjusted the vent so the cool air blew directly on her, then crossed her legs. Deciding it would be in her best interests to start—and therefore hopefully control—the conversation, she asked, "How big is Heartbreak?"

"A better question is how *little* is it. I believe Paulette likes to refer to it as 'a wide spot in the road.'"

"Yeah, I heard that phrase from her a couple of times."

He grinned. "You don't need to spend much time with Paulette before she starts repeating herself. She can be annoying, but at heart she's a good person." At the end of the lane, he slowed almost to a stop, then turned east onto the dirt road. "Heartbreak...let's see.... It has an elementary school, middle school and high school, though if the number of students keeps dropping, they'll have to close them and bus the kids to Buffalo Plains. There are a couple of cafés, a hardware store, a five-and-dime, a grocery store, a part-time doctor and lawyer, a post office—oh, and a boot-and-saddle maker. If you want to take home a one-of-a-kind souvenir, you should see her. There's also a couple of small junk stores—pardon me, antique stores—and a consignment store. That's about it."

"All the necessities of life," she said with a faint smile.

"If you're not looking for anything fancy. If you are, you have to go to Tulsa or Oklahoma City."

At the intersection where they would have turned left to go to Buffalo Plains, he turned right instead, then asked, "Get any writing done today?"

So much for controlling the conversation. "A little."

"After you write the book, what happens then?"

She stared out the side window for a time, some part of her brain registering pastures dotted with cattle, occasional houses, barbed wire fences and acres of the scraggly trees Paulette had identified as blackjacks. Finally, when the expectant silence began to gnaw at her nerves, she gave him a narrowed look. "Didn't we agree yesterday that I didn't want to talk about my career?"

His laughter was warm and unexpected. "Oh, honey, we haven't agreed on anything yet except that my mom's a good cook. Besides, you said that about the book you're currently writing. I'm just asking about the process in general."

"Why?"

He gave the same answer he'd offered in regard to the Wanted posters. "I'm curious."

"Why?"

"I haven't met many writers before, and most of them were newspaper or TV reporters."

She grabbed the chance to turn the conversation back on him. "Now you've made me curious. How does a small-town Oklahoma cowboy manage to run into so many newspaper and television reporters? They do many stories on branding and castrating around here?"

Now it was his turn to think before he answered. "Nope, not many. But if there's a reporter around, they seem to lock in on me. Must be my charm."

Must be female reporters, Cassidy thought dryly.

"Okay, we'll drop that part of the discussion. Can you at least tell me what kind of research you did before coming here?"

Absolutely not. She'd chosen Buffalo Lake the same way

she'd chosen every other place she'd temporarily lighted in the past three years—spread out a map of the U.S., closed her eyes and pointed. "Just general stuff," she fibbed. "Climate, topography, industry." Please don't ask, she silently prayed, but of course he did.

"And what did you learn about the climate?"

In the outside mirror she watched dust clouds swirl behind them. Looking ahead she saw heat waves shimmering in the air. "That it gets hot in summer. Damn hot."

"And?"

She gave him another of those narrow gazes. "Why are you quizzing me? I'm not a student and you're not my teacher."

"I bet I could teach you a few things," he said, his voice huskier than normal. Then he gave her a long, intimate look. "And you could teach me a few."

Her throat had gone as dry as the road they were traveling. She couldn't think of a response, though, until he turned back to the road, when the air rushed out of her lungs and she sank back against the seat.

As if the moment had never happened, he gestured toward the house ahead on the left, identifying it as Easy and Shay Rafferty's place, where he helped out occasionally with the horses. Farther down the road on the right was Guthrie and Olivia Harris's ranch, where he helped out occasionally with the cattle. Two young girls were playing in the yard. One, dangling upside down from a tree branch, waved so enthusiastically Cassidy feared she might fall. The other, sitting primly on a quilt underneath the tree, raised her hand without so much as a wiggle of her fingers.

"That's the Harrises' twins. Elly's the tomboy and Emma's the prissy one," Jace remarked. "Which were you as a kid?"

"I wasn't prissy."

"Did you play with dolls?"

"Of course. That's what little girls do."

"Let me rephrase that—*how* did you play with dolls? Did you play house with them, like Emma, or cut them open and stuff them with firecrackers to see if you could blow them to bits, like Elly did last week?''

She'd played house, but she wasn't about to admit it. Instead she folded her arms over her chest and pressed her lips together.

''That's a clear enough answer,'' he said with a chuckle. ''Did you ever climb trees? Collect spiders? Make a pet of a mouse and keep him in your pocket? Or did you like to sit in the air-conditioning with your dollies and books and not get dirty?''

''I climbed trees,'' she said in her defense. And she had, too. At least, a time or two. Until she'd fallen from an unstable limb and broken her arm when she was eight. After that, she'd kept her feet on the ground.

''And the rest?''

''I kill spiders and the only mouse I want around is attached to my computer.'' Her expression slid into something that felt remarkably like a pout. ''Besides, what's wrong with staying cool and clean and reading?''

He laughed again, not a chuckle this time but a full-throated laugh. ''So you were prissy. Of course, I could tell just by looking at you.''

''How?'' she challenged.

''Because girly girls always grow up to be such womanly women.'' Again that low, husky tone. Again the dry throat, the air rushing from her lungs, the general weakness spreading through her body.

Spending the next few hours with him couldn't hurt, could it? she had convinced herself back in the Honda. Not just this one time.

She would have snorted in disdain if she could have found the breath. He was a dangerous man, and his relentless questions were only the half of it. Questions she could avoid. Emotions, though… She couldn't escape them no matter how she tried. Feelings in general were okay. Feelings for other people weren't. Those were the rules that governed her life.

The sooner she remembered and acted on that, the better.

* * *

Jace parked in downtown Heartbreak, climbed out of the truck and waited on the sidewalk for Cassidy. As she got out and walked toward him, her gaze was swiveling from side to side and around. Looking for anything in particular or just trying to take the whole town in at once?

He'd never tried to see his hometown through someone else's eyes. It was so familiar to him that he wasn't even sure he saw it through his own eyes, but rather through the eyes of the kid who had once lived here. He usually didn't notice that the buildings looked pretty shabby, that the sidewalks were cracked, that half the buildings on the next block were boarded up. He didn't pay attention to the paint peeling from old wood or the crack that had extended through the insurance agency's plate-glass window for as long as he could remember. He looked and saw home.

What did Cassidy see?

He gestured toward Café Shay—really the Heartbreak Café, owned by Shay Rafferty—and they started in that direction. Just two days ago he hadn't wanted Reese and Neely to see Cassidy, and now here he was taking her to lunch in Gossip Central. Somebody would be on the phone to his mother before they made it to the grocery store across and down the street.

But he didn't even consider taking back the offer.

The bell over the door announced them and several dozen pairs of eyes turned their way. About half the customers greeted him before speculatively looking back at Cassidy.

Hell, they probably wouldn't even be through with lunch before someone called his mom.

They'd just claimed the only empty booth when Shay showed up, balancing a chubby-cheeked baby on one hip. She set down two glasses of water, then two menus. "Hey, Jace, how's it going?"

"Not bad. Shay, Cassidy." He gave the briefest introductions possible, then reached for the baby, who came to him with a toothless grin and a drool. "And this is Liza Beth."

"That's her name today because she's in a good mood,"
Shay said, "but we're thinking of changing it to something
like…oh, I don't know. Difficult. Tough."

"Nah, she's too pretty for a silly name like that," he responded, directing his words to the baby who was gazing with
great interest at his finger closest to her mouth. "Besides, one
unconventional name per family is plenty."

Shay smacked him on the shoulder. "Who are you calling
unconventional? Easy or me?" Then she smiled across the
booth. "It's nice to meet you, Cassidy. Are you visiting from
K—"

Jace shot her a look and she smoothly shifted. "Or are you
making your home here?"

"I'm just here for a while."

Cassidy gave him a vaguely curious look over Liza Beth's
head, no doubt wondering what Shay had been about to say.
To distract her, he announced, "Cassidy's a writer. She's finishing up a book."

"Really?" Shay's blue eyes brightened. "That's so cool!
What kind of book?"

A flush flooded Cassidy's cheeks, so Jace answered for her.
"She writes romance novels. The one she's working on now
is set in this area."

"How wonderful. What is the name and when will it be
out?"

"I—I don't—" Cassidy broke off to take a sip of water.
"I haven't settled on a title yet, and I don't know
when…when it will come out. Probably never, if the guy next
door doesn't stop interrupting my work time."

Shay grinned at Jace. "That would be you, I presume. He's
a terrible distraction," she said to Cassidy. "Wants attention
all the time. Just like Liza Beth."

"Hey, we resent that, don't we, Liza?" He moved the baby
to cradle her in his lap, and she snagged his finger at last,
guiding it into her mouth. "I'd've been perfectly happy not
having *any* attention last winter, but it didn't keep any of you
away, did it?"

"What happened last winter?" Cassidy asked.

Shay opened her mouth, looked from Cassidy to him, then closed it again and smiled. "I believe I'll take my child and send the waitress over to take your order."

"Nah, let Liza stay—at least until the food comes. She's happy enough for the moment."

"You don't have to say it twice," Shay said with a laugh. "Cassidy, nice meeting you. I'm sure I'll be seeing you around."

She left and a young waitress appeared. Without looking at the menu, Jace ordered a double cheeseburger and onion rings. Cassidy studied the menu for a moment, then asked for the lunch special. Then she folded her hands together on the tabletop and gave him a raised-brow look.

He ignored it as long as he could before faking a grouchy look of his own. "What?"

"What happened last winter?"

"Not much. Oklahoma winters can be really mild or really cold—but then, you know that, having researched the climate." He let a little good-natured sarcasm slide into his voice on the last words. "We had a couple ice storms that shut things down for a day or two, and we had a tornado in January. That's something you don't see a lot of."

She continued to look at him, her expression unchanging.

"They have tornadoes where you come from?"

"Occasionally."

"In San Diego? I wouldn't have thought so."

"Lemon Grove," she corrected him. "And none of that answers my question. What happened with *you* last winter?"

He leveled his gaze on her, as steady and measuring as hers was, then smiled coolly. "I'll make you a deal. You answer all those questions of mine you've danced around, like what your pen name is and what your book is about and what kind of research you did, and I'll tell you about last winter."

She smiled, too, a bright smile that involved her whole face without bringing one bit of warmth to it. "It would serve you right if I agreed."

He shrugged.

"Fair enough." Then she lowered her gaze to the baby. "She doesn't look anything like her mother."

"Nope. She's the spittin' image of Easy, except she's prettier and has all her fingers. He's only got seven."

"Jace! You shouldn't joke about that."

"Hey, I'm just repeating what he said. Besides, I think we're distantly related. I'm mostly Osage and he's mostly Cherokee, but a few generations ago somebody from his father's side married somebody from my mother's side."

"So you're probably tenth or twelfth cousins."

He grinned. "It still counts as family. At least, when you want it to."

"You like kids," she commented, her gaze lowering to the baby.

He looked down, too, at Liza Beth's dark skin, eyes and hair, her fat cheeks and the mouth that managed a grin in spite of her gnawing on his finger. "I like most people." Even some of the people he'd arrested over the years. Civilians tended to think that cops and crooks were mortal enemies, but that wasn't always the case. Sure, most bad guys weren't anxious to go to jail, and some would do *anything* to avoid it, but a lot of them didn't hold grudges. They were doing their jobs and he was doing his. No hard feelings.

"Then why were you trying to avoid attention last winter?"

He gave her a steady, censuring look. "We agreed, remember? If you don't answer questions, I don't. No fair trying to sneak around the back way."

Her only response to his rebuke was a nod, then she glanced at Liza Beth again. "Why aren't you married and raising a houseful of kids?"

"I always figured I would be, but..." He finished with a shrug, then studied the faint wistfulness in her expression. "You want to hold her?"

Her hands flexed and came up off the tabletop, a prelude to reaching for the baby, then she caught herself. She dropped her hands into her lap, put on a taut smile and shook her head. "I keep my distance from kids."

"Why? You don't like them?"

"I like them fine—at a distance."

There was that itch again. Jeez, why lie about liking kids? It was about as inconsequential as things got in the bigger scheme of things. About the only time not liking kids mattered would be when she already had them. Otherwise, so what?

Maybe she regretted not having any, so she pretended not to like them. Maybe she *couldn't* have any, so pretending eased the pain. Maybe she had one or two or three, and had lost them for some reason, so it was guilt she was easing.

His wondering was interrupted by the waitress with plates of food. She set them down, then reached for the baby. "Her daddy just came in to get her, so I'll take her now."

"See you, sweetheart," Jace said, brushing a kiss to Liza Beth's forehead before handing her over. The kid didn't want to give up her pacifier, and sucked hard enough to make a *pop* when his finger pulled free. Immediately she screwed up her face as if to cry, then she caught sight of her father and was all smiles again. How could anyone not want to brighten a kid's world like that just by walking into it?

He waited until Cassidy had taken a bite of the chicken-fried steak that was the day's special, then asked, "What made you pick Buffalo Lake for your vacation—uh, work?"

After studying him a moment she levelly replied, "I told you—the book I'm working on takes place here."

"Here, specifically? Or in the general area?"

Her only response was a shrug.

"The state's got some really nice resorts, places where you could find the privacy and quiet you want, along with all the conveniences and a few luxuries…but not around here. I'm having a hard time picturing you sitting in your apartment in Lemon Grove, saying, 'I think I'll rent a run-down cabin on the shore of a small lake no one outside Canyon County, Oklahoma, has even heard of.'"

As he expected, she chose to answer the wrong part of his comment. "The cabin's not run-down. It's rustic."

"You're playing with words."

A smile flashed across her lips, then disappeared. "That's my job."

And his job was finding out the truth...at least, it had been. For the first time since the disciplinary hearing last winter, he was tempted to do a little cop work. As temptations went, though, it was a mild one, just a passing thought that he *could* find out her truth if he wanted. If he cared enough. Since he neither wanted nor cared...

She surprised him when, after a moment of paying proper attention to the potato-and-cheese casserole accompanying the steak, she actually offered him some information. "You're right. I didn't leave Lemon Grove with the intent of coming to Buffalo Lake. I knew I was coming to Oklahoma, but I didn't decide on an exact destination until I got here."

"Why here? Why not Shangri-La or one of the other resorts?"

"Do you know how much rent the Davison family is charging for the cabin? Two hundred bucks a month. Furnished. I can spend six months there for the cost of—what?—maybe a few weeks at one of those resorts. Besides, conveniences and luxuries are just a distraction I don't need."

"That's redundant, isn't it? Or is there a distraction you do need?"

Her face colored, making him wonder if she was remembering Shay calling *him* a distraction. *Wants attention all the time,* she'd said, which wasn't exactly true. He didn't want everyone's attention—just Cassidy's at the moment—and he didn't even want that all the time.

Just more than was wise.

Without waiting for an answer that he really didn't think was forthcoming, he polished off the last bite of his burger, then drained the last of his pop. "What do you do on a hot summer day in Lemon Grove?"

"I sit in my air-conditioned office and work."

"All the time? You don't go to the beach or into the mountains? No drives north to L.A. or south to Tijuana?"

"I'm not an outdoor sort of girl. What can I say? I'm dedicated to my job." That much was one-hundred-percent true, Cassidy reflected. Her job was staying alive, and she was committed to it twenty-four hours a day.

She took one last bite of tender, battered steak, then pushed the plate away. As if alerted by some sixth sense, the waitress immediately appeared. "Did you save room for dessert? Manuel baked up some dewberry cobblers this morning."

Though she didn't know what dewberries were, Cassidy was tempted. "Cobbler" was enough to do that to her. Peach, cherry, blackberry—she wasn't finicky. She loved them all, especially warm from the oven with a scoop or two of vanilla ice cream melting over them. But she'd stuffed herself on chicken-fried steak, potatoes and creamy cucumber salad and didn't have room left for one single berry.

"None for me," she said politely.

"How about a couple servings to go?" Jace suggested, giving the waitress a smile that made her melt like the ice cream Cassidy had been fantasizing about.

While the woman left to get his cobbler, Cassidy let her gaze slide around the restaurant. The fixtures showed a lot of hard wear, much like the customers. Even so, it held a certain homey appeal. It was a place to meet friends, to catch up on news, to enjoy good food at good prices, to connect with other people. Once upon a time she'd had favorite restaurants where she'd been greeted by name, where the waitresses knew her favorite dishes, where she'd connected.

She missed that.

"You ready?"

Refocusing her attention, she saw Jace was holding a foil pan and their ticket and was about to stand. As she slid to her feet and slung her purse over one shoulder, he dropped some ones on the table, then gestured for her to precede him to the cash register near the door. There she withdrew her wallet, but he gave a shake of his head.

"I can pay for my own lunch."

"It was my invitation." He handed a twenty to the waitress, pocketed his change, then followed her outside.

Though the grocery store was only half a block away, they drove. Jace parked in the shade of a huge oak, then glanced back across the street when he got out. "I need to make one stop," he said when she joined him at the back of the truck. "Why don't you go on in, and I'll catch up with you."

"Sure." She was *not* disappointed, she told herself as she crossed the parking lot. She always did her grocery shopping alone and there was no reason to mind it today.

Always shop on a full stomach, her mother preached. The theory, as Cassidy recalled, was that she wouldn't make impulse purchases based on hunger. The downside was that, with her stomach so full, she couldn't work up much enthusiasm for any of the foods available.

It was going to be a salad kind of week, she decided as she gathered the ingredients for chicken salad, pasta salad, garden salad and potato salad. She added a few staples—cereal, milk, ice cream and chocolate—along with a paperback from the limited selection, and was finishing up on the pop-and-potato-chip aisle when a man near the checkout caught her attention. Jace, she thought with a rush of warmth that was more pleasurable than was good for her.

No, not Jace. The clothes were a match, but this man's back was to her and there was no long, silky black ponytail to be seen. His hair was short, as short as hers.

Then he turned, saw her and started toward her.

"You cut your hair," she blurted when he was still fifteen feet away. Damn! As if he hadn't been handsome enough before. He was a dangerous man, she'd decided on their way into town. Now she amended that to *very* dangerous.

He combed his fingers through it, dislodging a few stray hairs. "It's getting too hot to wear it long. I never liked it that way anyway."

"Then why let it get so long?"

"It was easier than getting it cut."

She wanted to ask when he'd last cut it. Back in the winter, she would bet, when he hadn't wanted anyone's attention. What had happened? Had he undergone some personal crisis, been depressed or sick or in trouble?

He would tell her...if she answered all his questions first.

She didn't want to know that badly.

Instead of getting his own shopping cart, he turned hers back from the register and took it—and her by default—on a quick sweep through the store. Though he wasn't working from a list, he knew what items he wanted and in what brands and sizes. He gathered twice the amount of food she had in less than half the time, then steered the cart to the checkout.

The cashier was a pretty woman with auburn hair and a name tag identifying her as Ginger pinned to a snug-fitting T-shirt. "Hi, Jace," she said warmly before turning her attention to Cassidy. Her gaze narrowed and her smile slipped a bit, but when she finally greeted her, it was with almost the same warmth. She rang up Jace's purchases first while a teenage boy in baggy denim shorts sacked them.

"Are you visiting Jace?" she asked as she started on Cassidy's groceries.

Cassidy glanced at Jace, talking football with the bagger and paying them no mind. "No. I'm renting the Davison cabin out at the lake."

"Oh, you're the one—the writer from Alabama." Ginger smiled. "I go out with Buddy Davison from time to time. He mentioned it."

"Actually, it's South Carolina," Cassidy corrected her. *Ask the same question ten times and she would give ten different answers.* That was one of her methods of survival.

"No, I'm pretty sure Buddy said Alabama. He says you write history books."

Had she told Paulette Fox that? Cassidy wondered. Maybe. Hell, she'd told the woman she was from Alabama, when she'd never set foot in the state. She'd gotten in the habit of not paying a great deal of attention to her lies. After all, she was rarely in one place long enough for her untruthfulness to catch up to her, and this place wasn't likely to be any different. "Not history books. Historical novels."

As soon as the words were out she inwardly grimaced. That was dumb. If she knew little about writing books in general, she knew *nothing* about writing historical books. The only history she was intimately familiar with was her own, and it had always been fairly innocuous...until six years ago. *Then* it had gotten interesting. Three years after that it had become movie-of-the-week material. Now it was boring and lonely, but tempered by the certain knowledge that it could all blow up at any moment.

Baseball, her father liked to say, was a game made up of long stretches of tedium broken by brief spurts of excitement. It was an apt description of her life.

"I don't read much," Ginger said, "but I always thought it would be cool to write a book. Of course, I just barely squeaked through senior English, and I don't have a clue what I would write about, and really I don't think I have what it takes. I can't even bring myself to write a letter from time to time, so I think a book is pretty much out of the question."

That was something else Cassidy had learned in her brief "career"—not only was everyone planning to write a book someday, but they equated completing a four-hundred-page novel with writing a one-page letter to Grandma. It was as if they defined *write* in its simplest form—putting words to paper—and never acknowledged the difference between that and telling a logical, compelling, cohesive story.

She had learned the difference all too well in her past few days at the computer.

Ginger read out the total of her purchases and Cassidy handed over three twenties. She glanced up as Jace moved to her side again, but he wasn't looking at her. Instead his gaze was on her open wallet. The wallet where a Wisconsin driver's license was half revealed behind an old photograph. Abruptly she snapped the wallet shut, accepted her change and dropped it, coins and all, into the bottom of her purse.

"See you, Jace," Ginger said, then added to Cassidy, "Nice meeting you."

Cassidy murmured something appropriate—she hoped—then followed the bagger toward the door, Jace right behind her. Her jaw was clenched as she waited for him to say something about the license, but when he finally spoke, the subject was harmless.

"You like to fish?"

The relief that rushed over her was enough to weaken her knees. It must have been the photograph he'd seen and not the driver's license, or surely he would be questioning her about it. He'd never hesitated yet to ask whatever came to mind, and surely a license in a different name from a different state would rouse a curiosity too strong to resist.

"I don't know," she replied, hoping her tone was as casual as the question deserved. "I've never tried."

Naturally that wasn't entirely true.

There had been the time with her dad, when she'd impaled a fish hook in her foot and required a trip to the emergency room to remove it. And the time with her brother, David, when she'd knocked his precious hand-tied lures overboard and he'd tossed her after them. And the time with Phil, trying to impress him by removing the ugly creature she'd caught quite by accident from its hook. It had latched onto her finger the way Liza Beth had claimed Jace's, and in her resulting hysteria, that time it had been Phil who'd gone overboard. Not surprisingly, none of the three had ever invited her fishing again.

"It's not a bad way to spend an afternoon. We'll give it a try sometime...when you don't mind being distracted."

She frowned at him and saw he was giving her a sidelong look and grinning. He was entirely too handsome when he grinned, with all the mischievousness of a boy run wild...and all the sexiness of a man full grown. It made her want to blurt, *How about now?* Thankfully she managed to keep the words inside and politely said, "That sounds like fun."

And for once, she thought as she climbed into the truck and turned the air-conditioner vents her way on full blast, that was the honest truth.

Chapter 4

"You lied to me."

Jace backed away from the door the next afternoon as Neely opened the screen door and walked into the cabin as if she had a right. Technically, since her husband was half owner, she did have that right. He kept backing, not stopping until the sofa was behind him, then folded his arms across his chest and scowled at her. He knew it wasn't a very good scowl— he loved her too much to ever get really annoyed with her— but he pretended anyway. "About what?"

"Your neighbor. You remember, the one who's this tall, round, old enough to be your mother and not your type?" She copied his position, then added a tapping toe to it. "I happened to stop by Shay's yesterday and the waitress said you'd been in for lunch with your new neighbor. Then I went to the grocery store and Ginger said you'd been in there, too. They said she's pretty, blond, about her age, and Ginger said you looked... How did she phrase it?" She raised one hand to tap a fingertip against her chin, then feigned enlightenment. "Smitten. She said you looked smitten with her."

"Smitten. That's a good old-fashioned word. Sounds like something my dad would use, or maybe Uncle Del, but not Ginger. I'm kind of surprised that she even knows it."

The hand belonging to the chin-tapping finger smacked his shoulder lightly. "You must be smitten, or why would you lie to us about her?"

"Why wouldn't I? Jeez, Neely, look at the facts—I took a woman to the grocery store because she'd never been to Heartbreak before and we had lunch while we were in town and now everyone thinks it means I'm hot for her. Under those circumstances, I'd have to be crazy *not* to lie about her."

Her head slightly tilted, she studied him a moment before giving in. "I guess." Then... "*Are* you hot for her?"

Define *hot,* he was tempted to say. But Neely would recognize that for the delaying tactic it was and she would have her answer.

"Okay," he said, sliding out from between her and the sofa and heading for the kitchen. "Yes, she's pretty and blond and young, and yes, I'm...attracted to her." *Attracted* wasn't a word he ordinarily used, but between it, *smitten* and *hot,* it seemed the better choice. "Am I going to sleep with her? Maybe. Am I going to get serious about her? No. No way."

She followed him to the kitchen, accepting one of the diet pops he kept in the refrigerator just for her. "You can't live the rest of your life without a woman just because Amanda did you wrong." She spoke in that sympathetic-but-tough-advice-between-good-friends voice they'd used with each other on more than one occasion. There'd been the time years ago when Reese broke her heart, and the time some lowlife scum had tried to kill her, and when Jace had blown one of the most important cases in his career.

"I appreciate your concern, but, honey, I have no intention of being celibate the rest of my life because of Amanda. She screwed me, just like the department did, but...so what?" It was over and done with—his career as a cop, his relationship with Amanda. All that was left were some good memories, a whole lot of bitterness and a determination that he wouldn't join the crowd and screw himself. No more police work, no more protecting and serving, and no more making commitments to a woman until he was convinced beyond a doubt that *her* commitment equaled or exceeded his own.

"Then bring your neighbor to dinner Saturday night."

He leaned against the counter, his own pop can cold and wet in his hand. "I don't have to prove anything to you, Neely. You're my family, not my conscience."

"Oh, come on. You said you want to go to bed with her. Taking her out for a nice dinner and pleasant conversation can go a long way toward accomplishing that."

"I know better ways to seduce a woman than that," he said scornfully. "Besides, if I decided to go that route, it wouldn't be dinner with family. I'd take her someplace in Tulsa or Oklahoma City and do it right."

Though for someone as alone as Cassidy said she was—no parents, brothers or sisters, aunts, uncles or cousins—family very well might be the way to seduce her. She struck him as the sort who would place a lot of value on family, whether her own or someone else's.

So why didn't she have one? Why hadn't she married some guy with siblings and cousins out the wazoo? Why was she thirty-something and still single?

Not a fair question to ask unless he was also willing to ask its counterpart—why was *he* thirty-something and still single?

Because the department had seen fit to sacrifice him for the greater good. Because Amanda had cared more about the uniform than the man who wore it. Because his job had been the most important part of his life. Now that it was gone, there wasn't much left to take its place.

If he'd put things into perspective sooner, if he'd made time to get married and have a family, would things be better now...or worse? Instead of losing a career and a prospective wife, would he have lost the career plus a wife and kids?

"Earth to Jace. Helloooo."

Slowly his gaze focused on Neely's hand, waving lazily in

front of his face. She was grinning. "Lost somewhere in the thought of seducing Cassidy?"

"Far from it," he said dryly.

"What about dinner tomorrow?"

"Do I have to bring a woman?"

"That's the price of admission."

"Does it have to be Cassidy?"

"I suppose not," she said with an exaggerated put-upon sigh. "If you don't want to bring her, I can always come out here and introduce myself."

His matchmaking cousin alone with Cassidy—not a very comforting thought. Neely would tell everything there was to know about him, from birth right up to the day Cassidy had moved in, only she would make him sound better than he really was. Like a real prize.

He wasn't anyone's prize...except in bed, and he didn't need any help there.

As far as dinner, though... It couldn't hurt, as long as he set up a few ground rules with Neely and Reese first. And who knew? Maybe he could learn something new about Cassidy. After all, the sheriff and the lawyer had almost as much experience getting to the truth as he did. Surely, Cassidy, with her lies and evasiveness, wouldn't stand a chance against the three of them.

He looked at Neely, waiting expectantly as if she knew he couldn't turn her down. And he didn't, at least not flat-out.

"I'll think about it."

And that was how he found himself on his way to Reese's house Saturday evening, with Cassidy sitting quietly across the truck. He figured he'd caught her in a weak moment with the invitation, when the book wasn't going well or the solitude was closing in on her or something. She had automatically turned him down, but there had been such longing in her eyes—the same that had been there when she'd looked at Liza Beth the other day. It hadn't taken much cajoling at all to get her to change her answer, if not her mind.

She wore a dress this evening, pastel flowers that ran together in a swirl of soft color, with no sleeves and a hem that flirted with her calves. Her shoes were sandals, and her toenails were painted pale pink. Dark shades covered half her face and silver bracelets jangled on her wrist when she moved it. Other than that, she wore no jewelry, not even earrings.

She sat primly, legs crossed, hands folded in her lap, gaze on the dirt road ahead. She looked remote, untouchable, yet his fingers itched to do just that. Nothing intimate—just a squeeze of her fingers, a brush along her bare arm. Something to warm her and to remind her that he was there.

As if reading his thoughts, she suddenly looked at him. "Tell me about your cousins."

"You have to be specific, or I could spend the next few days catching you up on their life stories."

She was silent a moment before asking, "How did Reese get to be the sheriff?"

He'd been following in his older cousin's footsteps, Jace thought with a humorless smile. Of course, he couldn't tell her that. Not yet. "He went to college on a baseball scholarship, then got drafted by the Kansas City Royals. He was well on his way to becoming the best pitcher to ever step onto the mound when he injured his shoulder. A couple of surgeries and a lot of physical therapy later, he was looking for a new career."

"So he just said, 'I think I'll be a cop today'?"

Jace shrugged. "He was already used to wearing a uniform. Adding a gun was no big deal."

"And he met his wife through his job?"

Another shrug. "They were both new in town—he'd just joined the department and she'd just passed the bar."

"She defended the people he arrested? Must have been interesting."

"It was, for as long as it lasted. They broke up after a year or so, didn't see each other for nine or ten years, then got back together last year."

What he could see of her expression was thoughtful. Did

she find it odd that after such a long time apart—and she didn't know the half of that—two people could put things back together as good as new? If she'd known Reese and Neely when they'd first gotten together, it wouldn't seem strange at all. In spite of the problems caused by their jobs, they'd been perfect for each other. All those years after they'd separated, Jace had kept in touch with both of them, but he'd never gotten used to the idea of them not being together.

And now they were.

Of course, the romance novelist inside her probably found it too romantic for…well, not for words. As she'd told him at the café, words were her job. She probably never ran out of ways to use them.

Though she could certainly be stingy with them where he was concerned.

"Does she still defend the people he arrests?"

"Sometimes. It's not a problem now, though. He's grown up."

"Did you ever have any desire to be a cop?"

He kept his gaze on the road, though they hadn't passed a single car since leaving the cabins. It wasn't a hard thing to say, *Yeah, sure, I was one for seventeen years*—or at least, it shouldn't be. But it would lead to questions—*What happened, why aren't you still on the job?*—and in some way, it would change the way she looked at him. She could be part of that segment of the population who didn't like cops for whatever reason or, worse, she could be like Amanda, who did like them.

Interchangeably.

If he slept with Cassidy—or if he didn't, for that matter— it would be because it was what they both wanted. Not because he'd once been a cop.

"And give up this life that suits me so well?" he asked, laying on the drawl.

"Oh, yeah, sleeping until noon, fishing when you feel like it, watching the clouds when you don't—the life every young man aspires to."

The faint censure in her voice rankled. "Don't forget working when the mood strikes and being thankful when it doesn't."

A blush crept across her cheeks. "I wasn't criticizing."

"Sounded like it."

"If this lifestyle suits you, it's no one's business but yours."

"I know that. It just didn't sound as if you did." He waited a moment for the barb to sink in, then asked, "Did you ever hold a real job before you started writing?"

"I taught yoga for a while, worked as a secretary and was a salesclerk in a gift shop, a shoe store and a one-hour photo store. I've been a receptionist for a doctors' group, a lawyers' group and a dentist. I worked in a nursery school for a while—" fleeing just before the owner was due to find out that her references were as bogus as she was, Cassidy thought "—and I spent a while longer in a plant nursery. In the past few years, I've done everything but wait tables." And teach school. That was the career she'd trained for. She'd taught fourth grade for four years and loved it.

Then her world had fallen apart.

To be more accurate, Phil had torn it apart.

"So many jobs. Were you looking for new experiences or do you just have a short attention span?"

She laughed at the idea of seeking out new experiences. Not her. She would have been perfectly happy living a perfectly routine life in the town where she'd grown up. A cozy, modest house a few blocks from her parents' home, walking to her job at the elementary school while Phil took the train into the city, home in time to grade papers, go over lesson plans and fix dinner, helping their kids with homework and chores, taking them on an occasional vacation that was educational as well as fun—that was the life she'd wanted. The only new experiences she'd wanted were childbirth and motherhood.

Not widowhood.

Certainly not being constantly on the run.

"That laugh isn't an answer," Jace remarked.

"Maybe I was just lousy at everything I tried, or I lack ambition."

"Speaking as someone who lacks ambition, I doubt that."

She doubted the same about him. There was a lot more to Jace Barnett than met the eye.

Deliberately she turned the subject back to him. "Are you and Reese close?"

"Closer than brothers."

She gazed out the window, recognizing the Rafferty and Harris ranches as they sped past. A few miles down the road was the Stephens' place, owned by Shay Rafferty's parents, and a few miles beyond that was Heartbreak. It was a strange feeling—knowing names, identifying places. Usually she didn't stay in a town long enough to learn more than the most superficial details about it.

"Have you noticed," she began conversationally, "that people say that as if it really means something—about being closer to someone than brothers or sisters? When the truth is, an awful lot of people wouldn't have anything to do with their family if they *weren't* family. If I said I was closer to someone than to my brother, it wouldn't mean anything at all, because I'm not close to my brother at all."

"That makes sense, considering you don't *have* a brother."

"I have one," she responded automatically, then heard her own words and inwardly winced. This was a fine time to tell the truth, she chided herself. If Jace had any questions about her honesty, they were answered now.

But so what? The sooner he found out she was a first-class liar, the better. After all, what could he do about it? Tell his cousin, the sheriff? And what could *he* do? Reese Barnett would have to have a reason for investigating her, and being on shaky footing when it came to separating truth from fiction didn't qualify.

Jace didn't say anything until he'd brought the SUV to a stop at a dusty, faded stop sign. Then he shifted first his gaze, then his head, in her direction. "I thought you were an only child."

She resisted the urge to fidget, to look away guiltily, to blurt out an apology. Instead, just to be perverse, she removed her sunglasses and met his gaze head-on. "No. I said I come from a long line of only children." That was half true. What she'd actually told him was *I'm an only child from a long line of only children.* Better some truth than none at all.

He didn't look convinced. Hopefully he hadn't paid close attention to their conversation that day—after all, they'd just been making small talk, saying nothing important enough for him to remember.

Even though she remembered everything *he'd* said.

"You said you have—"

"No family." Again, partly true. "I haven't seen my brother in years. I don't know what he's doing, whether he's married, how his life is going. I don't even know where he is. He doesn't count as family."

"But you went on to specify no parents, brothers or sisters."

"No, I didn't. I said no parents, no sisters." Those had been lies, too.

"You said—"

"You must have misunderstood."

He gazed at her a long time, the expression in his dark eyes making it obvious he damn well hadn't misunderstood. But instead of forcing the issue, abruptly he looked away, rolled his shoulders as if easing an ache between them, then put the truck into motion again.

The tension in the air was so thick she could cut it with a knife, if she had one available. Slowly, with great deliberation, she put her sunglasses back on, sliding them to the bridge of her nose, turning the world outside a darkened blue-gray version of its real self. She crossed one leg over the other, then crossed her arms across her chest and wondered what the silent man beside her was brooding about. His fingers gripped the steering wheel tightly. His eyes were steely and as cold as stone as the muscle in his jaw twitched, relaxed, twitched again. He looked like some noble warrior, sculpted in hard

marble, his chiseled features smooth and cold yet amazingly
perfect, from the broad forehead to the aquiline nose to the
sensuous lips and the square jaw that bespoke stubbornness.
The soft folds of clothing obscured the hard, muscular planes
of his magnificent body and made her wish for the knowledge
of how he looked unclothed, with nothing but warm, soft,
smooth, bronzed skin stretched over long, solid, powerful mus-
cle and…

Don't even think about that, Cassidy warned. *No, no, no,*
no, no. She wasn't looking for love—or lust—but if she was,
he would definitely be the wrong man.

The dirt road they were following became paved a few
blocks before it reached Heartbreak's Main Street. As Jace
stopped to wait for traffic to pass before turning onto the street,
she spoke. "If your misunderstanding bothers you, you can
forget dinner and take me home. I don't mind either way."

At least, she wouldn't mind *too* much. Granted, once he'd
talked her into coming this evening, she had looked forward
to it. It was such a man/woman thing to do—have dinner with
friends, talk, laugh, return home when the evening was over.
Such a *normal* thing, and she hadn't done normal in more
years than she wanted to remember.

But she could spend the rest of the evening alone. She was
good at it. She could play games on the computer, and when
she got tired of that, she could read or even go outside and sit
near the water in the warm dark evening, listening to crickets
chirp and fish plopping and even wishing on stars. Then she
could go to bed early and cry herself to sleep, because, even
though it didn't happen often anymore, the disappointment and
discouragement could turn her that blue.

He drove several blocks before finally glancing at her. "I
guess I did misunderstand," he said in a voice that made it
clear he knew otherwise. "Besides, I promised you dinner and
entertaining company tonight, and I always keep my promises."

The last words stung, as he'd no doubt intended. She kept
her promises, too, she wanted to protest. She just hadn't made

any since the day she'd promised herself she would do every-thing in her power to keep herself alive and to not get anyone else hurt.

Reese and Neely Barnett lived on the east side of Heart-break. Their house was set off the road between a stand of blackjacks and a big weathered barn, with a manicured lawn bordered by pasture. Horses grazed in the shadow of the barn, glancing up with a marked lack of interest as she and Jace climbed out of the truck.

The house itself was relatively new, a log cabin on the out-side, elegant and homey on the inside. They were met at the door by Reese, who looked nothing like his cousin but had the same easy, friendly manner as Jace. Closer than brothers, Jace had said. Cassidy could see that for herself. The affection between them was obvious, and neither man seemed the least bit uncomfortable with it. David had never been very good at showing affection for anyone other than the then-current woman in his life, and neither had Phil. This was a refreshing change.

Reese led them into the great room that filled the center half of the house. The colors were muted—soft greens, roses, tans and blues—and the furniture was oversize, overstuffed, and great for relaxing in front of the big-screen TV. A stone fire-place filled one wall and large bay windows took up another. A rustic oak table separated the living area from the kitchen, where Neely was restuffing twice-baked potatoes at an elab-orately tiled countertop.

After Jace performed the introductions, Neely smiled. "Cas-sidy McRae...is that a good Irish or Scottish name?"

Cassidy didn't have a clue—she'd picked the name the way she'd picked every name she'd used, made up out of thin air—so she returned the smile and gave a nonanswer. "Yes, it is. I appreciate the invitation to dinner. I've been busy since I moved here, so it's nice to finally get to meet someone. Can I help you with anything?"

"What's up?"
Jace was leaning against the railing on the back deck, a

bottle of water in hand, his gaze on the row of arched windows that looked into the kitchen. He couldn't see much, just occasional glimpses of Cassidy and Neely as they passed a window on the way someplace else, but on a warm night with the sun low on the horizon, steaks cooking on the grill and the occasional nicker of horses behind them, it was enough.

"Nothing's up," he replied, glancing at Reese, who stood in a similar position a few yards away. "My life is normal and routine—"

"—and dull."

Jace shrugged. "What's dull to one man can be satisfying to another."

"What's up with Cassidy?"

"Your wife invited me to dinner, then after she stirred my appetite, she added the stipulation that I had to bring a woman. Since Cassidy was handy…" It was a bad attempt to downplay his interest in his neighbor. Neely wasn't so great in the kitchen that Jace would put himself out to eat her cooking, and Reese knew it. He had come because he wanted to, and he'd brought Cassidy because he wanted to.

"I see she grew a few inches, lost a few pounds and discovered the fountain of youth since we were out at your place Tuesday."

"Yeah, she cleaned up pretty good, didn't she?" Too bad she didn't seem to know the other meaning for clean, as in *coming clean.* He had an excellent memory for details, and he *knew* there had been no misunderstanding about her having a brother, just an outright lie on her part. Why? Whether she had a brother didn't matter to anyone in the world, except maybe the brother himself. Why lie about it? And what else had she lied about? Was she really a writer? Were her parents really dead? Was she really from Lemon Grove?

He could find out. All it would take was one phone call to an old buddy in Kansas City—or hell, one request to Reese. Within twenty-four hours they could tell him everything there was to know about Cassidy McRae.

But he didn't make the request of Reese, and he wouldn't make the phone call. It smacked too much of police work and he wasn't about to get tangled up in that again. Besides, what did it matter that she'd lied about having a brother? And about not liking kids. And had gotten a little shaky on her story of living in Lemon Grove. And was evasive about everything having to do with her work. Maybe she was just a very private person who saw no reason to share any details of her life with someone she'd just met.

More likely she was just one of those people who lied, whether it benefitted them or not, whether it would cause trouble, whether it would be easier to tell the truth. God knew, he'd run into plenty of those folks in his seventeen years in the department. Honesty was the first virtue to make it onto the endangered list. He knew that better than most.

Besides, he'd lied, too, when he'd described her to Reese and Neely. He'd had his reasons, but presumably she did, too. That didn't make him any nobler than her.

"Find out anything about her?" Reese asked.

"What makes you think I'm trying?"

His cousin's only response was a snort.

"Hey, I know all I need to know about her. She's pretty, she's single and she's not going to be around long."

"And that's all that matters?"

"I'm not looking for anything permanent, bubba. What else do you need to know before you sleep with a woman?"

Reese gave him the sort of look his father would have given had he been here. There had been a time when Reese's only real interest in women had been sex, too, but you couldn't tell it from the way he acted these days. Of course, that time had been a *long* time ago—before Neely. It had been a long time ago for Jace, too—before Julie, who'd come before Lisa, who had come before Amanda—but he was looking to get back into that mode. Sex, he could handle. Anything more didn't interest him at the moment.

Reese checked the steaks on the grill, then added one more. Three mediums and one medium-rare coming up. Stepping away from the heat, he took a long swallow from his pop, then asked, "You remember Troy Littlejohn?"

"Graduated the year after us? Smart kid? Lazy as hell?"

Reese nodded. "We busted up a meth lab out at his folks' farm yesterday. His mama was so mad at him, I don't think he would make bail if he could. He's gonna have to find someplace else to live for a while."

"Yeah, like Lexington," Jace said dryly. That was where newly incarcerated guests of the Oklahoma State Department of Corrections went to be processed, evaluated, then assigned to a prison. "You gonna seize the property?"

"Nah. The Littlejohns didn't know what was going on. Their only mistake was treating Troy like family when he'd already proven a few dozen times he didn't deserve it, and there's no crime in that."

A lot of people wouldn't have anything to do with their family if they *weren't* family, Cassidy had said. Jace figured it was true of the Littlejohns. Troy had been nothing but trouble since he'd been old enough to walk, but they'd still let him come around. They owed him. He was *family*. Too bad that sense of obligation hadn't run both ways. Then Troy wouldn't have used his parents' property for his drug manufacturing operation, and they wouldn't have risked losing the land that had provided a living for a hundred years' worth of Littlejohns.

"I always thought Troy was too lazy to get into any serious lawbreaking," Jace remarked as Reese removed the steaks from the grill.

"He had partners. He provided the place and they did the work." Reese turned off the gas to the grill, picked up the serving plate and tongs, then glanced at Jace. "How long did you work drugs?"

"A couple years. Too long." He'd preferred just about every division he'd worked. At least in the others, there was a clear-cut right and wrong, victim and bad guy. In narcotics, like prostitution, the victims were willing and not much, if any, more righteous than the bad guys.

"We're running into more drug cases every week. We could use someone with some experience to help out," Reese said as he opened the back door.

"Advertise," Jace replied sarcastically as he walked inside. "You'll find someone."

"Not for the salary we can pay."

That was no joke. Sheriff's deputies in the majority of Oklahoma's seventy-seven counties were notoriously underpaid and overworked. Most of Reese's deputies were people with solid ties to the community that kept them close to home. The single deputies kept their expenses down, and the married ones could count on their working wives' contributions to make up the shortfall. The only exception was the undersheriff, Brady Marshall, who'd come to Buffalo Plains from Texas, whose family money and wealthy wife—Neely's younger sister, Hallie—made the pay issue a nonissue.

"If I wanted to bust my butt for less than minimum wage, I'd hire on with Dad to run the ranch," Jace remarked.

"You're gonna have to go to work sometime. Your savings aren't gonna last forever."

"No, but it'll last a while longer. Then I'll think about getting a job." But it wouldn't involve carrying a badge and a gun or busting up meth labs. He really would rather take over his folks' ranch or even help out in the garage his dad owned in Buffalo Plains with Reese's dad.

Cassidy and Neely were sitting on opposite sides of the oak table, where four places had been set. A cucumber salad, a towel-wrapped loaf of bread, twice-baked potatoes and ears of early corn filled the center of the table, along with tall glasses of iced tea. Jace took the seat next to Cassidy as Neely fixed her gaze on him.

"What were you two talking about?" she asked.

"Reese was telling me about Troy Littlejohn."

She wrinkled her nose distastefully. "No discussion of my client at the dinner table, okay?"

"You're representing him?" Reese's grimace was distasteful, too, as he sat down. He forked the medium-rare steak across to Jace's plate, then passed the remaining steaks around.

"That must make life interesting," Cassidy remarked.

"Sometimes more than others," Neely replied with a droll smile. "There was a time it was a huge problem, but now we have a few rules. We don't discuss the cases we're both involved in, and whoever's side wins doesn't get to rub it into the loser."

There was more to it than that, Jace knew. Neely was selective about the few criminal cases she voluntarily took on. She had to believe the defendant's claims of innocence or extenuating circumstances, she didn't represent repeat offenders, and she didn't represent men who raped or beat their wives, or anyone who mistreated children.

Of course, those restrictions couldn't be applied to the defendants the court appointed her to represent. He would bet next month's grocery bill that Troy Littlejohn was such a case.

"Not that anyone's asked," Neely went on, "but Cassidy and I were talking about the Founder's Day barbecue next weekend. It's about as much fun as a body can have in Heartbreak, and, Jace, I told her you would prove it by bringing her. We'll meet here around eleven, then drive over together."

He glanced at Cassidy, who seemed to find that cutting her steak required one-hundred-percent of her attention. Even so, a pink tinge crept into her face. "Sure," he agreed. "I was planning on going anyway." Probably. Alone. In the evening, when the carnival atmosphere gave way to a band and dancing. Not that he objected to the idea of spending the better part of another day with Cassidy or showing her what constituted a good time in a tiny place like Heartbreak. Coming from the San Diego metropolitan area, she would probably find it quaint, amusing and ripe for big-city disdain.

As soon as the thought took form, though, he dismissed it. She'd had plenty of chances when they were in town on Thursday to make snide remarks about the shabbiness of the town, but she hadn't said a word. Just because the women he'd brought for a visit—Amanda and, before her, Julie—had scorned his hometown didn't mean Cassidy would. After all, she'd chosen to come here, hadn't she? No one had twisted her arm to get her here and no one was making her stay.

Maybe, because he didn't say anything else on the subject of Founder's Day, it was still on Cassidy's mind when they headed home a few hours later. Little more than a shadow in the dim lights coming from the dash, she kept her gaze directed out the side window as she politely said, "You don't have to take me to the barbecue Saturday. I'm perfectly capable of going on my own. It's just…Neely thinks you need a social life."

"Did she say that?"

She glanced at him then, shaking her head. Her blond hair was a pale tousle of light in the darkness.

"No, she would have been more blunt and said I needed a woman." He did, too. Just not in the way Neely thought. She wanted him happily married and settled down, doing what he did best—being a cop—and raising a family. He wanted sex.

"Would she be right?"

The question surprised him, and not just because there was a sensual, seductive huskiness to her voice. It was a leading question, suggestive for a woman who'd shown little interest in getting close to him, or anyone else.

A glance her way as they reached downtown Heartbreak and the regular illumination of streetlights showed that the question had surprised her, too. He couldn't see for sure that she was blushing, but he would have bet she was—would have bet she wished she could call back the words or, failing that, could brush them off as not even worth a response.

He had a response, all right—one that necessitated turning up the air conditioner a notch and shifting position in the seat. Doing his best to ignore the sudden discomfort, he shrugged and carelessly said, "Man is not meant to sleep alone." Woman, either.

"That sounds like a big yes," she murmured.

And getting bigger with each passing moment.

Since he saw little reason to get hot and hard over a woman

who'd given him zero encouragement so far—reluctantly accepting a few invitations to meals didn't count—he forced his attention back to the subject. "If Neely had given me a chance, I would have asked you to the barbecue myself. There are crafts for sale, games, carnival rides for the kids and plenty of food. It's like going to the fair, only the food's better and you don't have to deal with all the crowds to get to it."

"Sounds nice."

"Nice. Now there's a big endorsement."

She smiled unexpectedly. "Wow, that really sounds great! It'll be so cool! I can hardly wait!"

"Now you sound like Elly Harris. Everything in her world is great and cool and fills her with anticipation." Which wasn't a bad way to live. It beat the hell out of disillusionment and misapprehension.

Apparently, Cassidy felt the same. "I remember a time when my biggest worry was finding the patience to wait. Christmas, birthdays, holidays, vacations—I wanted everything *now*. My mother used to tell me to quit wishing my life away because time passed quickly enough and I'd never be able to get it back. And you know what? She was right. Time does pass quickly, and once it's gone, all you have left are the regrets."

Once again she was gazing out the window, as if they were passing something more interesting than open pasture and clumps of woods. She seemed lost in the past that had gone by too quickly, so unaware of him for the moment that when he spoke, she startled. "What are your regrets?"

She turned away from the scenery, crossed her legs, smoothed her skirt, then shrugged. "The usual." Then she added a less-than-convincing smile. "Everything about me is as usual and normal as can be."

Except that she was about as alone as anyone he'd ever met. And that she was keeping secrets by telling lies.

"I don't know what constitutes 'the usual' in regrets. My regrets are different from Reese's, whose are different from Neely's, whose are different from yours."

Not unexpectedly, she shifted the conversation from herself. "What are your regrets?"

His grin was braced with a cockiness he didn't feel. "I don't have many."

"So what are they?"

He regretted devoting seventeen years of his life to a job, only to be betrayed by the people he answered to. He regretted getting sucked into believing Amanda's sweet lies. No matter how good she was at them, a damn good detective should have suspected *something*. He regretted not having more of a life— getting married somewhere along the way, having kids, non-cop friends, a life that would have been there for him when the department screwed him over.

He didn't offer any of that in response, though. "I regret not becoming an astronaut and living in space with a few pretty Russian *babushkas*. And not joining the Navy and becoming a pilot, going 800 miles per hour with my hair on fire. And not breaking the four-minute mile."

Her snort sounded remarkably like Reese's, despite the fact that she was half his cousin's size and delicate as spun glass. "You never even *tried* to do those things, did you?"

"Only the four-minute mile. But not trying doesn't mean you can't have regrets." For example, if he didn't try to kiss her good-night when they reached her cabin, he would likely regret it when he was alone in his bed and trying to sleep. And if he hadn't done more than just think about sex with her before she packed up and returned to California, he would regret that, too.

"To be an astronaut or a Navy pilot, you need a college degree. Do you ever regret not getting that?"

He gave her a sideways look. "What makes you think I didn't?"

The question, or maybe the sharp undertone, flustered her. "I—I just thought—" She shrugged apologetically. "You said yourself you lacked ambition and worked only part-time as a cowboy. I assumed..."

"What? That I can't get a better job? That I'm stupid, lazy or both?"

She hugged her arms to her chest, the posture looking more defensive than defiant, but said nothing.

"Oklahoma State University. Class of '87."

"Sorry," she murmured.

He forced his fingers to loosen their grip on the steering wheel. She thought he was a dumb, lazy cowboy. A *cowboy,* for God's sake. Even when he'd lived on his folks' ranch, getting up before dawn and working past dusk, dealing with four-legged critters all day, wearing cowboy boots and a cowboy hat as naturally as breathing, he'd never thought of himself as a cowboy. In his very young days, like when he was *eight,* he'd considered himself a rancher in training. By the time he'd turned twelve, he'd changed that to a rancher's son doing what was necessary until he got out on his own. Even when he'd worked for Guthrie Harris and Easy Rafferty this past spring, it hadn't been a job so much as a way to break up the monotony of his days and helping friends who'd needed it.

"I take it from your superior attitude that you went to college, too," he said.

"University of California," she murmured.

"Which one?" When he felt her gaze on him, he glanced her way. She looked as if she'd been caught off guard and didn't quite know what to say, and the itch started again between his shoulder blades.

"Uh...Los Angeles."

Big school. Well-known. Easy name to pull out of thin air, especially for someone living—or claiming to live—in Southern California.

"What was your major?"

"Education."

"You don't like kids so you got a degree to teach them?"

"Maybe," she said primly, "the not-liking-kids came *after* the teaching degree. Besides, teaching doesn't automatically mean kids. There's middle school, high school, college, adult ed...."

"What did you teach?"

"Mostly English and history. No math, though. Creative people often aren't mathematically gifted."

He raised one hand to his back to scratch absently. When he'd asked her about her prewriting career on the way to Reese's, she'd listed everything under the sun *except* teaching. Was she lying then or now?

Damned if he wasn't tempted to find out.

Chapter 5

He parked beside his cottage, the truck's engine coughing spasmodically before sputtering into shuddering silence. The pale thin moonlight gleamed on the silvered wood of the house, hiding the myriad flaws that came from cheap construction, lack of maintenance and old age, giving it a certain charm, a sense of enchantment almost, that was lost in the bright light of day.

The night had a sense of enchantment, as well, the air cool and only faintly moist with humidity, the sky dark and velvety soft, the sounds of the forest muted and peaceful, as if all its inhabitants were settling in for a night's rest. It was the sort of night that made Cassidy want to open her arms wide to embrace it, to slowly twirl in the dew-damp grass in a lazy dance with the sky, the stars and the moon, or to strip off her clothing and dive into the still-warm water of the lake, naked and sleek, just another of its myriad creatures.

What if she did just that? she wondered. What would *he* do? Shake his head at her foolishness and go inside, leaving her to herself? Take a seat in the damp grass and watch? Shuck off his own clothing and join her in the water? And when their limbs grew tired, would he help her out of the water? Would he pull her close and look at her through those midnight-dark, mysterious eyes of his and make heat stir in her belly and dampness pool at the juncture of her thighs as he reached out to caress the firm globe—

"Hey. Are you coming?"

Startled, Cassidy gave a shake of her head to clear it, took in a deep breath, then moved away from the SUV. Jace had parked next to his own cabin and was now waiting to walk her across the footbridge to her house. She went as far as the steps that mounted to the bridge, then turned and faced him, forcing him to stop abruptly to keep from running into her.

"You don't have to walk me to the door."

"I know." But he showed no sign of backing off.

She appreciated the gesture. Her father was a gentlemanly sort who had always required such courtesies of David and, later, Phil. She was comforted by men who opened doors, gave up their seats in crowded places and met a woman at and returned her to her door. Besides, going home alone after dark ranked near the top of her Things I Hate list. She'd left a light burning in the living room, but the reassurance of a lamp was a poor substitute for that of a living, breathing man.

Deciding to be gracious for once, she nodded, then turned again. The boards on the bridge creaked and shifted but held steady under their combined weight. Still, she felt a bubble of relief when her feet were on solid ground again.

A breeze quickened as they climbed the steps onto the deck. She tested the doorknob to make certain it was still locked before fitting the key, then swinging the door open. The lamp illuminated the living room and a good portion of the kitchen and showed nothing out of place. The computer was still turned on, the screen saver adding its own pale light. Her tea glass still sat on the coffee table on a cork coaster, the ice melted and warmed enough to avoid condensation.

The place appeared undisturbed. No one had visited while

she was gone. No one—*please, God*—was lying in wait for her.

She tossed her purse on the sofa before turning to say thanks and good-night to Jace. Without making a sound, he'd moved from the threshold where she'd left him and was standing next to the dining table. He nudged the computer mouse enough to make the screen saver disappear, then studied the photograph that served as wallpaper on the screen. ''Who is this?''

Quickly she crossed to his side, intending to push down the screen. Anticipating that, he stopped her by catching her hand. ''I'm not asking for details. Just generic information. 'This is my sister and her husband'...but you don't have a sister, right? So 'It's my brother and his wife'...but a few days ago you didn't have a brother, either. Maybe they're total strangers whose pictures you got off the Internet and claimed for your own—you know, like keeping the picture that comes in a new frame.''

His fingers were loosely clasped around her hand—long, slender, warm, deceptively gentle. They gave the impression she could pull away with the slightest effort, but she had no doubt she would free herself only if he let her. She suspected he wouldn't do that until she answered his questions, one way or the other. Truth or lie.

''That's me,'' she said, gazing at the photograph. Younger, happier, more innocent, more naive, more trusting—more everything that was good.

Jace looked from her to the screen, then back again, his gaze sharp, shrewd. She had the uncanny certainty that in those few moments, he'd cataloged every difference between her past self and the present. She was ten years younger in the photo and twenty pounds heavier. Her brown hair reached halfway down her back, heavy and smooth, and her eyes— She studied them intensely, wondering if their blue shade was really so noticeable or if it seemed so only because she *knew* they were blue.

She looked so young, so full of hope and expectancy and joy. Exactly the way a woman *should* look on her honeymoon.

The poor fool that she'd been hadn't had a clue about the turns her life would soon take, or she would have run off screaming into the ocean behind her to drown.

"You're prettier now," Jace remarked thoughtfully. "Though I like the brown hair, too."

Despite its throwaway nature, the compliment warmed her more than was reasonable. It had been such a long time since any man had told her she was pretty—since any man had even noticed her as a woman. She'd missed that. Missed the relationship stuff, the someone-to-snuggle-with-on-cold-nights, the comfort of a lazy morning with someone who didn't require conversation, the knowing someone was waiting for her at home and missing her when she was gone.

She *really* missed the sex stuff.

"Who's the guy?"

And she would continue to miss all those things. Because *the guy* was a reminder—to not get involved. To not let anyone into her life. To not risk such sorrow again.

"He's…" Would it be an obvious untruth if she claimed him as her brother? Was there too much affection in the way they looked, the way they touched?

Drawing a breath for courage, she quietly replied, "He was my husband."

Jace's dark gaze cut to her. "But you said—" Then his expression gentled. So did his voice. "He's dead, isn't he?"

Finally she pulled her hand from his, grabbed the mouse and clicked through the steps to shut down the computer. As soon as the screen went dark, she walked into the kitchen, wishing for a good stiff drink, settling for water instead.

It had been stupid to leave that photo on the computer, but in three years, Jace was the first to see it, and she'd thought she needed the reminders. Of course, she hadn't. How could she forget that her husband was dead? That, thanks in part to her, two more people had died? How could she ever forget that people out there wanted her dead, too, and wouldn't hesitate to kill anyone who got in their way?

"What happened?"

She knew from the sound of his voice that Jace was standing at the entrance to the kitchen, blocking the only exit, and she figured from experience that he wasn't about to politely move aside and let her walk away just because she asked. Gripping her water bottle tightly, she turned to face him, the refrigerator at her back, the length of the small kitchen between them, and she formed her words deliberately, harshly. "He was murdered."

His impassive expression didn't change. He didn't look surprised or horrified or shocked. He didn't exclaim, "Oh, my God!" or "I'm sorry" and he didn't drop the subject. He simply, quietly, asked again, "What happened?"

She could refuse to answer on the grounds that it was too upsetting, or she could lie. Telling the truth wasn't an option, and this time, neither was a lie. Creating a lie of this sort would be best done in bright sunlight, when she had things to do or places to go, when she didn't face a long, lonely night of heartache and might-have-beens. She needed strength to lie about Phil's death, and at the moment she was feeling just a tad vulnerable.

"Someone shot him. He died." And she had been on the run ever since.

She shrugged, but there was nothing of the casual fluidity she'd been aiming for in it. The movement was taut, jerky, uncontrolled, and made her feel uncontrolled, as well. "I really can't talk about this right now."

She closed the distance between them, hoping he would move, go home and leave her alone, resigned to the fact that he probably wouldn't. He had more questions than anyone she'd ever known who didn't wear a badge or have a byline in a newspaper.

As she approached, he took a step back, then another. Pivoting on his heel, he headed for the door. "Thanks for having dinner with us this evening. I'll see you later." An instant later the door closed behind him, and an instant after that, the sound of his footsteps faded as he moved from steps to ground.

His giving in so easily and leaving so abruptly took her by

surprise. She stood rooted to the kitchen floor, water bottle still clutched in one hand, and stared at the door. She was relieved, she told herself. Glad he was gone. Glad this long evening was almost over.

But the emotion swirling in her belly and tickling around her spine felt suspiciously like disappointment instead of relief. Had she secretly hoped he would stick around and ask more questions—display more interest? Had she subconsciously wanted to extend their time together, to delay the time when she would be alone—*again*? Had she *wanted* him to coax her into telling him about Phil? Not everything, of course. She couldn't tell anyone everything. But just…what had he called it? Generic information.

Had she wanted, in some dark, lonely, empty place inside, to think he *cared?*

She was as big a fool as the twenty-one-year-old bride on the computer screen. The last thing she needed in her life was to confide even generic information to anyone, and the last thing she could have in her life was caring. Not unless she wanted more deaths on her conscience…including her own.

After an hour or so—more likely, a few minutes—she forced herself one step at a time into her nightly routine. Lock the door. Retrieve her book and glasses from the coffee table. Shut off the lamp. Brush her teeth. Wash her face. Change into her cotton gown. Remove the contacts that turned her blue eyes brown. Open the windows.

Before lying down, she slid one hand under the edge of the mattress, made contact with the items hidden there, then crawled into bed. She stuffed the pillows behind her back, then tried to get involved with the book, but it was tough to get swept away to 1812 England when her attention kept wandering across the inlet.

Finally she set aside the book and the glasses and shut off the light. She curled up underneath the sheet and pretended, as she had for years, that it was just the normal end to another normal day, that tomorrow would be just one more normal day with one more normal end. It was how she made it through. Pretending. Faking. Lying.

It wasn't much of a life, but it beat the alternative.

Tired but unable to sleep, Jace shut off the television at two-fifteen and booted up the computer in his bedroom. When he turned on his cell phone, the message flashed that he had new voice mail, but he made no effort to retrieve it. The only people he wanted to talk with knew where to find him and knew he wouldn't bother with his messages. Everybody else could go to hell.

He connected the phone and the laptop, then signed on to the Internet. He had e-mail, too, which he also ignored in favor of typing a name into his favorite search engine. *Cassidy McRae.* He wasn't sure what he wanted to find—truth, he guessed. A mention on some book review site, a newspaper article about her husband's murder, something connecting her to UCLA or Lemon Grove.

He didn't find anything of the sort in the handful of entries that popped up.

Okay. If she wrote under a pen name, maybe she'd managed to keep her real name so private that none of the book sites associated it with her. So to find out her pen name…he did a search of the Library of Congress Copyright Records and came up empty. Either she had incorporated her writing career under a name other than her own or she'd never registered a copyright.

He wasn't up on copyright law—those were federal statutes enforced by federal agents—but he supposed it was possible she'd chosen not to register her copyrights. As far as he knew, it was an option, not a requirement, though he didn't understand why an author would decide against it, since it was for the writer's own protection.

It was little time spent, but all of it wasted. There was no telephone listing, no address information at all. He couldn't check UCLA's alumni list for her without calling the registrar's office, which would have to wait until Monday. Though the search didn't turn up a single news article about her, the list of free searchable newspaper archives was far from extensive. It looked as if he would have to call an old cop buddy who was now an FBI agent and had access to the Lexis-Nexis database. If it didn't have anything on her, she didn't exist.

He' smiled faintly as he signed off. She existed, all right, though possibly not in the world she claimed as her own. Dissatisfied with her real life, she could have created an entire fantasy life, from the career to impress people to the murdered husband to gain sympathy. It was entirely possible that not one single thing about the woman next door was real.

Except the fact that he wanted her. Whether she was who or what she said.

Was that proof of what an attractive woman she was? he wondered.

Or how boring and empty his life had become?

Sunday morning Cassidy watched out the kitchen window as Jace putted past in his boat, the space beside him filled with a rod and reel and a tackle box. Remembering his offer—*We'll give it a try sometime when you don't mind being distracted*—she sighed heavily. She would have appreciated a distraction this morning to drag her away from the computer and the old memories trying to escape through her fingertips onto the screen.

After refilling her glass with peach-flavored tea, she returned to the table, sat and read what she'd written.

Like so many brides, my wedding day truly was the happiest of my life. If I'd had any hint how thoroughly the mere exchanging of I do*s would change my life, that it would lead to betrayal, death, deception and heartbreak, would I have gone through with the ceremony?*

She wished like hell she could say no, that she would have kissed Phil goodbye, mourned him for a while, then gotten on with her life. She just couldn't be sure it was true. She had *loved* him—truly, committedly, permanently. Didn't the past prove that?

But she'd hated what he'd done to her—the danger he'd put them in, the unbearable situation she found herself in after his death. If only he hadn't died...if only he'd taken her advice...if only he'd admitted just once that his judgment was flawed....

She could spend the rest of her life lamenting *if only*s, but it wouldn't change anything. It wouldn't magically solve her problems and put her life back to normal. Nothing would, short of a miracle.

She positioned her fingers on the keyboard, smiling faintly. When she'd learned to type back in ninth grade, she'd thought she would use the skill only to get through school, typing reports and papers. What use did a fourth-grade teacher have for typing, beyond occasional letters? She'd never imagined that someday she would use her less-than-competent typing abilities to write her life story. Hell, she'd never imagined she would even *have* a life story.

But here she was, doing just that. Even if no one ever read it, she would feel better for doing it.

She passed the next few hours typing, getting lost in the memories, then typing again. When she heard a boat approaching, she glanced at the clock, realized it was past lunchtime, then went to the kitchen to find some food. Not to watch as Jace steered the boat toward his cabin.

There was no dock or beach over there. He pointed the nose toward a grassy spot, increased the power and ran the front half of the boat onto the shore before cutting the engine. Once he climbed out, he dragged the boat a few feet farther onto land, then picked up his tackle box, a string of fish and his pole and turned.

For a moment he looked toward her cabin, forcing Cassidy to automatically take a step back. She couldn't begin to guess whether he could see her through the window at that distance, but if he could, she didn't want him to think she had nothing better to do than to watch him.

Though watching him was certainly a pleasant distraction. Today he wore ragged denim cutoffs that made his legs look ten miles long and a white T-shirt that fitted snugly and all but gleamed against the dark bronze of his skin. The Royals baseball cap looked as if it had survived a few dunks in the lake as well as a few close encounters with the ground. It hid his eyes and nose in shadow, but revealed the thin, flat set of his mouth and the strong, square lines of his jaw.

He had the long, lean look and the grace of a runner, but she had yet to see him do anything so physical. He was probably one of those lucky few blessed with a great body by nature and not through his own hard work. Phil had been like that, too, eating everything he wanted, sitting behind a desk all day, but never losing the muscles he'd earned as a high-school football player. Her brother, David, on the other hand, had the tendency to go soft if he slacked off on his workouts even occasionally.

As Jace disappeared inside his cabin, she turned away to the cabinet where she stored the canned and boxed food, taking down a package of pasta and jars of artichoke hearts, olives and pimientos. She didn't even know where David was, she'd told Jace the night before, but that wasn't true. She hadn't spoken to him for six years, and the last time they'd talked had ended in a terrible argument, but she knew right down to the street and number where he was living. She knew the phone number, too, though she'd never dialed it.

Some days she wanted to so desperately she could hardly stand it. But she did stand it. She held off, stayed strong and made it past one more temptation.

But it got harder every time.

The pasta was cooking on the stove, the artichokes and pimientos waiting in a bowl, the olives draining in a colander and awaiting chopping, when a knock sounded at the door. Jace, she thought, her pulse quickening. She popped an olive into her mouth, wiped her hands on a towel and headed for the door. On the way, she closed the file she'd been working on, hesitated at the sight of her honeymoon picture, then shut down the computer.

She expected her neighbor to greet her with a fish or, at

least, an invitation to a fish luncheon. Instead, she found his cousin and another woman on the deck.

"Hi, Cassidy." Neely Barnett gave her an easy smile. "I hope we're not interrupting your work."

"Uh, no, I was just…fixing lunch."

"Good. We came to see if we could entice you into coming to an organizational luncheon for the Founder's Day barbecue. It's at Olivia Harris's house, and it would be a perfect opportunity for you to meet most of the younger women in Heartbreak."

The blond woman beside Neely made a face. "Don't be fooled," she warned good-naturedly. "Bribing you with great company and better food is Neely's way of persuading you to volunteer for an hour or three or five Saturday. She's in charge of finding enough volunteers and she's running short this year."

Neely elbowed her. "Hush, Hallie, she's not supposed to know that until it's too late to say no. By the way, this is my sister, Hallie Marshall. She lives in Buffalo Plains with her husband, Brady, and my two gorgeous nieces. Hallie, Cassidy McRae, novelist and friend of Jace."

Interesting introduction, Cassidy thought. Though *novelist* was supposed to be the part that impressed, she suspected *friend of Jace* carried more weight with the blonde. As she murmured something appropriate, she tried to think of a way to politely turn down both the invitation and the unasked request for her time Saturday. Going to the celebration was one thing. Having to deal with the people there was another entirely.

But it was hard to turn down the offer of pleasant company, especially friendly women. She'd had girlfriends before things got shot to hell, close friends with whom she'd shared practically every intimate detail of her life until six years ago. She missed the companionship, the closeness, the laughter, the having-someone-to-turn-to. She couldn't replace those things with Neely Barnett, Hallie or their friends—couldn't let them into her life for their safety or her own sanity—but oh, she

96 One True Thing

was tempted, and after a day spent so far remembering better times, she was weak.

"You really don't have to volunteer," Neely said. "We'd love to have you come with us anyway. The meeting part will be over in no time and then it's just a big, friendly ladies-only party."

How close could she get to a group of women in only a few hours? How much danger could she put them in, when she'd been relatively safe herself for the past eleven months?

"Let me put a few things away," she said at last, stepping back so they could come inside. While they waited in the living room, she drained the pasta, dumped it and the olives into the big bowl and snapped a lid on it, then put it in the refrigerator. She took a few minutes more to change into navy shorts and a red-and-white top, to touch up her makeup and run a brush through her hair, then returned to the living room.

After locking up, she followed the two women to the car parked beside hers—a sleek little convertible with the top down. So much for the brush through her hair.

"Hey, Jace," Neely called, drawing Cassidy's attention to the cabin she'd been deliberately ignoring.

"Hey, Jace," Hallie added as she slid behind the steering wheel.

He was sitting on the deck, his chair shaded by the overhang of the roof, his feet propped up on another chair. "Neely. Hallie." He waited a moment before adding, "Cassidy."

Her smile of acknowledgment felt more like a grimace.

"Where are you guys off to?"

"The Harrises' house. We're having a Founder's Day committee meeting," Neely replied, stepping easily into the back seat. "Hey, call your mother. She's wondering about you."

He raised a hand, but said nothing else. Instead he watched as Cassidy slid into the passenger seat and buckled her seat belt. She felt his gaze, narrow and intense, until they rounded the first curve. Why intense? she wondered. Because he believed/suspected/knew she'd lied to him? And why that definite pause before speaking to her, as if…as if he hadn't *wanted* to acknowledge her but felt he'd had no choice?

With some effort, she put him out of her mind and focused instead on the two sisters. Conversation was difficult with the wind rushing around them, snatching away every other word, but she'd learned one thing by the time they'd parked behind a row of cars at the Harris house. She could like Neely and Hallie…a *lot.* More than was safe. She should keep her distance, should come up with some excuse to return to the cabin right away and refuse any further contact with them.

Unfortunately, doing what she *should* didn't always come easily to her. For months at a time, she did exactly that, no matter how hard, but then the time came when she *had* to do something to satisfy the emptiness inside her or go nuts. This, apparently, was one of those times.

The Harris house was like countless others she'd seen in her travels—average size, two stories, white with dark green trim, a porch stretching across the front with rockers and a swing for enjoying cool evenings. It sat in the center of a large yard with trees for climbing for the tomboy daughter and plenty of shaded grass for being prissy for her twin, and the usual outbuildings in the back. A half dozen horses were lazing near the barn, but there was no sight of the cattle Guthrie Harris raised.

Cassidy trailed up the steps behind Neely and Hallie, breathing deeply of the warm, flower-scented air. It was a perfect day for being lazy, warm enough to sap a person's energy but not so warm that resting in a shady spot with a bit of a breeze was uncomfortable. That was exactly what Emma Harris was doing. Wearing a chambray sundress, with her long hair pulled back in a French braid, she sat primly on the porch swing, a book open in her lap and a well-loved doll beside her.

"Hey, Miss Neely, Miss Hallie," she greeted in her little-girl-soft voice.

"Hey, Miss Emma," Hallie responded. "What are you doing out here?"

"There's too much noise inside and all the babies are asleep, so I come out here to read." Emma glanced curiously at Cassidy before turning back to Hallie to hopefully ask, "Did you bring Brynn?"

"No, hon, she stayed home with her daddy and Lexy. Sweetie, say hello to Cassidy."

"Hey, Miss Cassidy."

"Hi, Emma. It's nice to meet you."

"Likewise," the girl said, sounding for all the world as if she were forty-eight instead of closer to eight. "You'd better go on in or the food'll all be gone. Daddy says no one can cook like these women, which is a good thing because no one can eat like 'em, either."

"See you, Emma," Neely called as she reached for the doorknob.

Just as she touched it, the door flew open and Emma's twin screeched to a surprised stop. "Hey! What're you doin' standin' out here? The food and the air conditionin' are inside."

This time Neely performed the introductions. Instead of a prim, *Hey, Miss Cassidy,* Elly Harris strode forward and stuck out her hand. "Howdy. Pleased to meetcha, ma'am," she said in a bad movie cowboy parody, even going so far as to tip her cowboy hat before plopping beside Emma on the swing.

"Pleased to meet you, too, partner," Cassidy said.

It was a curious experience, seeing the two of them side-by-side, so very much alike and yet so very different. They had the same bodies, the same faces, but where Emma's pale brown hair was elegantly braided, Elly's was cut short and stuck out from under her cowboy hat as if she'd grabbed the business end of a cattle prod. Where Emma's sundress was neat and unwrinkled, Elly's purple denim shorts and lime-green T-shirt looked as if she'd dug them from the bottom of the laundry basket and clashed almost painfully with her yellow socks and red tennis shoes. The tan hat was the only thing that didn't make Cassidy's eyes hurt to look at it.

They were adorable, and the sight of them together stirred a longing deep inside that Cassidy hadn't let herself feel in more months than she could remember. She was grateful when Neely led the way inside the house and the closed door blocked her view of them. She could come here, she counseled herself as she followed Neely and Hallie into the living room. She could spend time with these people and treasure every moment of it. She could envy their normal lives, their husbands, their friends and especially their children.

And then she could go back to her own life, because she couldn't be a part of theirs. She couldn't be their friend, couldn't pretend for even an instant that she was like them in any way. She couldn't have what they had.

No matter how desperately she wanted it.

Chapter 6

Around noon Monday, Jace picked up the phone to call the registrar's office at the University of California at Los Angeles. He didn't get past the area code before disconnecting. He made it as far as looking up the number for the Kansas City FBI office, but stopped there. He already knew honesty wasn't Cassidy's strong suit. Did he really need proof?

Besides, what would knowing accomplish? Finding out that she'd never graduated from UCLA wouldn't tell him why she'd lied about it. Ditto for finding out that she didn't live in Lemon Grove. As for the details of her husband's death...okay, so he was curious, but he didn't need to know the facts. Deep inside, he didn't *want* to know. Didn't want to be touched even peripherally by the effects of violent crime. Didn't want to feel obligated to somehow help her, to make things right for her. Yeah, it sounded selfish as hell, but hey, he could *be* selfish. He wasn't a public servant anymore. He could stand by and do nothing, and not be responsible.

Besides, the whole process of checking out her story smacked entirely too much of an investigation, and he was out of that. He fully intended to *stay* out of that, so much so that he'd rather have suspicions about her than proof.

Though, for a man who'd spent his entire adult life seeking out proof, settling for suspicions was a difficult thing.

On Tuesday he took half a dozen frozen perch to his mother, deflected her questions about his new neighbor and returned home with two brown paper bags filled with frozen casseroles.

On Wednesday he went to Tulsa, for no reason other than to get away from the cabin. He ate lunch, saw a movie and passed an hour or two in a bookstore before returning home.

On Thursday he took the john boat to the northernmost point on the lake where his uncle Ronald lived, borrowed his Jet Ski and spent the next few hours with the wind in his hair, working muscles he hadn't used in too long, pretending to enjoy the laziness of the day.

On Friday he did nothing.

Unless watching Cassidy's cabin counted.

And on Saturday he talked himself out of taking off for Tulsa again. In the past six days he'd caught only glimpses of Cassidy, and he was fine with that. He didn't miss her at all. Didn't consider crossing the bridge and knocking at her door just to see her up close, to hear her voice, to smell her subtle fragrance. He didn't even think about her…much. She wasn't the least bit important, which made it all right, therefore, to spend more time with her.

When he pulled into the clearing in front of her cabin shortly after ten o'clock, the passenger-side door of her car stood open and she was on her way down the steps with a plastic-wrapped plate in both hands. She stopped abruptly, pink tinting her cheeks as a guilty look spread across her face. As soon as it formed, she wiped it away, then continued toward her car.

He shifted into Park, climbed out and folded his arms across his chest as he leaned against the fender. "Sneaking off without me?"

If her hands hadn't been full, she would have shrugged carelessly. As it was, only her shoulders lifted. "I'm walking upright in broad daylight. How does that qualify as sneaking?"

"We had a—" *Date,* he'd been about to say, but it was the wrong choice, implied the wrong thing. "An agreement, remember? I would pick you up, and we would meet Reese and Neely at their place at eleven?"

"I remember. I just wasn't sure you did. You've been keeping your distance this week."

"I thought that was what you wanted." Not, he admitted grimly, that his decision had had anything to with what *she* wanted. His only priority these days was to look out for himself. If Cassidy had any needs that were sexual in nature, he would be happy to volunteer. Anything else, though, and she was out of luck, at least with him.

She looked as if she knew that what she wanted had played little part in his decision, but she didn't press the issue. Instead she shifted the plate to one hand, then tucked a strand of hair behind her ear. "I told you last week this isn't necessary. I'm perfectly capable of going by myself. That's how I do most things."

Sounds lonely, he thought, but caught himself before saying so out loud. "It's pointless for both of us to drive into town in our own cars when we can go together. Besides, if I show up without you, I'll get the third degree from Neely, and I try to avoid that when I can."

For a moment her face tightened—because he'd made it sound as if his only interest in taking her was to appease his cousin?—then she shrugged. She scooped her purse off the front seat and slammed the door before walking around to the opposite side of his truck.

Now that he had her in the truck, he didn't know what to say to her, so he settled for silence instead, filled only by the music from the stereo. The CD was one of his favorites—an old Trisha Yearwood—but it seemed to only increase the stiffness that held Cassidy upright in her seat.

"You don't like country music?"

"Not so anyone would notice."

He pressed the button that switched the stereo from CD player to radio. More country music spilled out of the speakers before he turned it down a few notches. "What do you like?"

"A little of everything, except country. And classical. And rap. And bluegrass. And I'm not fond of—"

"Whoa. You can't say you like everything, then make all those exceptions. About all you've left is rock, jazz and blues."

"Exactly." Her smile was all the brighter for being unexpected. She'd been so pissy this morning that he'd figured they were in for one long and uneasy day...unless he chose to charm her out of her wary mood, and he wasn't sure at the moment that fit in the category of *looking out for himself.*

He gestured toward the stereo, giving her permission to find her own station, then pretended to watch the road while watching her from the corner of his eye. She leaned forward, pressing the scan button, letting it slide through five or six stations before stopping it on a Tulsa oldies station. She didn't turn the volume up, though, but left it at background level as she settled back in the seat.

"How was the meeting Sunday?"

"Fine." She glanced at him. "Did you tell them to invite me?"

"*Me* tell Neely and Hallie what to do? Their husbands barely get away with that...sometimes. They're strong-minded—and friendly—women."

"I like them. I liked everyone."

She sounded...not surprised. Wistful. Did she have any friends back home, wherever that might be? He imagined, working alone and at home as she did, making friends could be tough. Where was she likely to meet anyone? At the bookstore? The grocery store? Maybe the office supply store? Of course, there was the Internet, with support groups and special interest loops for every subject under the sun, but virtual friends couldn't meet you for a margarita at the local Mexican restaurant.

"Folks around here are easy to like," he remarked as if he

hadn't taken a brief detour into feeling sorry for her. "Most of them, at least. Be wary of any females you meet today with the last name of Taylor, though. Inez, her daughter, Chris, and her sister are the self-appointed arbiters of taste and propriety around here, and they love to sharpen their tongues on the unsuspecting."

"Every town has someone like that. Back home it was this woman named Mardelle Simpson. My father called her a viper and my mother referred to her as 'that woman.' She could broadcast gossip up the entire east coast faster than the airwaves."

That damned prickle down his spine came again. "I thought you were from California."

Her cheeks turned pink again. For a woman who liked to lie, it was a shame her involuntary blush response betrayed her so often. "I live there now. I'm from... Virginia."

"Can I give you some advice?" he offered, deliberately keeping his tone conversational. "Don't hesitate when you're about to tell a lie. You shouldn't have to think about where you're from, so it's like waving a red flag."

Now the pink turned deep crimson and her fingers knotted together in her lap.

He continued as if they were discussing something as unimportant as the weather. "Why lie about it anyway? You don't live there now, and naming the state doesn't narrow it down much. Most of them are big places. Why bother with a lie?"

"I have my reasons," she said stiffly.

Like maybe she suffered from some psychiatric disorder characterized by the compulsion to lie. Or maybe she was wanted back there in some East Coast state other than Virginia. Maybe she'd been a witness to her husband's murder— if there had been a murder, if there had been a husband—or maybe she was the one who had killed him. Maybe he was alive and well and looking for her as they spoke. Maybe she'd stolen from him, or hidden his kid, then disappeared, or his favorite form of entertainment had been knocking her around.

He knew too well from the domestic cases he'd worked that abusive men hated losing their victims.

All those *maybe*s added up to one thing—trouble. She was trouble in its most dangerous form—walking, talking, smiling. Sweet, delicate, pretty, tempting.

So tempting he was at risk of forgetting that he'd sworn off trouble for good.

Rolling his shoulders to ease the tension there, he changed the subject to one that hopefully couldn't lead them into unstable territory. "Did your research into the area tell you how Heartbreak got its name?"

She shook her head.

"In the early 1900s, there was nothing around here but a few cattle ranches and some oil fields until an oil man by the name of Philbert Stephens—Shay Rafferty's great-great-grandfather—turned it all into a town, named Flora in honor of ol' Bert's fiancée. Once he'd made his fortune and built a grand house, he brought Flora out from South Carolina for the wedding. She took one look around and decided no way was she going to live in such an uncivilized place and hightailed it back East, breaking Bert's heart in the process. The townsfolk, who were none too fond of the name to start with, renamed it Heartbreak to commemorate the event."

"Poor Bert had to live with that reminder the rest of his life, huh?"

"Nah, he got over it pretty quick. He married three times, produced fourteen children and died at the ripe old age of eighty-three."

"So his heartbreak was short-lived but the name stuck anyway. I would have called it *Heartbroke,* though. It sounds more Oklahoma-y and cowboyish and small-townish. Isn't there a country song about being heartbroke?"

"Only about a million," he said with a snort. "If you listened to the music instead of turning your nose up at it, you'd know that."

"I don't turn my nose up at it. I'm not a snob."

Again he snorted. "You're the one who assumed I didn't go to college because I'm a dumb, lazy cowboy."

"I didn't—!" She cut off the protest with a deep breath. "I never said you were dumb or lazy, though I plead guilty to calling you a cowboy."

"You said I lack ambition." He baited her.

"*You* said it first. You're obviously very intelligent, and God knows, you've got enough curiosity for any ten people. And as for being lazy..." She opened her mouth a time or two, but found nothing to say. As he broke into laughter, she clamped it shut.

"Okay. We'll strike the *dumb,* disagree about the *cowboy* and ignore the *lazy.*" Immediately, though, he disregarded his own words. "I'm not really lazy. These past few months I've just been..."

"Recuperating?" she suggested when he fell silent.

He gave her a sharp look. "What makes you think that?"

She responded with a shrug. "You're obviously intelligent. You haven't isolated yourself out there at the lake for nothing, and you're obviously not a loner by nature. Presumably you're out there for a reason, presumably getting over something that happened, presumably last winter."

He remembered the curiosity she'd shown at Shay's café when the past winter had come up in the conversation. *You answer all my questions,* he'd told her, *and I'll answer yours.*

Neither of them had gone for it.

"Is this a writer thing—observing people, analyzing them?"

The mention of her work had the desired effect—made her back off. She gazed out the window, realized they were approaching Reese's driveway and said with fake cheer, "Saved from having to change the subject *again,* aren't we?"

For the moment, he thought as he turned into the drive. But maybe not much longer.

The Founder's Day celebration was held in a small park bordered with woods on one side, baseball fields on another and tennis courts on the third. The street on the fourth side was clogged with cars on both sides, which Reese drove past to the park entrance. Being the sheriff and on duty entitled him to a space near the center of activity, Cassidy assumed as they climbed out of his SUV.

Neely, in her sleeveless cotton dress with its muted floral print, fit in perfectly with the women in the park. Except for Reese and the half dozen deputies wearing the Canyon County Sheriff's Department uniform, most of the men wore jeans and work shirts, the majority of them with gimme caps or straw cowboy hats. Cassidy and Jace, each in tailored shorts, a T-shirt for her, a polo shirt for him, looked like tourists who'd taken a wrong turn somewhere. He didn't seem to notice, though, and she…well, she was accustomed to being the odd one out.

Without today's festival, the park would have little to offer in terms of entertainment. There were a few picnic tables scattered around beneath giant oaks, two swing sets that were each missing one or more swings, a merry-go-round and a teeter-totter with the ground worn away underneath in such a way that it would turn to mud when it rained. Mostly there was grass, lots of it, nowhere near manicured but mowed, and lots of big, shady trees. For imaginative kids who made their own fun, it was a great place. For kids who relied on structure and guidance, it wasn't.

Today, though, there was plenty to do. Grills and smokers were set up to one side to provide the barbecue, and flanking them, long tables groaned under the weight of the accompaniments. They headed that way first, to drop off Neely's and Cassidy's contributions to the meal—a large container of tabouli from Neely and Cassidy's own favorite cream cheese/caramel/pumpkin spice cake. Then they strolled toward the booths that faced each other across a wide, grassy aisle, the women leading, the men following.

''Are you a crafty person?'' Neely asked as they stopped to examine the items at the first booth.

Cassidy glanced up sharply, feeling the sting of the question, only to find the other woman holding up an adorable hand-painted flower pot. "Oh…uh, no. I'm not."

"Me, either. I look at these things and think, 'I can do that.' It's just a clay pot, some paints and some sponges. But either I never try, or if I do, it turns out awful. I have no artistic sense whatsoever."

"Me, neither," Cassidy murmured as she returned her gaze to the display of goods. She wouldn't have been so quick to read Neely wrong if Jace hadn't so casually confronted her on her propensity to lie—and to do so badly, in his opinion. She didn't care if she was a bad liar—preferred it, in fact. She rarely stuck around long enough for people to realize how seldom she told the truth, and even if they did realize it, so what? They could either live with it or keep their distance. Whichever they chose didn't matter to her.

Those options were open to Jace, as well, and his choice didn't matter, either.

Not very much.

They examined jewelry, ceramics and paintings on every surface imaginable. There were myriad angels and puppy dogs, cow-spotted foot stools and chairs and pot holders, horsey things, toys and dolls. There were dozens of things she was tempted to buy, but in the end she didn't open her purse for any of it. If she had a home of her own, that would be one thing, but there was no point when she might have to flee on a moment's notice. Given five minutes to load her car and hit the road, she would grab clothing and her computer, not a cow foot stool or a whimsically decorated wicker basket.

Though some part of her yearned for those meaningless decorations to clutter up her life. More accurately, she yearned for the sort of life that allowed for decorative clutter.

"Are you normally this controlled when you shop?"

She glanced over her shoulder at Jace, who was standing close behind her, while Neely debated the choices for a gift for her mother. "I can spend money with the best of them."

"But not on handmade crap like this?"

Her gaze narrowed as she moved away from the booth and

strolled past the next one, a fish-to-win-a-goldfish game, to the one beyond that. "I like handmade stuff." Then she glanced at the Southern belle dolls, their long crocheted skirts concealing toilet paper rolls or tissue boxes, and amended that. "A lot of it, at least. But I have to make room in the car for anything I buy, and then I have to find room for it in my apartment when I get home. So, yes, I tend to restrain my buying impulses."

She picked up a carved wooden bowl, little bigger than her fist, and ran her fingers over its smooth surface. "I take it other women you've brought—" No, bad choice of words. That implied an invitation supported by a desire to share her company. Though he'd claimed he would have invited her given the chance, the fact was, Neely's order had taken away his choice. "The other women who have accompanied you to these events haven't been as appreciative of the selection."

"What makes you think I've brought other women?"

"I assume previous experiences are causing you to expect the worst of me, or maybe you're still laboring under the delusion that I'm a snob." She gave the delicate bowl one final caress before regretfully replacing it. It was gorgeous, but thirty-five dollars for a bowl whose sole function was to be gorgeous was a bit pricey for her. And that—money—was the real reason behind her restraint. She had a nice little stash, thanks to Phil, but who knew when she might need it? When she might regret every penny she'd spent on nonessentials?

She turned to leave the booth for the one across the aisle, but paused a moment, facing him. "Or maybe you're just determined to be mean to me," she remarked before taking advantage of a break in the crowd to reach the other booth.

The booth was being run by Olivia Harris, a true Southern belle who'd planted her roots in Heartbreak. At the organizational meeting, Neely had given Cassidy the short version of Olivia's history—finding herself flat broke after her husband's death, forced to uproot her daughters to move halfway across the country, making a new life for herself on the Harris ranch, marrying Guthrie, giving him two sons in addition to the twins and living happily-ever-after. She was lovely, serene, the easy, drawling way she talked matching the easy womanly way she moved. She greeted Cassidy as if they were really friends, making her wish fervently they were, making her wonder how foolish it would be to pretend, just for a while.

They'd chatted for several minutes before Jace joined her. "I haven't been mean to you," he announced defensively.

She responded with a sniff and started to move on, but he caught her arm. "You were right. When I brought Julie to the barbecue a few years ago, she was condescending and rude. She called all these people hayseeds and made fun of the crafts and criticized the food and insulted just about everyone she met, thinking her put-downs were so clever and they were too stupid to recognize them. And when Amanda spent last Thanksgiving with us, she said she'd come and done what was expected of her, and I'd better not ever ask her to do it again."

Julie and Amanda, Cassidy mused. So that was his type— shallow, none too bright, wrongly convinced of their own superiority. Beautiful, for sure, and probably city girls, with that disdain so many city dwellers felt for small towns.

Where had Jace hooked up with two city girls? Did he seek his fun in Tulsa or Oklahoma City, only an hour or so to the east or west? Or had he lived someplace else and neglected to mention it?

Gee, wouldn't that be a surprise? she thought dryly, considering all the little things *she'd* neglected to mention.

"Julie and Amanda." She couldn't resist shading the names with a bit of her own smug superiority. "Let me guess—tall, anorexic, beautiful, IQs smaller than their bust sizes, sexy, great in bed, material girls. Am I right?"

He looked rueful. "Close enough."

"You have lousy taste in women."

His fingers tightened around her hand. "It's improving."

Her breath caught in her chest and her skin warmed as if someone had turned the sun overhead to full strength. He didn't mean anything by that, she warned herself. *Couldn't* mean anything. He valued honesty in a relationship, and knew she was nothing but lies. He was a laid-back sort, while danger followed wherever she went. He was home, and she had no home.

No home. No permanence. No family. No friends. No kind of life.

Gently she pulled free of him, called goodbye to Olivia, then resumed her browsing. She was acutely aware of him right behind her, but he did nothing to force her attention to him and she did everything to keep it away from him.

They'd made it through about half the booths when Neely and Reese caught up. "My poor baby's starving," she announced, giving her six-foot-plus baby a sympathetic glance. "You guys ready for lunch, or do you want to meet us later?"

Jace looked to Cassidy to answer. All it took was one deep breath filled with the smoky aromas of ribs, brisket and sausages to decide for her. While Neely claimed a newly vacated picnic table in the shade, Cassidy and the two men got in line. She filled her plate with small samples of everything and still wound up with way too much, she lamented when she slid onto the concrete bench across from Neely.

"It's once a year. You're allowed to overindulge," Neely said with a laugh. "Besides, Guthrie Harris was right the other day. These women sure can cook. The barbecue sauce is Aunt Rozena's specialty—that's Jace's mother. I'm sure she'll come wandering over to meet you as soon as she gets a chance. The ribs and brisket are Hallie's contribution, though she left the smoking to others. If Brady couldn't cook, the Marshall family would live in starvation mode."

"I heard that," Hallie retorted as she passed by, a baby in a sling against her chest and a tall, handsome, stern-faced man at her side. He wore a sheriff's deputy's uniform with a large pistol on the gun belt—not necessary at all, Cassidy was sure. He could intimidate the most hardened crook with nothing more than a look from that hard, dark gaze.

The gaze that softened tremendously when he glanced down at his wife and daughter.

"Hey, Cassidy. Having a good time?" Hallie asked.

"Yeah, I am." The lukewarm tone of her response reminded her of a conversation with Jace the weekend before, when he'd told her about the festival. *Sounds nice,* she'd remarked, and he had dryly responded, *Now there's a big endorsement.*

She really was having a good time. This very well might be the most comfortable and relaxed she'd gotten in public in three years. The only times she had looked over her shoulder had been to locate Jace or Neely and Reese. She hadn't scrutinized the faces of every farmer, cowboy or deputy for familiar features, hadn't scoped out hiding places or the quickest exits. She had simply enjoyed.

And that was a habit she couldn't fall into. She had to stay alert and ready. That and luck were the only things keeping her alive.

Jace and Reese delivered three overflowing plates to the table, then left to get drinks from a nearby booth. When they returned, they took a few minutes to make a good start on their meals, then Reese shifted his attention to her. "Paulette tells us you're from Alabama, but Jace says it's California and Ginger says South Carolina."

Lie like a dog—that was her motto, and she did so with a smile. "Actually, I'm from Maryland, but I live in Southern California now. Maybe Ginger heard the *southern* and confused California with Carolina, though I don't know where Paulette got Alabama. I don't believe I've ever been there."

Underneath the table, Jace bumped his leg against hers. His idea of a subtle warning?

"And you write historical romance novels, right?" Reese continued.

"Oh, no. That's way too much work for me. You have to research every little detail of life—clothing, speech, food, everything. I prefer to stick to my own time, where I know those things automatically."

"Do you write under your own name?" That came from Neely as she cut a slice of tender brisket.

"No." Cassidy knew they were waiting for more, but she

politely ignored them and cut her own meat into bite-size pieces.

"She's probably the only writer around who doesn't want people to know her pen name," Jace said at last before glancing her way. "Which I could understand if you were writing porn—"

"If I were, it would be erotica." Not that she had a clue how to go about that. She liked reading steamy books, but she didn't have the imagination to write hot, kinky sex scenes—especially considering how long it had been since she'd had even lukewarm, sleep-inducing sex.

"Then you would *have* to hide behind a pen name," Neely said, "to keep your mother from freaking out."

"Exactly," Cassidy agreed. "And she *would* freak." Along with a few other people.

"Except—" Jace's gaze narrowed as he stared at her a long, still moment. Then he blinked, let the tension ease and stabbed a piece of smoked sausage on his fork.

He'd been about to say, *Your mother is dead.* Instead he settled for eating, no doubt to keep his mouth full so he wouldn't call her a liar in front of his cousins.

"I read romances when I get a chance," Neely said, either not noticing Jace's reaction or being kind enough to ignore it. "Maybe I've read some of yours. Please, please—" she went into wheedling mode "—tell me your pen name."

Cassidy pretended to consider the request while, in reality, she was mentally sifting through all the names she'd used in her lifetime, settling on two she could easily remember. "Okay...but I would really appreciate it if you wouldn't tell anyone else." She waited for Neely's nod, took a breath, then announced, "Shauna Cassidy."

"Hmm...it doesn't sound familiar," Neely said apologetically. "But I'll definitely be watching for it in the future."

Could she be lucky enough that there might really be a Shauna Cassidy out there writing romance novels? Probably not. But that was okay. Before long, she would leave

Oklahoma, just as she left every place, and soon after Neely would forget she existed. They all would, including Jace.

That was a fact she couldn't bear to face, not in the middle of a warm, relaxing, pleasant day. In the middle of the night, when she couldn't sleep for the fear, the depression, the tears…then she would face it. But not today. Today was a time to enjoy, and she intended to do just that.

How many ways could you spell Shauna?

Jace sat in front of the computer, the search engine cursor blinking patiently, waiting for another attempt. He'd tried Shauna, Shawna, Shahna, Shanna, even Seana. The closest thing he got to a hit was on the actor Shaun Cassidy. He'd found a Cassidy who wrote romance novels, but her first name was nowhere close to Shauna.

She'd lied again.

His first impulse was to do whatever it took to find out why—call his cop buddies, run her tag number, check out each and every bit of information she'd given him. Put more simply, *investigate* her. It was easy enough to do, even for an ex-cop. Even without the access he'd had before quitting the job, he still had all the necessary resources.

His second impulse was to blow her off. She wanted to live in fantasyland? Who cared? He sure as hell didn't have to live there with her. He just wanted to spend a night or two there.

Third time around, his instincts said wait and see. She had her reasons for lying, she'd said on the way into town that morning. In her mind, at least, they were good ones, even though he couldn't automatically agree. More importantly, he couldn't care. Reasons for lying, good or bad, were a clear signal that she was the wrong person for him to get involved with—even for sex.

Or maybe except for sex.

As he shut down the computer, a line from an old tune flashed through his head: *We gotta get you a woman*. Sad, but true. If he threw some clothes into a bag, he could be in Kansas City by 1:00 a.m., could be too exhausted by two to lift his head off the pillow, much less think about sex with *any* woman for at least a few hours. Hell, he could skip the road trip and get lucky in Buffalo Plains. Then maybe he could get Cassidy out of his system…though he seriously doubted anything less than several very long, very intense go-rounds in her bed would accomplish that.

They'd left the park around five o'clock and made a fairly silent trip back to the lake—a tired kind of silence that was more comfortable than he'd wanted it to be. Amanda had been a talker, and so had Julie and Lisa. Cassidy didn't find it necessary to fill every silence with chatter, no matter how inane. He hadn't realized how much he liked that until they'd said goodbye at her door and he'd headed back across the bridge to his own door.

After taking a bottled water from the refrigerator, he stepped out onto the deck. There was no moon and the stars seemed a million miles away. The only light came from his living-room windows, as well as Cassidy's, and the only sounds were the usual ones—whippoorwills and bobwhites, tree frogs croaking and fish plopping, water lapping against the shore. He'd become so accustomed to the quiet that he wondered sometimes if he would ever be able to live in the city again. Usually he cut off that line of thought as soon as it occurred to him, but as Reese had pointed out not too long ago, his savings weren't going to last forever.

What could he do besides be a cop?

The answer was as elusive as all those stars a million miles away.

As he considered thinking about it, a man-made sound disturbed the stillness…or, to be accurate, a woman-made sound—a soft sigh that seemed too heavy with its own burdens to do anything but hover in the night air. He searched the shadows on the opposite side of the inlet and saw what he should have noticed the moment he stepped out of the door— Cassidy, sitting near the edge of the water, knees drawn up, blond head bowed. She looked as forlorn and blue as her sigh.

He could pretend he hadn't seen her, go back inside and

watch TV or read. That would be the smart thing. So, of course, it didn't surprise him that when he moved, it was toward the steps, not the door.

She didn't notice him until the footbridge creaked beneath his weight. Hastily, she straightened her shoulders and wiped one hand across her face. Drying tears? He didn't want to know.

He sat a few feet away and watched as a thin sheet of lightning crackled across the distant sky. He hadn't heard a weather report this evening and wouldn't have paid any attention if he had. Summer in Oklahoma was fairly predictable— warm temperatures or hot, humidity, rain, thunderstorms or drought, with the occasional tornado. He'd never actually seen a tornado himself, though he'd lived his entire life in Tornado Alley. He was smart enough to take cover when one threatened. He would stick around for a good old-fashioned thunderstorm, though.

The moments passed slowly, one after another, before he finally turned his head to look at her. "You're not really from Maryland, are you?"

An expression of regret crossed the half of her face he could see, then her mouth tightened as she shook her head.

"And your pen name isn't Shauna Cassidy."

Another shake of her head.

"Do you even have a pen name?"

"I have several pseudonyms."

He wondered if there was a fine distinction between pen name and pseudonym. All he knew was they were both fake names, but then, he didn't earn his living with words. He could be missing some subtle nuance there.

"And you're not going to tell anyone what they are."

She shook her head once again.

"Why not?"

"Why does it matter?"

Her tone was so casual, her question so incredible. Why did the truth matter? No one had ever put such a question to him before. It mattered because it *was* the truth. There might be additional reasons, but none were needed. Truth mattered, period.

"When I leave here," she went on, not waiting for an answer he couldn't adequately explain to someone who didn't already grasp it, "you people are never going to see me again. After a few weeks, you're never even going to think of me again. What will where I'm from or where I live or what name I use matter then? What difference will any of it make?"

"You really believe that? That truth and honesty and trustworthiness don't matter?"

"In a perfect world, sure. But my world's not perfect." She was using that meaningless tone again, accompanied this time by a shrug.

"So you just lie about anything, everything, without reason."

"I told you, I have my reasons."

"What? An aversion to the truth? Lying's more fun? It lets you change the things you don't like in your life? It keeps people at arm's length?"

She stretched out her arm and her hand rested against his shoulder. There wasn't enough room between them for her to straighten her elbow. "Some people," she replied flippantly.

He scowled hard at her. "That's not funny."

Abruptly her voice turned cold. "So go home. I didn't invite you over here. I have never once encouraged you to even speak to me. You're the one who keeps coming around, who's invited me to lunch and asked me to go places. If my dishonesty bothers you so much, stay away. I promise, I won't come looking for you if you do."

Was it that simple for her? He would live on his side of the inlet and she would live on hers, each pretending the other didn't exist? She wouldn't think about him, wonder what he was doing, miss him?

Probably not.

While he would probably think of nothing *but* her.

He looked at her, and she turned so he could see her entire face. Her maybe-brown eyes—with her track record, that was probably a lie, too—were steady and cool, her mouth relaxed, her face expressionless. If he got up and walked away without another word, she wouldn't care.

At least, that was what she wanted him to believe. He was trying, but the nagging tingle between his shoulder blades made it tough.

He searched her face for *something,* and found it in the convulsive tightening of a muscle in her jaw, the stiff way she swallowed, the unsteady movement of her lips. "Tell me one true thing," he demanded. Just one.

She looked as if she wanted to refuse, but after a moment she smiled thinly. "All right. I'm a habitual liar. You can't believe a word I say."

That was two true things, and probably the only things she possibly could have said that he would have believed.

For now, it was enough.

Chapter 7

Where Heartbreak was just a speck on the map, Buffalo Plains was an honest-to-God dot. Not much of one, but still a dot. Cassidy parked across the street from the courthouse, shut off the engine and sat there a moment. What was she doing here? Dallying around town didn't make her list of Smart Things to Do. She didn't need to do any shopping, didn't need to be spending any money indiscriminately, and she surely didn't need to see anyone who might make the mistake of being friendly to her.

She hadn't had to worry about that last part in the past few days. After her *one true thing,* Jace had gone home without a word and he'd ignored her since. Stay away, she'd told him. *I won't come looking for you if you do.* And she hadn't. Even though she'd spent more time watching his cabin than reading, trying to write or playing Free Cell combined. Even though she'd been sorely tempted to walk across the foot bridge and offer him a compromise—*Pay attention to me, and I won't lie to you.* She wouldn't tell the truth and nothing but the truth, but she would stop lying.

Somehow she didn't think he would see that as any great offer on her part.

He'd stayed gone all day Sunday, had had company she didn't recognize Monday and had gone out Tuesday evening, wearing khaki trousers and an olive drab shirt. The light wind had carried the tune he was whistling across the inlet, along with the earthy scent of his cologne. Going out on a date, she'd suspected, and the thought had depressed her more than she'd expected.

It wasn't that she was jealous, she insisted as the temperature climbed in the car. Well, of course, she was, but not of *him*. Of the date. Ten years had passed since she'd been out on a date, twelve years since she'd been out with anyone besides Phil. She missed the whole ritual—the anticipation, the dressing up, the conversation, the dining, the dancing, the parties, the hand-holding, the kissing, the possibilities.

She missed the possibilities. Her life was so empty of them. She couldn't go out on a date. Couldn't spend the night with a handsome man. Couldn't make friends. Couldn't even dream about falling in love, getting married, having children. It hurt too much.

A bead of sweat trickled down her face, jarring her out of her thoughts. She pulled the keys from the ignition and climbed out, finding it not much cooler outside.

Antique shops, the kind that carried "old stuff" rather than genuine antiques, lined the block in front of her. She decided to start at one end and work her way to the other. As she reached for the door to the first shop, it swung open and the man coming out stopped abruptly.

"Cassidy."

She looked at him, blinked, then looked again. She hadn't met him before, she was sure of that, but she was equally sure who he was. His was Jace's face, with twenty-five or thirty years added and the Osage blood taken away. It was disconcerting to see Jace's features in a white man's face. "M-Mr. Barnett."

He stepped back so she could enter, then let the door swing

shut again. "Oh, call me Ray. Everybody does—except Jace, of course. Rozena and I wanted to get an introduction to you Saturday at the barbecue, but her father took sick and we had to leave early. Did you have a good time?"

"Yes. Yes, I did. The food was incredible. She should bottle that sauce and sell it."

"I'll tell her you said so. She prides herself on her cooking. Like you can't tell that just looking at me." With a laugh, he patted his rounded belly. "Did Jace come into town with you?"

"No. I'm alone." She'd peered through the trees as she'd driven along the lane past his cabin, but the growth had been too thick to see the cabin, much less his truck parked toward the back. If he was there, he'd stayed inside. Just because? Or avoiding her?

"Rozena wants to have you two over for dinner sometime. I'll tell her to call him, and you tell him to listen to his messages, would you? He seems to think that cell phone is for *his* convenience and no one else's." He gave another friendly laugh. "I understand you're from…Georgia, is it?"

"California."

"Close enough," he said with a wink. "What with all the smog and people and earthquakes out there, you must think you've found heaven here."

She resisted the urge to point out that smog wasn't confined to California—she'd heard a few ozone-alert warnings on the Tulsa radio station she listened to, urging people not to drive, barbecue or even mow their lawns. As for people, all cities had them—it was part of the definition of the word—and she'd never experienced an earthquake, though places other than California had.

"You live in a nice place," she agreed.

"Perfect place for settling down and raising up kids to be spoiled rotten by their granddaddy," he said with another wink. "Guess I'd better get going, or the boss'll shorten my leash next time. Rozena'll call about dinner. Nice to finally meet you."

She watched out the plate-glass window as he crossed the street, strode past the courthouse and disappeared from sight, then turned her attention to the store. It was one large room, crammed with merchandise, and could use a few hundred watts' more lighting. It smelled of old things—wood, fabric, paper—and, over all that, a clean crisp citrus scent. Music came from a small stereo somewhere in the back, and a lovely, clear voice sang along and, judging from the accompanying sounds, danced along, too.

The owner of the voice did a slide-shuffle step around the distant corner of the main aisle. She was in her teens, Cassidy guessed, though she wouldn't even try to narrow it beyond that. Her brown hair was pulled back in a ponytail, a demure contrast to the multiple earrings that glinted in each lobe, and her white T-shirt and short denim overalls emphasized her long legs and golden-tanned skin. She was too cute for words, even with the hiking boots and the stud in her nose.

"Hi, I'm Lexy," she called, wiggling the feather duster she held in a wave. "Feel free to look around. If you need anything, yell." She glanced in the direction the music was coming from, then grinned slyly. "Loudly."

"I will," Cassidy replied as she turned into a small alcove filled with pressed glass. She'd heard the name once before— at Olivia Harris's house. So Hallie Marshall, who didn't look a day older than Cassidy herself, was mother to this womanly creature as well as the tiny girl she'd carried at the barbecue Saturday. Some people had all the luck.

She was examining a display of wooden bowls similar to the one that had caught her attention at the festival when Lexy joined her. "Aren't they pretty? The guy who makes 'em used to be the doctor here in town—Doc Walker—but he retired and turned his practice over to Callie—she's a midwife—well, actually, she's a nurse pract—a practicing nurse or something like that."

"Nurse practitioner," Cassidy supplied.

"Yeah. She delivered my baby sister, Brynn. She delivered everyone's babies until Doc Walker's grandson came to town, but a lot of women still want her instead of him. Anyway, Doc Walker took up wood turning to pass the time, and he makes these bowls. Isn't this one great?''

She handed Cassidy a delicately rounded bowl, the wood rich and dark except where a V of pale wood sliced through. ''It grew like that, in two different colors. Isn't it cool? And they're so smooth and pretty.''

Amazingly so, Cassidy agreed. Maybe thirty-five dollars wasn't so pricey for something whose purpose was to look pretty when she could also use it as her own version of a worry stone. A few minutes rubbing the unblemished surface might be as calming as a half hour of yoga.

Before she left Oklahoma for good, she promised herself as she returned the bowl to the shelf. She deserved a souvenir of at least one of the three dozen places she'd lived—something besides regrets.

''You're Mom and Aunt Neely's friend, aren't you?'' Lexy asked.

Not really. But she would like to be. Just as she would like to have dinner with Jace and his parents, and would like to cuddle Liza Beth Rafferty the next time she was in the café. She would like to stay in the cabin at the lake as long as she wanted, to pretend that life was normal and that the nightmares in her past wouldn't destroy her future.

''Yes,'' she lied, and felt a twinge of guilt for it.

''Mom says you're a writer. I bet people tell you all the time how they're gonna write a book someday.'' Lexy gave her a sidelong look. ''I really am…someday. I've kept a journal since I was ten, and I write some poetry and short stories.'' Suddenly she gave a self-conscious laugh. ''Don't worry, though—I'm not gonna ask you if you'll read my stuff and tell me whether it's any good. I don't let anyone read it yet. I figure the editor who buys it will be the first one other than me to see it. It's really just for me anyway.''

''I think that might be the key,'' Cassidy said. ''They say writers write because they can't *not* do it. It's part of who they are.'' Not that she had any great experience with writing anything other than checks, but the story she was working at putting into words was for *her,* no one else. Maybe someday someone else would read it, but that wasn't the important part. The telling was.

"Yeah," Lexy agreed. "Sometimes my friends ask me why I do it, and I'm, like, I don't know why. I just do. So…what do you think of your neighbor, Jace? He's awfully cute for an old guy, isn't he?"

Old? "Yeah, just like you're awfully cute for a baby."

"I'm not a baby." Lexy drew herself up to her full height and imperiously looked down her nose. "I'll be sixteen before too long." Then she let her shoulders slump a bit. "And six feet tall if I don't stop growing. I'm five-eleven now…well, five-eleven and a quarter, but we don't mention that. I'm practically taller than anyone else in school."

"There are lots of men who are taller than that."

"Yeah, like Mitch. He's a deputy who works for my dad and Uncle Reese. He is *so* cute, and he's a lot closer to my age…though not close enough to matter until I'm, like, twenty or older. With my dad, probably not even then. Anyway, speaking of cops…Jace is checkin' out your car." Lexy's voice turned singsong on the last words, accompanied by an ear-to-ear grin.

Cassidy turned to look out the window and saw Jace standing behind her car. If one mistook his dark skin for a tan, he looked like the quintessential beach bum in baggy shorts, a T-shirt and dark glasses that reflected everything back in iridescent shades. Of course, the nearest beach was the Texas Gulf coast and—

Abruptly she turned back to Lexy. "What did you say?"

"He's checkin' out your car. Probably trying to figure out where to find you—"

"Before that." When the girl frowned in an effort to remember, Cassidy gave her an assist. "'Speaking of cops…'"

"Yeah. So?"

"Jace isn't a cop."

"Sure, he is. Well, he was for, like, forever. In Kansas City.

But he quit his job last winter and came home. Uncle Reese and Aunt Neely have been kinda worried about him, 'cause he's just vegetating and not doing much of anything, and Uncle Reese is always offering him a job at the sheriff's office, but Jace says he's never gonna be a cop again. Uncle Reese says that's not possible. He says being a cop is like you describe being a writer. It's not what you do, it's who you are, and Jace is a cop.''

Cassidy glanced outside again. Jace had moved to the sidewalk and was sitting on the hood of the car. Absently she wondered if the hot metal didn't burn through the cotton of his shorts, then gave herself a mental shake.

So he had been a cop—and still was, according to his cousin, even if he'd quit the job. At least that explained all the questions and the suspicion. Heavens, if she'd known she was lying to a former cop, she would have done it with a little more finesse…not. Years of lying daily hadn't made her much better at it than when she'd started.

Was this good news or bad? Or was it nothing at all? A cop had that protect-and-serve bit down pat, so if trouble tracked her down, he could come in handy. But there was also that curiosity. He was accustomed to getting answers to his questions one way or the other—to sorting through lies until he uncovered the truth. Keeping her secrets could be tough unless she kept her distance.

But she *really* didn't want to keep her distance. Not this one time. She'd been so good, so careful, for so long. Couldn't she catch a break just once?

"You may as well go see what he wants," Lexy suggested. "As if that's such a hardship, him being so cute and all."

"Maybe if I keep shopping, he'll go away." And maybe he would go straight to the sheriff's office in the courthouse and ask cousin Reese to run her tag number. What would he think when it came back to Stacy Beauchamp? Or would it be Linda Valdez? She would have to check the registration to be sure.

Lexy laughed at her comment as if she'd told a great joke.

''Ain't gonna happen. He's a Barnett, and they're waaay more stubborn than that.''

He looked awfully comfortable sitting on her car, hands on the hood, feet propped on the bumper. Lexy was probably right. After all, she was related to one Barnett by marriage.

''I guess I'll go see what he wants,'' Cassidy suggested with a smile she didn't feel. When she faced Lexy again, the smile became sincere. ''I enjoyed talking to you, Lexy.''

''I'll see you around.''

Not likely… ''Yeah.'' As she started toward the door she gave the girl a wave, then took a fortifying breath and stepped out into the heat. She ignored the pleasure rising inside her at the mere sight of Jace waiting for her, tempered only by her new knowledge about him. A cop. Just her luck…and she didn't have a clue whether it was good or bad luck.

She stopped a few feet away and waited for him to speak. The shades he wore were an expensive brand, chosen as much for the camouflage they provided as for the protection from the sun, she suspected. His tennis shoes, worn without socks, were expensive, too, though they showed a tremendous amount of wear. If she checked the tag on his shorts, would she find they were pricey, too? Pricier than a part-time cowboy could afford?

''Indulging in another shopping spree, huh?'' he asked in that easy-going, heartland cowboy drawl of his, tinged with a bit of sarcasm.

She didn't respond to the remark. Instead she put her own dark glasses on, then slid her hands into her shorts' pockets and studied him. ''Fancy meeting you here, Officer Barnett…or should that be Detective?''

It was hard to tell, but she thought a crimson stain crept into his cheeks. He unfolded into a standing position, slid his hands into his own shorts' pockets and rocked back on his heels. ''Six months ago it would have been detective. Today it's not.''

Six months ago. Back in the winter, when he would have been happy not having anyone's attention. When he'd stopped cutting his hair. When he'd isolated himself from family and friends. When something had happened that he'd needed to recover from.

She could imagine a million things that could have gone wrong for a cop and driven him away from his job. She wanted to know about the one thing that had gone wrong for *this* cop, but damned if she could ask. They'd made a deal, he would no doubt remind her. Her truths for his.

"You have a problem with that?"

Cassidy gazed at the war memorial in the grass across the street. She hadn't decided the answer to that yet. She did know, no matter how irrational it seemed, that she felt...annoyed that he'd not only failed to mention a long career as a cop, but had, in fact, gone to some effort to hide it.

And that, she thought with a wry smile, was a prime example of the pot calling the kettle black.

Finally she looked at him again. "I'll let you know when I figure it out myself. Why are you in town?"

His response was a shrug and a question of his own. "Why are *you?*"

"I've been good, and I needed a break." She had spent a lot of time at the computer since Saturday evening, increasing her manuscript file to an impressive size. It was tough, writing about all the things she'd lost—the family, the husband and, worst of all, the dreams. She didn't dream anymore. Didn't hope.

At the same time, the writing was cathartic. For so many years, her life—her entire self—had been a lie. Being able to speak openly, honestly, even if only on a computer, felt freeing.

"So you're taking the rest of the day off?"

She nodded. Her comment about needing a break had been true, too. There was such a thing, she'd discovered, as too much catharsis.

"Let's get some lunch. I know this place on 51st that's got great burgers."

"On my first day here, I drove all over town, and I know for a fact that Buffalo Plains doesn't *have* fifty-one streets."

"In Tulsa. It's not far."

Not far was a reasonable distance to go for a great burger...unless the drive time was filled with more unanswerable questions. He was being pleasant enough at the moment, but who knew how long that would last? One badly told lie from her, or one suspicion that she was being less than honest, and the day could turn very unpleasant indeed.

On the other hand, she was expert at dealing with the unpleasant. Maybe the trip would surprise her. Maybe she would tell only the truth, or he would ignore her lies.

"Okay." Hearing her own agreement brought both a sense of anticipation and a clutch of apprehension. Good choice or bad?

Only time would tell.

The restaurant Jace took Cassidy to didn't look the sort of place a person would associate with great, greasy burgers. The location was too pricey—an elegant little shopping center—and the decor too upscale, with cloths on the tables and linen napkins. But the hamburgers were thick and fried with onions, the buns toasted with real butter, the fries crispy and dotted with salt.

They had finished their burgers and were picking at the last of the fries on the plate between them. They'd talked about nothing important—because she lied about the important stuff, he reminded himself. Of course, she lied about the unimportant stuff, too.

For today, at least, he wasn't going to care.

"I haven't seen you lately," he remarked as she took the last French fry, as if the fact were of no consequence. As if he hadn't missed seeing her, and talking to her, and thinking about having sex with her. Not that he'd stopped doing that last. Out of sight definitely did not mean out of mind.

She delicately wiped her fingers on her napkin. "I told you if you stayed away, I wouldn't come looking for you." Unexpectedly she smiled. "You wouldn't want me to make a liar of myself, would you?"

Though his jaw tightened, he managed a similar smile. "God forbid...especially with you being such an honest person and all."

A bleak look stole into her eyes, then in an instant was gone. It made him want to speak, though he couldn't think of a thing to say. Instead, he turned his attention to the other customers in the dining room.

The shopping center might be upscale, but the hamburger lovers weren't. The uniformed ones were easy to peg—phone repair guys, a delivery service driver, three mechanics from a garage down the street. There were a half dozen workers from a street maintenance crew, still wearing their reflective orange vests, a couple of men in suits and a group of women from a nearby doctor's office.

The only other couple sat a few tables away—a man in a cream-colored suit with a tie that was all wrong and a woman who looked the epitome of the rising young businessman's wife. The man seemed displeased with the way his day was going and the woman appeared anxious over his displeasure.

They made Jace and Cassidy look damn near lovey-dovey in comparison.

He was about to turn his attention back to Cassidy when a clatter sounded at the other couple's table. The woman's glass lay on its side, its contents splattered everywhere, and the man was on his feet, wiping at his trousers and swearing loudly. His wife—they wore matching bands, Jace could see now—looked small in her seat, her head ducked, her shoulders rounded.

Jace glanced at the bill, tossed down enough money to cover it and a tip, then started to rise. "You ready to go?"

Cassidy was watching the man, whose voice was louder now. He'd moved from generic curses to ones aimed specifically at his wife. He was standing so close to her that she had nowhere to look but at him, and she did it tearfully, her face as red as the tablecloth, apparently aware that everyone in the restaurant was staring at them.

"Cassidy." Jace gestured toward the door. He'd been involved in enough domestic disputes to know this one wasn't going to blow over any time soon, and he wanted to be gone before it escalated. "Let's go. Since it's not too—"

Too late. Furious now, the man had found an additional target—the teenage busboy who'd come to clean up the spill. The kid was leaning against the wall, apparently stunned after getting shoved there by the suit, and the dishes lay broken on the floor at his feet. The woman was starting to cry, silent tears that slid down her cheeks.

The girl at the cash register was on the phone, no doubt with the police. Everyone else in the place watched, edgy and uncomfortable, torn between stepping in and minding their own business. Doing what was right versus doing what was easy. He understood their indecision. Hell, he *shared* it. He didn't want to intervene, either. He wouldn't. It wasn't his job anymore, and it damn sure wasn't his responsibility.

Though he knew two people—the ones who had raised him—who would insist otherwise. Doing the right thing had nothing do with his job, they would say, and everything to do with who he was.

And who he was was the sort of guy who didn't get involved in other people's problems. The sort of man who would stand up—he did so slowly—and walk out the door.

The woman spoke, her voice audible for the first time. "Dennis, please…" She put out a trembling hand. "Please…p-people are—are staring. L-let's discuss th—this—"

He knocked her hand away. "Do you think I give a damn whether people are staring? I'll give them something to stare at, you stupid bitch!"

Reluctantly, Jace glanced at Cassidy, who was looking back at him. He couldn't read anything in her expression, but he identified expectancy in her gaze. She wanted him to do something—would be disappointed if he didn't. That shouldn't matter one bit to him, but damned if it didn't.

The guy drew his right hand back as if to strike his wife, and she shrank away as if she'd received many such blows. It took Jace two strides to reach him, to catch hold of his wrist and twist it behind his back. The angle was sharp enough to make the man yelp, to force him over the table in an effort to ease the pressure.

"Get your hands off me, you bast—" Twisting around, the guy caught his first look at Jace—a half foot taller, twenty pounds lighter and nowhere near as easy to intimidate as his wife. The curse died unfinished, and so did the struggles. "Hey, man, you're hurting my arm. Everything's cool now. Let go, okay? I'm cool."

Off to their left, the door opened and a police officer came inside. A second was following a few yards behind.

Jace released the man with a shove that sent him sprawling across the table. Before the guy could regain his feet, the first officer was handcuffing him. With nothing more than a glance at Cassidy, Jace walked out of the restaurant. He was sitting in the SUV, engine running and AC cooling, when she finally joined him.

He had thought he would give her the nickel tour of Tulsa after lunch. Instead, he turned onto 51st and headed for the nearest access to the bypass. He didn't say anything, and neither did she, until they reached the Arkansas River bridge.

"Is that why you quit being a cop? You got tired of being the good guy?"

Not the good guy, he wanted to say. The sucker, the sap, the fool. But he didn't bother as he changed lanes to take 75 North. Instead, he challenged her first question. "What makes you think I quit? Maybe I was fired."

"Maybe you were," she agreed quietly. "But if you were fired for cause, would Reese be so eager to have you working for him?"

"When the salary is low and the benefits substandard, you can't be too picky about who you hire."

She let another few miles pass before speaking again. "What happened?"

They crossed the Arkansas River once more, then merged onto the Keystone Expressway. He flexed his fingers around the steering wheel, then affected a careless tone. "I woke up one morning and decided I was sick to death of helping people. It doesn't ever last. The people you put in jail get out again. The victims you deal with this week will be someone else's victims next week. Witnesses refuse to testify, cases get thrown out, verdicts get overturned. The job's pointless."

And the people he'd done it for were self-serving, disloyal and ungrateful.

She let another few miles and most of Sand Springs pass before she asked once more, "What really happened?"

He could ignore her, as she often ignored his questions. He could lie, as she almost always did. He could give her some pat response that was true enough to count, but not the whole truth. He hadn't decided which—at least, not consciously—when he heard his own voice breaking the silence. "I was working Homicide, and one of my cases got ugly. The victim was a prostitute, the suspect the only son of a socially prominent family. I built a case against him, and at the same time his family built one against me. They made it look like I'd tampered with the evidence. They paid off a witness to say I'd threatened them into incriminating him. I got jerked off all my cases and reassigned to a desk pending investigation. Internal Affairs couldn't find a damn bit of proof that I'd done anything wrong—because I *hadn't*—but the chief wanted to make an example of me, wanted to prove how tough he was on his officers. He let everyone believe I was guilty, that I'd covered my tracks so well they couldn't prove it. I got demoted and suspended, the son of a bitch got away with murder, and the chief got a hefty contribution from the guy's family to his gubernatorial campaign."

For a time the silence between them was sharp enough to sting. Then she quietly said, "I'm sorry."

"Yeah. Sure." With a shrug to ease the tension in his shoulders, he flippantly added, "And that's why I'm no longer interested in getting involved with other people's troubles."

Before he looked away, he saw the muscle in her jaw tighten and realized that she was likely applying his words to herself, too. As she should, he thought, ignoring the guilt that nagged at him. He wanted to sleep with her, not fight battles for her. He wanted a nice, uncomplicated affair—no strings, no baggage, no responsibilities beyond behaving decently, using a condom and having no regrets.

Especially the *no regrets*—that was the most important part.

They were almost at their exit when she shifted to face him as much as the seat belt would allow. "Feeling the way you do, why did you interfere back there?"

He would have called it—*had* called it intervening. Interfering smacked of nosiness, doing something you shouldn't, being wrong. The difference rankled. "Given the difference in their sizes, that's felony assault. Besides, if I sat back and did nothing while a man hit a woman, my father would tan my hide."

"But your father wasn't there. He would never know."

"*I* would know."

"So you can't just quit being the good guy." She said it with some measure of satisfaction, but changed the subject before he could disagree. "Your mother's going to call you to invite us to dinner. I'm supposed to tell you to be sure and check your messages."

"And you got this little tidbit from...?"

"Your father. I met him this morning on my way into the store. He seems much too nice to ever have resorted to physical violence with you."

Jace had been grateful Saturday that they'd avoided meeting his parents at the barbecue. He owed his grandfather, the worst hypochondriac alive, for having another of his heart attacks—in reality, just another bout of indigestion—and calling Ray and Rozena out of town. For feeling as poorly as Grandpa claimed all the time, he was the healthiest old goat Jace had ever known. Rozena knew that, too, but she couldn't ignore one of his calls. After all, as with the boy who cried wolf, from time to time the wolf really did put in an appearance.

He wondered what Cassidy and Ray had discussed, whether his father had said anything that would embarrass him and why she hadn't mentioned it sooner, but he focused on her comment about Ray resorting to physical violence. "He never did."

"Oh? Where I come from, 'tanning your hide' refers to getting a whipping."

"And where would that be?" he muttered. "Maryland? Virginia? California? Mars?"

"Men are from Mars. Women are from Venus...I think," she said primly.

"It refers to getting a whipping here, too, but that's not physical violence, as long as it's not taken to excess. It's discipline."

"So when you have kids someday, you'll show them that might makes right. That the punishment for hitting another kid is getting hit by an adult. That their misbehaving is wrong but yours is all right because you're the parent."

"Let me guess. Your parents didn't believe in spanking." That was an easier-to-accept rationale than the other strong possibility—that they'd believed in it too much. Not surprisingly, kids who'd been beaten for the smallest infraction often grew into parents who rejected even the most well-deserved of swats for their own kids. It made his gut clench to think of a young, defenseless Cassidy getting beaten for an innocent mistake.

"Oh, we got spanked," she replied with too much easiness in her voice to be covering up abuse. "But it was reserved for the really bad behavior. Mostly, we got grounded, which was sometimes worse. When you're ten and you have to miss your best friend's birthday party just because you cut your sister's hair, spankings start to look pretty good."

Damn. He'd thought they might actually make it back to her car in Buffalo Plains without any red flags waving. Careful to keep his voice level and unaccusing, he asked, ''Why did you cut her hair?''

''Because my hair was short and I—''

The silence in the truck was intensified by its suddenness. If he looked at her, he knew she would be blushing and thinking furiously of a way out. He didn't give her a chance to find it. ''So you have a sister, too, but you haven't seen her in years. You don't know what she's doing, whether she's married or how her life is going. You don't even know where she is, so she doesn't count as family. Does that about sum it up?''

''Yeah,'' she replied, subdued. ''Just about.''

''Is that the story you want to stick with? Maybe she's an imaginary sister, made up to go along with your imaginary brother. Maybe your name's not Cassidy and you're not from California or anywhere else because you're imaginary, too.''

She gave him an unamused look. ''If I were making up a name, don't you think I would choose something other than Cassidy? It sounds like a character on a TV show. Given a choice, I would be Elizabeth or Rachel, Jessica or Anna or Katherine.''

She didn't look like an Elizabeth or a Rachel, though he could see her as a Jess...or, in the middle of a long steamy night, Jessy. Not an Anna, but an Annie. Maybe even a Kate.

''Why did your parents give you a name better suited to a character on TV?''

''It's a family name. My mother's family are Cassidys.''

Maybe...if she'd ever had a mother. More likely she'd been brought to life full-grown in a laboratory somewhere, with the gene for honesty neatly excised and the one for believable prevarication badly damaged in the process. She *wasn't* a good liar—not that she hadn't had plenty of practice at it. It didn't come naturally to her...unless she deliberately lied badly to make him think so, in which case she might be the most accomplished liar he'd met.

Thinking about it all made his head hurt, and he'd told himself he wouldn't care today, remember? He was spending the afternoon with a pretty woman who'd crawled under his skin and tempted him in ways he hadn't been tempted in months. All he had to do was enjoy it. Relax. Pretend he had no reason to doubt every word that came out of her mouth. Pretend he didn't care.

Pretend. The way she did.

Too bad it was easier said than done.

Chapter 8

When the lights flickered, then went dark for the third time, Cassidy shut down the computer, rose from her chair and bent to touch her toes, stretching out taut muscles and easing kinks. The sky had been gloomy when she'd awakened that morning, and the thunder had started soon after, but it had taken more than three hours for the storm to blow in full-force. The first time the power had gone off, she'd unplugged the laptop and continued to work on battery power, but enough was enough. It was time to get up, move around and get a breath of fresh air.

Wind blew the rain sideways across the lake, pounding into that side of the cabin with a relaxing tempo. Unfortunately, it also meant all the windows on that side had to be closed, so the only fresh air came from the other side of the cabin—the side where she couldn't see her neighbor's house and maybe, if she was lucky, her neighbor.

She settled for leaning one shoulder against the doorjamb and watching the storm from there. As the mimosa swayed and bent under the force of the wind, she briefly considered trying to pick up a weather forecast on the radio. She'd never gotten caught in a tornado before and wasn't in the mood to try something new today. But the reception was iffy under the best of circumstances, and if they were under a tornado watch or warning, what good would it do her to know? She had no storm shelter to hide in. There wasn't even an interior room in the house away from windows—the next best advice the weather people gave.

Lightning flashed, quick and brilliant, as thunder rattled the cabin walls. The rain poured, covering the saturated ground, running in a thousand tiny rivers to the lake's edge. She didn't care one way or the other about storms. As long as she wasn't out in them, they could blow to their heart's desire. Phil, though, had hated them. They interfered with his work, his play, his sleep, his television-watching, his reading, his computing, he'd said. Privately she'd always believed he was afraid of them. She'd seen how tense he got, had felt him flinch a thousand times at a particularly loud clap of thunder or close strike of lightning. The same pressure systems that created the storms had created a disturbance of a different sort in him, with pressure building almost to the breaking point, then easing as the system moved through.

But if that was the biggest failing a husband had, his wife was a lucky woman. She'd *felt* lucky...until the last three years of their marriage. Even then, even with all the changes forced on them because of him, she had still loved him. Even when she'd resented him for all he'd cost her.

All he'd cost her.... That sounded so selfish. The price *he'd* paid had been so much higher than hers. He'd lost all the same things she had—family, friends, hope for the future—as well as his life. He'd been betrayed by people he trusted, murdered by someone who should have protected him. Even when he'd died, his last words had been for her. *Janey, get out!*

Janey...not a name she'd ever used, but Phil's nickname for her, similar, familiar, comforting. In return, she had called him John, as in Doe. Two people without identities.

She had obeyed his command and run, and three years later

she was still running. This was her eighteenth day at Buffalo
Lake. Another week or two and she would be setting a new
record for longevity.

It wouldn't hurt to be thinking about where she would go
next—how she would get there, who she would be, what she
would do. Her first lesson on the run had been borrowed from
the Boy Scouts—*Be Prepared.* If she had to leave Buffalo
Lake today, where would she go? Would she dispose of the
car before she left or once she'd arrived at her new destination? Would she sell it or simply abandon it? Would her hair
be red, black or shades of brown, her eyes blue, green, hazel
or lavender?

Too many questions, she thought with a thin smile as the
gusting wind blew raindrops through the screen door. Besides,
she didn't need to plan so carefully anymore. She'd fled
dozens of places. It had become second nature.

Movement across the inlet caught her attention as Jace's
SUV pulled close to the deck steps. She idly wondered where
he'd gone and why he hadn't waited out the worst of the storm
there as he took the steps three at a time, then paused under
the roof overhang to unlock the cabin door. Before stepping
inside, he glanced her way, but she guessed distance and
shadow prevented him from noticing her—along with the fact
that she was standing utterly motionless, barely even
breathing.

When he went in, he left the door open. No lights came on,
of course. Everything fell back into stillness, the storm the
only sign of life.

He hadn't come to see her or invited her anywhere since
they'd returned to her car in front of the antique shops on
Wednesday afternoon. *Stay away,* she'd told him. *I won't
come looking for you if you do.*

Did it bother him that all the interest, all the effort, in main-
taining some kind of friendship fell on him? That the only
time she'd walked across that bridge had been to accept his
invitation for lunch, never to offer one of her own?

It would bother her if the situation were reversed. If she did all the trying, all the giving, while someone else did all the taking, it wouldn't be long before she decided he wasn't worth the effort.

She glanced toward the kitchen. Figuring the power would go, she'd made potato salad and baked beans to go along with last night's leftover roasted chicken. She'd baked a batch of cookies, too, her favorite indulgence when things were good and consolation when they went bad. She'd made enough for today's lunch and dinner, and probably tomorrow's lunch, as well, so there was plenty to share. All she had to do was walk next door and offer it.

What if he said "no, thanks"? Or if the price of keeping her company was ten million questions for which untruthful answers wouldn't be accepted?

A shifting of shadows in his cabin door made her squint. It was impossible to be sure, but she thought he was standing there, looking out as she was. She turned away, shoved her feet into a pair of battered sneakers, bagged the food in a plastic Wal Mart sack, closed and locked the windows, then took her umbrella from its place near the door. Tingling as much with apprehension as anticipation, she stepped onto the deck, locked her door, then set off through the rain for the other cabin.

He *was* standing in the doorway, wearing nothing more than a pair of faded denim cutoffs that rode low on his hips, watching her with an utterly unreadable expression. Her expression felt the same as she looked back. How long had it been since she'd made a spontaneous friendly gesture? At least three years. Long enough to get rusty. To make it feel more important than it really was. All she was offering was lunch. Nothing more, nothing less.

Yeah, right.

When he didn't speak, she did. "I fixed lunch before the power went off. I thought you might like to share it."

He opened the screen door, then stepped back so she could enter. First she shook out her umbrella, then leaned it against the wall, out of the worst of the rain. She felt the need to give herself a shake, too, to shed the raindrops that had blown onto her shorts and legs, but she resisted, settling instead for discarding her shoes next to the umbrella before stepping inside.

As she unloaded the shopping bag on the kitchen counter, he came around the corner, tugging a T-shirt over his head. The part of her that missed love and lust was disappointed. The protective part was relieved. She had her weaknesses, and Jace bare-chested could very easily become one.

"Does it storm like this a lot?" she asked, more to break the silence than because she cared.

"You mean the intensity? Yeah, a lot. The duration? Often enough."

She took two plates from a cabinet and silverware from a drawer. "At least we can use the rain."

"Not particularly. It's coming down too hard and running off. What we could use is a good soaker rain." He paused a beat. "Of course, you probably know all about Oklahoma storms, having researched the climate before you came here."

It would serve him right if she'd taken the time since that earlier conversation to actually do just that. Then she could spout off something intelligent about storm systems or the effects of the Rocky Mountains on Oklahoma weather versus the effects of the Gulf of Mexico.

Instead, all she could do was dish up food while he got bottled water from the refrigerator. After he took his plate and cutlery, she picked up her own and started toward the dining table. He was headed for the living room, though, so she shifted direction. Once she was settled in on the couch, she asked, "What took you out in this weather?"

"I went to see my grandfather."

The ailing father whose illness had drawn the senior Barnetts away from the barbecue last weekend, the one Ray had mentioned briefly. "How is he?"

"Stubborn as a mule and sly as a fox. He's old, retired, bored and loves attention."

"So he wasn't sick so much as feeling neglected last weekend."

He nodded.

"My grandmother was like that. She had a different complaint every week, usually based on whatever she'd seen on television. Everyone was shocked when she really did get sick. It wasn't nearly as much fun for her as the pretend illnesses. We were relieved when she died." She repeated the last sentence again in her mind and grimaced. "That sounds cold, doesn't it?"

"No. No one wants to see someone they love suffer, especially when there's no cure for what ails them. If death is the only possible outcome, better to go quickly than to linger on in agony."

She plucked a piece of chicken from her plate and chewed it before asking, "What did your grandfather retire from?"

"He was the superintendent of schools in their county." He smiled cynically when her eyes widened. "You were thinking cowboy or farmer or maybe laborer, weren't you?"

"No." Though she could have been forgiven if she had, considering that she was smack-dab in the middle of ranch and farm country.

"You were, too. Because he's Indian or rural folk or, hell, maybe you just don't think highly of Oklahomans in general, you assumed he was an uneducated hick, just like you assumed *I* was."

"I didn't even know he *was* Indian or rural folk, and I don't make sweeping generalizations about anyone," she argued. Then she breathed. "Truth is—"

He snorted derisively, and her gaze narrowed.

"*Truth is,* I was a little surprised. You don't meet many school superintendents, though I lived with one for eighteen years."

"Your father?"

"My mother," she said with a smug smile, then turned his accusation back on him. "You were thinking 'highly educated professional' equals man, weren't you? That my mother must be a housewife or secretary or something better suited to a woman, weren't you?" She enjoyed watching the dull flush that reddened his face, enjoyed making *him* feel backward for once, but then she relented. ''Actually, you're right. It *was* my father. I just wanted to make the point that I'm not the only one who makes assumptions.''

He scowled at her. ''And where was your father superintendent? Virginia? Maryland?''

''Pennsylvania.'' Stabbing a forkful of potato salad, she slid it into her mouth. For once she'd told him the truth, though he didn't realize it.

''What about your mother? Did she work?''

''Not at a paid job. She took care of the house, the family and did volunteer work at school, church, the hospital. She was the best fund-raiser Mil—our town had ever seen.''

He studied her a moment, debating whether to be suckered in, she was sure. Guiltily she dropped her gaze to her plate, scooping up the last of the potato salad, then turning to the baked beans. When he finally spoke, though, it wasn't to challenge anything she'd said. ''Did she teach you to cook?''

''Yes.'' They'd spent a lot of hours in the kitchen, doing not just the usual cooking but baking and experimenting, creating their own dishes and tinkering with old recipes. Her mother had done the same growing up with *her* mother, and Cassidy had planned to duplicate the experience in the future with her own daughter.

Until she'd found out she *had* no future.

''She done good.'' He leaned forward, setting his empty plate on the coffee table and picking up the napkin with cookies there. ''We're invited to dinner at my folks' house tomorrow night.''

Still considering the offhanded compliment, Cassidy blinked. ''Are we going?''

''I'm planning on it. Are you?''

''Oh...well...sure. Why not?'' she responded with a weak smile. Immediately she could have kicked herself. *Why not?* Because dinner with his parents was a relationship sort of thing. She'd known when Phil invited her home to meet his parents that he was *serious* about her, and her acceptance had given the same message.

But that was then and this was now. Jace wasn't serious about her at all. He could go days without seeing her and never miss her, probably not even think of her. When she moved on to a new safe place, he would have no regrets and no memories worth holding on to. While Mr. and Mrs. Barnett would no doubt like to see their son married and raising a family—Ray, at least, had a hankering for grandchildren—that happening with *her* wasn't even a remote possibility. He didn't want it, and she couldn't have it...not that *she* wanted it, either, she hastily assured herself.

This would just be neighbors, friends of a sort, having dinner with one's parents—no different from Reese, Guthrie Harris or Easy Rafferty going with him to his folks' for dinner. She could handle that.

She set her own plate next to his on the table, then sat back, looking around the room. He had an impressive home entertainment system to go with the satellite dish up on the roof, and the furniture was nice—she could grow seriously attached to the buttery softness of the leather couch where she sat— but the place had an impersonal feel. She recognized the cause of it—the lack of any personal items—because she lived with it herself. "Is your decorating style always so austere?"

"Austere," he repeated. He looked around as if noticing the empty walls and shelves for the first time. "My style is easy-to-clean. Nothing unnecessary to dust or vacuum around."

"Photographs are worth dusting."

"Then why don't you have some?"

"I do at home," she lied. She *had* had a box of photographs when she and Phil had moved to Oregon, but she'd been forced to leave them behind when she fled. She'd been too traumatized to think about anything but saving her life. She hadn't remembered the pictures until days later. "You can't expect me to pack them up and move them with me for a short trip like this."

"If they're worth dusting, they're worth taking along. Who

do you have photos of? Family? Friends? Or are all the people in your photographs strangers?''

In all fairness she couldn't hold his cynicism against him. God knew, she'd given him plenty of reasons to doubt her. Still, it stung. She was an honest person by nature. It had been honesty that had led Phil to the decision that changed their lives—that ended his life—and honesty that had led her to support him one hundred percent. She didn't *like* lying or giving people cause to think poorly of her.

But she shrugged as if the pain didn't exist and carelessly answered, ''Family. A few old friends. Whatever good-looking men I've come across in my travels.''

''And your husband?''

That quickly, *careless* was no longer an option. She couldn't summon it up to save her life. She fixed her gaze on the stormy scene outside the window, wishing for one moment that she was out in it. The rain could wash her clean and the wind could carry her away, setting her down in a time and a place far from the troubles of the present. She doubted, though, that such a time and place existed, or that she could find them if they did.

What she meant to be a simple exhalation quavered too much like a sob. ''Yes,'' she replied. ''And pictures of my husband.'' A few snapshots had been stored on her laptop and she'd carried another in her wallet. That last night in Portland, she had been juggling groceries and mail and had left her purse and laptop in the car, intending to return for them. It had turned out lucky for her, since all she'd had time to do once she got inside the house was scream in horror, drop everything—grab one thing—and run.

''How long were you married?''

She drew her feet onto the seat, tucking them beneath her, then rested her arm on the sofa back, her head on her hand. ''Seven years.''

''Was it a mugging? A robbery? A random shooting?''

She shrugged. ''They never caught the person.'' For months she'd checked the Portland newspapers every chance she got, praying she would see a story about the killer's arrest. When she'd never found a word, she had tried to convince herself the authorities *had* arrested him but were keeping it quiet. Then one day she'd seen him, and the terror streaking through her had left no doubt that he was looking for her. She had disappeared again that very afternoon, and she'd become smarter about covering her tracks. She would love to believe that, after all this time, he no longer considered her a threat, but another close call nearly a year ago had robbed her of that luxury.

"What happened? Was he shot at work? In his car? On the street? Did he walk in on a burglar? Had he been involved in an altercation?"

His questions were prompted by natural curiosity, she knew—more natural for him with his law enforcement background. Her reluctance to answer was prompted by the strongest instinct she possessed these days—the one for self-preservation. If she told him too much, he could prove her right or wrong. He could poke around, as cops tended to do, and fill in a few blanks. He could uncover some of her secrets.

The last thing he needed—the last thing *she* needed—was for him to know her secrets.

So she made the one comment she was fairly certain would turn him away from that line of questioning. She settled a measuring gaze on him and evenly remarked, "You sound like a cop."

Sure enough, that made a muscle in his jaw tighten and narrowed his gaze. He shoved to his feet, took their dishes in the kitchen where he set them in the sink with more force than necessary, then returned with the paper plate filled with cookies. She took one when he set it on the coffee table, then settled back again to watch as he paced to one of the side windows.

"Who told you I was a cop? Dad?"

Though he couldn't see her, she shook her head. "Lexy Marshall."

He grunted. ''Kid thinks because she's practically family she doesn't have to be afraid of me.''

''I don't believe I've met anyone yet who's afraid of you,'' she said with a smile. Tiny Liza Beth Rafferty certainly hadn't been, and neither had any of the other small children who'd greeted him at the barbecue last Saturday. Not that she doubted he could put the fear of God into a person, given the right motivation. ''I'm not sure it's occurred to Lexy to be afraid of anyone or anything. She's a very self-assured kid.''

He turned, leaning against the windowsill, feet crossed at the ankles. ''She is now. A year ago, when she showed up here, she had spiked purple hair, a dozen or more piercings, tattoos and an attitude with a capital A. Brady couldn't decide whether to put her in the lockup or to ship her back to Texas where she came from.''

''I thought she was his and Hallie's daughter.''

''Nah. They've only been married a year or so. Lexy's mother is Brady's first wife. Sandra's not real maternal and was doing Lexy more harm than good, so when Brady and Hallie got together, they got custody of her.''

''Her own mother just gave her up?''

His smile was thin and cynical. ''Not exactly. Hallie gave her a few good reasons. About fifty thousand of 'em.''

''She *sold* her own child? Jeez, my mother would *give* fifty thousand bucks to see me—''

The room was gloomy, but she didn't need light to see that his gaze had hardened, his expression sharpened. Her breath caught in her chest as she waited for him to pounce on her slip, to accuse in that sarcastic, scornful tone. *You said your mother was dead. You said you have no family, and now you've got a brother and a sister and your mother's been miraculously resurrected from the grave.*

But he didn't voice any of the accusations. Instead he shook his head with a derisive grin. ''You're something, Cassidy McRae. Damned if I know what, but *something*.''

After fifty years of regular clearing, the Barnett ranch con-
sisted of eighteen hundred and fifty acres of good grassland

with a minimum of timber and was home to a sizable herd of
cattle. Not being in the cattle business, Jace preferred the red-
and-white Herefords—the breed he'd grown up with, the ones
that always came to mind when he thought of cattle and ranching. Looking to get the best bang for his buck, Ray liked the
black baldies, born to a Hereford bred with an Angus or Bran-
gus bull, and the Brafords, a Brahman-Hereford mix.

What Jace *really* preferred, he thought as he drove along
the narrow lane that led to his parents' house, was not being
in the business. He wasn't the first Barnett who didn't have
ranching in the blood, and he wouldn't be the last. Hell, even
his dad only did it part-time. The majority of his workday was
spent at the garage he owned in Buffalo Plains with Reese's
father. He was fond of saying he preferred grease under his
fingernails to manure on his boots. He hired out the running
of the ranch to somebody else—had offered the job to Jace
when he'd first moved back from Kansas City. Jace wasn't
sure how desperate he would have to be to accept such an
offer. He hoped he would never find out.

"So this is where you grew up."

He glanced at Cassidy, her head swiveling to take in the
scene. There was no need. Once she'd seen one section of it,
for all practical purposes, she'd seen all of it—gently rolling
hills covered with grass, occasional arroyos created by hard
rains and erosion, even rarer stands of trees. Except for the
few acres surrounding the house, that described the entire
ranch. "Yep, this is it."

"It's lovely."

"Yeah. A bit open for my tastes."

She smiled. "You prefer the privacy of the forest and the
lake?"

"Oh, honey, that's not a forest. It's just a few thousand
acres of timber that no one's cut down 'cause they've gotta
have *someplace* to go hunting."

"How far off the road do your parents live?"

"About a mile and a half. It's just over that hill." He nodded ahead and to the right. "I've always thought that was why I took up running. I had to catch the school bus back at the county road every morning. My folks never had time to take me, and I never wanted to get up early enough to walk it, so I ran."

Again with that faint smile. "I thought you looked like a runner."

"I was, but not anymore."

"You gave it up last winter?"

He scowled at her as they crested the last hill, but she wasn't paying any attention to him. The valley stretched off to the horizon, dotted in the distance with trees and cattle, broken up in the foreground with the house and the ranch buildings. The house was on the small side, one story and built of native stone with a sharply pitched roof and tall windows stretching across the front. "My great-grandfather built the house—quarried the rock himself from a place a couple miles from here. Mom never really liked it, so as soon as more kids came along, she intended to build a new one right over there." Slowing to a stop, he gestured west toward a clump of catalpa trees. "Unfortunately, more kids never came, so she learned to make do." He gave Cassidy a sidelong look. "Some of us who claim to be only children really are."

She sat primly, legs crossed, chin raised, offering zero response to his dig. Instead she gestured into the distance with one graceful hand. "What are those buildings?"

"Barn, equipment shed, chicken house, manager's house. Manager's my cousin, Jimmy. His wife, Kristin, is his right-hand man. They'll probably be at dinner tonight."

She got an uncomfortable look at that, but didn't say anything. "Do they have horses?"

"Of course they have horses. It's a ranch, isn't it? Though they do an awful lot of work with trucks when they can." He removed his foot from the brake and the truck started rolling forward. "You like to ride?"

"I never learned."

"Don't they have horses back east?"

"Not where I lived."

"Tell me again where that was."

She frowned at him as he parked beside his mother's car. "Halfway between the middle of nowhere and the end of the line."

"Wrong, darlin', 'cause that's right *here*." He got out of the truck and took a few steps toward the door before realizing that she wasn't behind him. Turning back, he watched her slide to the ground, close the door as if trying to do so silently, then sidle toward the front of the truck. She looked nervous. Because she thought meeting his parents meant something? Because she thought *they* might think it meant something? Maybe it was simpler. Maybe lying to him, Reese and everyone else was one thing, but doing it with his folks was something else.

But that would mean she had scruples about her lies, and he was pretty sure that was an oxymoron, along with *honest thief* and *innocent criminal.*

"They won't bite."

She slowly circled the SUV. As she continued toward the stoop, he fell into step with her. "I know," she said with a dry look. "I was just thinking about how long it's been since I've had dinner with a man's parents."

"Your husband's parents?"

She nodded.

You sound like a cop, she'd told him the day before, shutting off his questions like a tap shutting off water. He still had the questions, though—dozens of them. Some were important, like *What did he do?* and *Why did he die?* and *How did you deal with it?* Others were important in other ways, like *Do you still love him?* and *Are you still grieving for him?*

He settled for one question. "What was his name?"

She climbed the two low steps leading to the stoop before facing him, stopping him at the bottom. The difference in height put them eye to suspicious, wary, maybe-brown-probably-not eye. "Why do you want to know?"

Because I'm curious. Because he was important to you. Be-

cause I want to know what I'm getting into. "Occupational hazard," he said with a shrug. "I spent seventeen years asking questions. It's a tough habit to break."

Suspicion and wariness faded into acknowledgment that he'd told her something—how long he'd been a cop—that he hadn't volunteered before. Just as quickly the distrust returned. Did she think it was tit for tat? He'd told her something, and so now she should tell him something in return? That hadn't been his intention, but if it worked....

"And if I tell you his name, are you going to get on the Internet or on the phone with Reese and check to see if someone by that name really was murdered and really did have a wife named Cassidy?"

That hadn't been his intention, either, not initially, but if she gave him the information, it would be too tempting to ignore. "Probably so," he admitted. Something that looked a lot like hurt flashed across her face and gave life to a twinge of guilt deep inside him, but he refused to accept it. "Hey, you want to tell lies all the time, you've got to get used to people not believing you."

She pressed her lips into a thin line and her jaw tightened. Then she took a deep breath and her face went blank. "And you've got to get used to not thinking you should be able to believe me."

The flat statement angered him. He wanted to shake her, to demand an explanation from her, to force her to tell him the truth, to confide in him, to trust him....

To trust him. That was what made him crazy—not so much that she lied, but that she lied to *him.* He was one of the good guys, honest, truthful, principled, above reproach, but she didn't trust him.

Why?

They were just looking at each other, neither willing—or daring?—to speak, when the door opened suddenly, followed by his father's booming voice. "I told your mother I thought I heard your truck, but she didn't believe me. Says I'm too hard of hearing to hear her tell me to run the vacuum when she's standin' right beside me, so I sure couldn't hear a truck pull up outside.''

With one last look at Cassidy, Jace stepped past her and stopped at the door. ''Doesn't she know by now that you've got selective hearing?''

Ray grinned. ''She'd rather forget that than think I could possibly not want to listen to what she has to say. Cassidy, it's good to see you again. Come on in and let me introduce you to Jace's mother.'' With a hand on her shoulder, he ushered her inside, gave Jace a wink, then followed.

Alone on the stoop, Jace rolled his gaze heavenward, then stepped inside.

The house was cool and smelled of…well, good things he couldn't quite identify. Orange-scented cleaning solutions, vanilla-and-citrus potpourri that Rozena mixed up herself and incredible food aromas. His mother's cooking was always good, but on special occasions she really knocked herself out—and his bringing a woman for dinner rated with his parents as the most special of occasions. They were always hopeful, in spite of having been disappointed every time in the past. They'd disliked Julie and Amanda practically from the moment they'd met—a mother had instincts about these things, Rozena had told him later—and though angry on his behalf when the relationships ended, they had also been relieved.

It seemed his father had taken an immediate liking to Cassidy. Was that good or bad? Good, he guessed, as long as Ray understood that nothing serious could come of it, that she was leaving soon, that Jace didn't want anything more than sex from her….

Sure, he would tell his dad that—when he wasn't standing in striking distance.

Though there was no sign of his cousin, the dining table was set for six, confirming his expectation that Jimmy and Kristin would be joining them. His mother was using her favorite china, tablecloth and napkins, handed down from some great-great on his father's side—a sign of how significant this dinner was to her. If Cassidy hadn't agreed to come, the invitation would have stood for him alone, but they would have been eating at the smaller kitchen table off the everyday dishes and with paper napkins.

He sighed before he followed the voices into the kitchen. Rozena, wearing an apron over her dress, stood at the stove, dividing her attention equally between the cooking and Cassidy, and she was smiling—not the polite-but-hating-it smile she'd offered the other women in his life, but an honest-to-God, genuine smile. Oh, boy.

"Hey, Mom." He slid his arms around her from behind, kissed her cheek, then lifted the lid on the pot on the front burner. She slapped his hand away before he got more than a whiff of fragrant steam.

"Don't interfere with the artist at work," she admonished him. "It's about time we saw your face around here. Do you know how long it's been?"

"I come every time you invite me."

"And since when did visiting your mama and daddy require an invitation?" She gave a sniff, then patted his cheek even as she pushed him to arm's length to study him. "Thank heavens, you finally got that hair cut. Was that your idea, Cassidy?"

Standing against the wall near the kitchen table, Cassidy looked startled by the question. "Oh, no. He just did it."

Rozena grinned knowingly. "Uh-huh. And here I've been nagging at him to cut it for months."

"She was afraid I would start braiding it with leather and feathers, the way her people used to do," Jace teased. "Then who knows how far behind the war paint and breechclout would have been?"

His mother swatted him, and he moved out of the way, copying Cassidy's position against the side wall. The table there held a napkin-lined basket, waiting for bread, and a bowl filled with sliced strawberries buried under sugar. The first meal he and Cassidy had shared had ended with strawberry pie, and she had all but gotten orgasmic over it. Lucky guess for Rozena on tonight's dessert.

After a few minutes of idle conversation, his father gestured. "Why don't you come out into the shop with me, son, and let the ladies talk. Your mother will give us a holler when dinner's ready."

Ordinarily, Jace was happy to hide out in the shop—it was filled with power tools, and what man didn't like that? It was the letting-the-ladies-talk part that made him reluctant this evening. He didn't want his mother taken in by Cassidy's lines, but he couldn't very well warn Rozena on the way out not to believe a word she said. All he could do was trust Cassidy to stick to the truth whenever possible.

As he followed his father from the kitchen, he gave her a narrow stare that he hoped conveyed that message. Then he grimaced. That was a stupid expectation. If sticking to the truth was possible, she wouldn't be a habitual liar, would she?

Chapter 9

"I understand you're a writer."

Cassidy kept her smile in place even though her jaw clenched hard. She wished she'd given Paulette Fox any other reason in the world for coming to Buffalo Lake, but, no, she'd gone with one that was guaranteed to spark interest in everyone who heard it. At least, instead of being a huge, all-encompassing lie, now it was only a semihuge lie, because she really was writing, with pages, chapters and everything. She probably wasn't writing well, but she couldn't have everything, could she?

"Yes, I am," she replied at last, mentally cringing in preparation for the next question.

"That's nice. You enjoy it?"

"Yes."

Rozena nodded thoughtfully. "Everyone should be able to make a living doing something they like. Where are your people from?"

"My—" Relief shivered through Cassidy. That was it? One simple question that could have as easily been asked of a doctor, a preacher or a prostitute? Obviously the interrogation skills in the Barnett family belonged to Jace. "My family lives in Pennsylvania." As she answered, she wondered if Jace would compare notes with his mother and realize that was twice Pennsylvania had come up in her responses. Would he suspect that once, at least, she'd told him the truth?

"Pennsylvania. I've never been there. Ray and I have always planned to do some traveling once he retired from the garage, but that's never going to happen. He may cut back on the hours he works someday, but he's never going to quit completely. He wouldn't know what to do with himself. More importantly, *I* wouldn't know what to do with him."

"Maybe Jace could give him some pointers."

Rozena looked at her over one shoulder, her expression serious. "That boy," she murmured. "It just makes me crazy to see him wasting his life like this. Things didn't go the way he wanted. So what? You don't just crawl off somewhere and be a bum for the rest of your life. I don't know how he stands it…though I have to admit, I'm glad he gave up the police work. But if he would just do *something* besides lie around watching television all day…."

Cassidy smiled politely. "I'm sure he'll find a job when he's ready."

"That's what Reese said…six months ago."

"People deal with things in different ways. Maybe he needs more time than you expected to get a handle on what went wrong." Cassidy's method of dealing with Phil's death probably hadn't been exactly conventional. Of course, unlike most widows, she hadn't gotten the chance to cope. She hadn't been able to plan and attend the funeral, to lean on family and friends, to focus on her grief, to accept and mourn, then rebuild her life. Her priority had been staying alive. She'd left the funeral plans to…well, whoever, and she hadn't had anyone to lean on but herself. Instead of drawing strength from her and Phil's families, she'd wondered if they would ever even know he was dead. Instead of mourning, she'd been learning the ins and outs of life on the run. She'd been cold, strong and focused during the days, but at night...for two years, she'd cried herself to sleep, wishing through the hurt that Phil was still with her.

"I suppose he can't live like this forever," Rozena said with a sigh. "I just don't know what he might find to do, though. All he ever wanted to be was a policeman, ever since he was a boy. I hated that job. I know he was very good at it, but being good isn't always enough. A mother worries, you know."

She flashed an apologetic smile at Cassidy, who returned it. If she had a son, she would worry, too, she was sure, just as her mother worried about her. On the other hand, though, she'd developed something of a fatalistic approach to life in the past few years. What happens, happens. When it was her time to die, she would die. That didn't mean she could come out of hiding, go home and start using her own name again. She had to exercise reasonable caution, but in the end, that was *all* she could do.

Phil had exercised reasonable caution, a small voice whispered in her head, *and look what it got him.*

Maybe her fatalistic approach was more a sanity-saving measure than a true belief, she thought wryly. If she laid the blame for everything on Fate, then she didn't have to torment herself with the what-ifs, the could-haves and might-have-beens.

After a few minutes chatting on lighter subjects, Rozena turned from the stove and removed the apron. "Well, that about does it. All we need is for Jimmy and Kristin to get here—that's my nephew and his wife, they run the ranch for us—and then we can sit down and eat." The last word was accompanied by the peal of the doorbell. "Oh, great. If you'll fetch the men—the shop's through the door in the dining room—I'll let them in."

Cassidy walked into the dining room, circled the large table and went through the door tucked into the corner. It opened into a long narrow hall, obviously not original to the house, since the interior wall had once been the house's exterior wall.

At the end it opened into a large square room, brightly lit with half a dozen overhead bulbs, meticulously neat and filled with more tools than she could identify.

Jace and his father were standing on opposite sides of the central work table, with some kind of power tool laid out between them. She waited in the doorway until Ray finished speaking, then stepped forward. "Mrs. Barnett sent me to fetch you two."

"Oh, now I'm sure she told you to call her Rozena," Ray said, immediately heading toward her. "'Mrs. Barnett' would be…come to think of it, we haven't really had a 'Mrs. Barnett' since my mother died. It's just way too formal for folks like us."

With a polite smile of acknowledgment, Cassidy returned the way she came with both men behind her. When she stepped through the dining-room door, she found Rozena and another couple standing at the far end of the table talking. Both newcomers looked at her with undisguised curiosity, making her wish for one second that she could slip back through the door, then take shelter for her reentry behind Jace.

Not that she needed protection from these people, she sternly admonished herself.

Not that Jace had any interest in offering protection.

Jimmy and Kristin Greenfeather were in their midtwenties, she guessed, and about the same height—around five eight— but that was where the similarities ended. He was obviously Jace's cousin on the Osage side of the family, with black hair, dark skin and eyes, and was reed thin. Kristin was blond, blue-eyed and fair-skinned, and carried an extra thirty pounds or so. They were both, she discovered after the introductions and throughout the meal, very nice people…and very interested in her relationship with Jace. As were his parents.

It wasn't her place to tell them that their relationship was entirely a matter of proximity. If his cabin wasn't across the inlet from hers, she probably never would have met him. There wasn't anything romantic between them—couldn't be, not when he distrusted everything she said. Not when she would be leaving Oklahoma soon. Certainly not when getting involved with her could prove hazardous to his health.

She was glad responsibility for setting them straight didn't rest on her shoulders—not only because it could be an awkward prospect, but also because…well, hell, deep down inside she kind of liked the idea of being *involved*. Not the reality of it, just the possibility. These people who knew him well found it easy to believe that *she* could attract and hold on to a man like Jace. For a woman who had been as utterly alone for as long as she had, there was something very comforting in that.

After a wonderful dinner and an incredible strawberry meringue for dessert, Rozena and Kristin hustled everyone away from the table, then declared the kitchen off-limits. When Cassidy volunteered to help with cleanup, they brushed her off and left her alone with Jace.

"Want to see the horses?" he asked.

See the horses. Hmm, just the two of them, walking out to the corral in the cool evening dusk, away from curious eyes and sly smiles, alone in the night…. "Sure."

Ignoring his mother's declaration, he went into the kitchen, then returned with a handful of carrots. He opened the sliding door that led to the patio, then followed her out.

It wasn't cool exactly, but not uncomfortably warm. All that was left of the sun was a tinge of color on the western horizon and stars were slowly appearing amid the clouds overhead. Lights shone from the workshop windows, making elongated rectangular shapes on the grass. When she glanced that way, she saw Ray, wearing safety glasses and bent over some task, while Jimmy watched.

The stone patio ran about half the length of the house, with a gas grill, table and chairs at the end nearest the kitchen and overflowing flowerpots and a small stone fountain at the opposite end. Halfway between the two, Jace turned onto the grass, making a beeline for the corral that butted up to the barn.

It was darker out here, with only the dim light from a bulb

mounted above the barn door for illumination. Cassidy's eyes adjusted easily enough, though, as the horses jostled for space along the fence.

Jace offered her half of a broken carrot. "Want to feed 'em?"

"Will they mistake my fingers for food?"

"Not if you keep them out of the way."

He showed her how to offer the carrot, then steadied her hand as the nearest animal nuzzled it away. She wanted to jerk her hand back and wipe it on something—preferably something not hers—and go, *Ewww, horse slobber.* Figuring Jace would be amused, annoyed or both, she did neither.

"They're beautiful," she said softly, then shook her head when he held out another carrot. He fed one to each of the horses and for a moment the only sound was the crunching of powerful teeth.

"This one's mine. His name is Rogue." He petted and scratched the horse, blowing in his nostrils, damn near cuddling with him. "He's twelve years old and seventeen hands."

Years, she understood. Hands... "I assume that has something to do with how big he is." When he nodded, she gave a shake of her head. "They should come in sizes that make sense—baby, pony, big, bigger, biggest."

"Then Rogue would be 'monster.' Seventeen hands is *big*."

She could see that, comparing him to the others. Of course, even the smallest seemed awfully big to her.

"You want to come back sometime for a riding lesson?"

The horse to whom she'd fed the carrot gently butted his head against her and she reached out to pet him. Was there a point to taking a lesson when she wouldn't be around long enough to really learn anything? Even if she did actually learn, what were the chances she would ever have another opportunity to ride?

The point was, it would be fun, new, different...and a few more hours spent in Jace's company.

"I'd like that."

"Good," he murmured before turning to lean against the

corral fence. Raising one hand to scratch Rogue's neck, he fixed his gaze on her. "My parents like you."

"I'm a likable person."

If his wry look was anything to judge by, he didn't one hundred percent agree, but he didn't say so. Instead he stuck to the subject of his parents. "Don't do anything to hurt them."

She wanted to take offense, to defend herself, to snidely point out to him that she was an adult and thoroughly capable of comporting herself appropriately. Another part of her wanted to remind him that, dinner aside, they were nothing more than acquaintances and likely to stay that way. Still another part wanted to weep that life had brought her to the place where a man could reasonably and legitimately make such a demand of her.

Her only response to his words was to hug her arms to her chest and to announce, "I'd like to go home soon. I—I need to get some work done tonight."

Though she didn't look at him, she could feel his gaze on her for a long time before he pushed away from the fence and gestured toward the house.

They returned in silence, and found Rozena and Kristin sitting at the kitchen table with cups of coffee between them. "We're gonna head home, Mom. Cassidy's got to work tonight," Jace said as casually as if it was true.

"Oh, I was hoping we could sit a while and talk, but...I understand. Call your dad out here so he can say good-night, would you, son?" As he left the room, Rozena stood and slid her arm around Cassidy's waist. "I'm glad we got a chance to meet, Cassidy. Maybe sometime we can get together without the men and just gab a while."

"I'd like that." Cassidy's smile was half forced, half genuine. Rozena Barnett was such a motherly woman, and in the past six years Cassidy had missed that more than she could say. When she was a teenager, she'd looked forward to the day when she would be grown up and on her own, no longer just a daughter but a woman, her mother's equal. She'd since discovered she would *never* be her mother's equal. For wisdom, comfort and advice, no one beat a mother.

Jace returned with the other two men and the group gradually moved to the front hallway. Just before she and Jace walked out the door, his parents both hugged her, then him. "I love you," she heard him murmur, first to his mother, then to his father.

A lump formed in her throat as she walked to the SUV. She couldn't remember ever hearing a grown man tell a parent he loved him—not Phil, not her brother, not her father. Had they ever regretted it? When her grandfather died, had her father wondered if the old man had known how he felt? Had Phil ever wished he'd said it to his own parents before he'd disappeared from their lives?

She had never been one to say it a lot herself, except to Phil. She was struck by the irrational urge to ask Jace to stop at a pay phone on the way home, to dial her folks' number, then her brother's, then her sister's, and blurt out the words in an emotional rush before hanging up again. Of course, she couldn't. That was one of the things she and Phil had been sternly warned against. Phone records could be monitored. Any out-of-state calls could provide a starting point to look for them.

Not that the man who killed Phil had needed anything so inconsequential as phone records to find him.

She stared out the window, seeing little in the darkness, until abruptly she became aware that they weren't moving. Blinking, she looked around but could see only shadows. Then the moon appeared from behind the clouds, glinting off the land, a broad creek, a pile of sandstone boulders taller than the truck. "Where are we?"

"My favorite of the Barnett eighteen-hundred-plus acres." Jace cut off the engine, then climbed out. After a moment she warily followed, moving to stand beside him at the front of the truck. "This is where I spent most of my summers growing up. There's a good swimming hole down there, and good fishing up that way fifty yards. Reese and I used to pitch a tent right here and stay two, three days at a time. We only went home for more food before coming back.''

''Didn't your parents worry?''

He shrugged. ''We're only about a half mile from the house as the crow flies. Besides, I think my dad used to sneak out and check up on us.''

''Sounds like a great way to grow up.''

''Better for me than for Reese.''

Raising her brows, she looked at him, and he leaned back against the truck, crossing one ankle over the other. ''Reese's parents weren't married. Uncle Del wanted to get married—hell, he wound up doing it four times—but Lena always wanted more than he could give, so she was in and out of their lives on a regular basis. Each time she left, they never heard from her until she popped up again. It was tough on Reese, not having a mother most of the time and knowing she didn't give a damn about him even when she was here. That's one reason he spent so much time with us growing up. My mom mothered him just like he was her own. It wasn't the same, but it was better than nothing.''

''That's sad. I don't understand bad parents. With all the options available, why bring a child you don't want into the world? Use birth control. Give him up for adoption. Learn to be a good parent.''

''You want kids?''

''I would love to have—'' Too late she remembered telling him first that she liked children only from a distance, then that she didn't like them at all. She had no doubt he remembered it, too.

If so, he gave no sign of it. He just continued to gaze at the creek. ''Is there any reason you can't have a couple?''

She couldn't restrain a snort. ''Yeah. No husband. No stability. No family to help.'' And no future. How unfair would that be to a child?

'''No husband' can be remedied—find a guy, get married. Other than your fondness for lying, you seem stable enough, and a husband would qualify as family. Besides, who knows? He could have plenty of family of his own.''

Like him. Like Rozena and Ray, Reese and Neely, Jimmy and Kristin, and his grandfather, and Paulette Fox and Easy Rafferty.

The thought started a tingle low in her stomach and spread warmth through her. Deliberately she moved away from the truck and toward the pile of rocks, seeking to put some distance between them. She was about to step onto the first low rock, intending to climb to the top and sit on the sun-warmed stone, when Jace caught her arm and tugged her back.

"I wouldn't advise that. Once the sun goes down, the copperheads come out, and they love warm rocks."

"Copperheads? Snakes?" She stepped back so quickly she stumbled over his foot, but he steadied her.

"Don't worry. Their bite's usually not fatal. It just hurts like holy hell. My mom used to plant great big flowerbeds all around the yard, and she was weeding one day when she reached in and grabbed a copperhead that had crawled in there to get out of the sun. It's hard to say who was more scared— her or the snake. Now all her flowers are in pots and she pokes around with a stick before she reaches in."

Cassidy shuddered. "I hate snakes."

"Most people do. It's too bad, too, because most of them are harmless. The few venomous ones give them all a bad name."

She gave him a narrowed look, then turned toward the creek instead. Before she'd gone a few feet, though, she glanced back. "Are there venomous water snakes around here?"

"Water moccasins." He laughed as she spun around and marched back to the truck. She climbed onto the hood, sat and smiled smugly when he said with feigned disdain, "City girls."

"Hey, it's got nothing to do with living in a city. It's common sense. I lived in a place that had cockroaches as big as small dogs, and I didn't freak out, but giant cockroaches can't kill you."

"Where was that?"

He asked the question softly, hesitantly, as if he didn't expect an answer—at least, not a straight one. Just as softly and hesitantly, she replied. "South Carolina." She'd gotten there, one short journey at a time, about a year after Phil died, before she'd realized that subconsciously she was making her way home. Since that was absolutely the one place she couldn't go, she'd immediately headed west again. Since then she hadn't gotten closer than five hundred miles to home.

There had been an old folk song about that, hadn't there? *Lord, I'm still five hundred miles away from home.*

"Were you researching a book there?"

"Yes," she murmured as she shook her head no.

He rested his arms on the hood on either side of her legs. "You're a pitiful liar, Cassidy. Is that even your real name?"

"I told you before, it's certainly not one I would make up."

"Yeah, but if you lied to me before, why would I think you wouldn't lie to me now?"

She waved one hand with a carelessness she didn't feel. "Those other lies had reasons. Why would I fib about something so basic as my name?"

He shifted his arms until they were pressing against her thighs, shifted his hand until his fingertip hooked in the belt loop on her shorts, creating a slight pressure at her waist, along with a significant heat. "You want to apply reason and logic to perjury?"

"That's the cop talking again. I think prevarication is a better description of what I do. Untruthfulness. Lying."

His other hand claimed a belt loop on her right side and he leaned closer. If she was sitting on her car, their position would be almost unbearably intimate, but the SUV had four-wheel drive and stood significantly higher off the ground. Even so, it was more intimate than she'd been with a man in three long years.

"Compulsive lying," he corrected her.

"It's not a compulsion," she disagreed. "I don't lie because I can't help myself."

"Then prove it. Just for tonight, swear you'll tell the truth, the whole truth and nothing but the truth, so help you God."

"Reese was right," she murmured. "Being a cop isn't what you do. It's who you are."

For the second time in a row, a reference to his former career didn't distract him from his focus. "Swear."

Swear. The evening was almost over. In a few minutes they would get back in the truck and drive home. He would deliver her to her door, say good-night and go to his own cabin, and she would spend the rest of the night alone. How difficult could telling the truth be for that short time? Besides, agreeing to tell the truth didn't mean she actually had to *tell* anything. She could always just refuse to speak.

"Okay," she said, then raised one hand as if taking an oath. "I swear."

She expected a question from him, sharp and immediate, but it didn't come. Instead he leaned closer at the same time his hands moved to her hips and pulled her toward the edge, and then he kissed her. He covered her mouth, stole her breath, made her hot and quavery and suddenly so needy that she literally throbbed with it. He stabbed his tongue inside her mouth, wrapped his arms around her, then lifted her from the hood, holding her tightly, sliding her slowly down the length of his body, holding her steady when her legs were too shaky to do so.

She wanted the kiss to go on forever. Wanted to rip off their clothes and to welcome him inside her right here. Wanted him to take her long and hard and fast and lazy until every minute of loneliness had banished from her soul. Wanted to jerk away and run screaming into the night.

She did none of that. When he raised his head, she dragged in a ragged breath that sounded half-sob, then dazedly tried to focus on him. His features looked hard—and his body felt it— as he rubbed one thumb across her mouth.

A kiss is just a kiss, another old song went. Yeah, right. Except that some kisses left you cold and some curled your toes. Some could make you forget common sense and safety and every means of self-protection you'd ever learned. Some could make you want. *Want*. Even when you couldn't have.

Some kisses could break your heart.

There were easily two dozen questions Jace wanted to ask, but he settled for the most inconsequential of them all. ''You want to go home?''

''Yeah.''

And he thought about but didn't ask a variation of the same question. *You want to go home with me?* If he asked, would she give him the answer he wanted?

There was an air of expectancy between them as he followed the faint trail back to his parents' driveway, then turned onto the county road. He could take the paved road to Heartbreak and make pretty good time, but tonight he wasn't interested in making time—at least, not that kind. He was in no hurry to get to the lake, no hurry at all to say good-night to Cassidy, then go home alone.

Since she was apparently waiting for him to take advantage of her pledge of honesty, he asked, ''What's your brother's name?''

A hesitation, a tightening of her lips, then a response. ''David.''

She'd needed a moment to think about that—to debate whether that tidbit could help him learn anything about her. Obviously she'd decided it couldn't, and she was right. There were probably only a few million Davids in the country, many of them with sisters.

''Is he older or younger?''

''Older.''

''And your sister?''

The same hesitation, though not so long. ''Marcy. She's younger.''

''Did she ever let her hair grow back?''

Her mouth formed a rueful smile. ''Not until I'd moved out of the house to go to college.''

He let a mile go by in silence before asking, "Your parents aren't really dead, are they?"

In her lap, her hands clenched tightly, and her foot, dangling with one leg crossed over the other, tapped anxiously in the air. She was regretting her promise and he'd figured she was about to circumvent it by not saying anything at all when she suddenly exhaled. "No. But they might as well be."

"Why do you say that?"

She shrugged. "They're not a part of my life. I'm not a part of theirs. For all practical purposes, I have no parents."

"They cut you off?"

Another shrug that he could take for yes or no, whichever suited him. He didn't believe her newly resurrected parents had removed her from their lives. What had she said when they'd talked about Lexy Marshall's mother taking Hallie's cash to sever her paternal rights to her daughter? *My mother would give fifty thousand bucks to see me.* That didn't sound as if the estrangement had been Mom's idea.

Dad's, maybe? She'd had little to say about him, beyond the fact that he was a school superintendent. Had he booted her out, and her mother lacked the courage to stand up to him?

"What's your favorite childhood memory?" he asked, putting aside the topic she clearly didn't want to discuss in greater detail.

She was silent a long time before smiling. "Sunday dinner. Before we went to church every Sunday morning, Mom would get dinner started—usually pot roast, though sometimes it was roasted chicken or baked ham. As soon as we got home, she would put an apron on over her dress and finish cooking. Marcy and I helped when we were old enough, and pretended to before that. When it was ready, we all sat down in the formal dining room—Sundays and holidays were the only times we used it—and my father would say the blessing while we all held hands—corny, I know—and then we would eat. Maybe it was because we ate in the dining room or we all still wore our church clothes or we were just…together, but it was always the best meal of the week. None of us ever missed Sunday dinner until David went away to college, then I did.''

Jace wondered how many meals she'd eaten by herself since then.

After a time he went on to his next question. ''How long has it been since you saw any of them?''

''A long time,'' she replied, her voice so soft he could barely hear. ''Six years.''

''Because of your husband?''

Finally he'd hit on a question that she grimly ignored rather than answer truthfully, which made the answer pretty clear. *Was the guy worth it?* he wanted to ask. *Worth losing contact with your parents, your brother and sister? Worth having no family for love and support?*

Had her family disliked her husband, or had he been the one to force the break? How much would she have to love him to let him get away with that? Either way, now that he was dead, what was keeping her from going home? Pride? Shame?

''His name was Phil,'' she said unexpectedly. ''He and David were in the same fraternity. That's how I met him.''

How difficult would it be to locate a school superintendent back east—he believed that much of what she'd told him before—with two daughters, one named Marcy, and a son named David who'd had a frat brother named Phil? Pretty damned difficult...but not impossible. Some Internet time, a few calls to old buddies....

Unbidden, her earlier words echoed in his mind. *And if I tell you his name, are you going to get on the Internet or on the phone with Reese...?* At the time he'd refused to feel guilty about the hurt that had crossed her face when he admitted he probably would. As he'd told her, when you lied all the time, you had to get used to people not believing you.

But she had reasons for lying, she had insisted—good ones in her mind. And she wasn't hurting anybody. She was frustrating the hell out of him, but so what? Women often achieved that effect on him without resorting to deception.

The bottom line was, no matter how accustomed he was to being trusted by everyone, no matter how repugnant he found her lies, he had no right to demand the truth from her. They were neighbors. Sort-of friends. Might-be lovers. But nothing more than that. Nothing serious. Nothing permanent.

Nothing that gave either of them any rights over the other.

And that was all he wanted, right? Right.

And maybe more than *she* wanted.

The official first day of summer arrived with a vengeance. The warm days Cassidy had come to expect gave way to a thermometer reading of eighty-six before the sun had even finished rising, and it kept climbing. By the time she gave up, closed the windows and turned on the small window air conditioner, it was miserably hot and muggy. Welcome to summer in Oklahoma.

Unable to concentrate with the racket from the air conditioner, she shut off the computer and stretched out on the couch where the cooler air washed over her. Her body temperature had dropped somewhere close to normal and she was seriously considering a nap when a knock at the door startled her. She hadn't heard footsteps, though with the AC running, she wouldn't have heard a locomotive pulling into the driveway.

Not that there was any reason to be concerned. No doubt it was Jace, since he was the only one who'd ever come here. Oh, except for Neely and Hallie. Or maybe it was his mother, ready for the male-free chat. Or Paulette Fox, wanting to know how things were going.

Making a face at herself for wasting time wondering who it might be when it was easier by far to open the door to see, she did just that. She'd been right the first time. It was Jace.

He looked past her, saw the computer was off and grinned. "Good. I'm not interrupting."

"Would it matter if you were?"

"I would say I'm sorry."

"But would you mean it?"

''Sort of. Change into your swimsuit and come out on the lake with me.''

She leaned one shoulder against the jamb and crossed her arms. ''To do what?''

''Enjoy the day. Cool off. Get some color.''

Slowly her gaze slid down his body, over arms and shoulders exposed by a basketball jersey that had seen better days and long, long legs that extended past the cutoffs he wore. ''You have plenty of color.''

''Yeah, but you don't. You give new meaning to the word 'paleface.'''

''I'm not that pale.''

''Pale enough. Go on. Change. I'll even buy you lunch.''

''Where on the lake can you buy lunch?''

''There's a little store on the north shore near the public boat ramp that sells gas, bait, fishing licenses and the best barbecued pork sandwiches in three counties. What do you say?''

When she was younger, she'd loved spending hot afternoons at the lake. The nostalgia tempted her almost as much as the prospect of another afternoon with Jace did. Besides, left on her own, what would she do but laze the afternoon away?

Instead of agreeing right away, though, she remarked, ''I don't have a swimsuit.''

''You're living twenty feet from the lake's edge and you don't have a swimsuit? City girl.'' Then he shrugged. ''So wear shorts and a T-shirt. If you decide to go in the water, you can strip down.''

''Yeah, right,'' she muttered as she turned away from the door. *Only if you do the same.* Though maybe not even then. The sight of him naked might leave her so dazed that she couldn't do a thing but stare.

Leaving it up to him whether he came in or stayed out, she went into the bedroom and changed into a shorter pair of shorts and a tank of her own. She shoved her feet into canvas sneakers, slathered sunscreen over her arms, legs and face, then returned to the living room, where she got her sunglasses and keys. "Okay, I'm ready."

After she locked up, they crossed the footbridge and by-passed his cabin for the grassy spot where the john boat rested upside down. The motor, two oars, a couple of life preservers and a small cooler sat nearby.

"I'd let you help me turn the boat over," Jace remarked even as she bent at one end, "but from time to time, I find a water moccasin curled up underneath it."

Without missing a beat, she straightened and backtracked a dozen feet, then waited. He flipped the small boat easily, though cautiously, slid it partway into the water, then gestured for her to climb in. After handing everything to her, he stepped in, then used an oar to push away from the bank. It took a little maneuvering to get the motor in place and started, then they headed for the main body of the lake with a soothing putt-putt.

The boat's top speed was probably a couple miles an hour. Using the life preservers for cushions, Cassidy settled in comfortably, facing Jace, to enjoy the leisurely trip.

"You smell like a piña colada," he remarked. "Like summer."

She sniffed the coconut-scented fragrance of the sunscreen. "I always loved summer when I was growing up. Going barefoot, being lazy, staying up late and sleeping in late. Picnics and barbecues and vacations at the shore. Rain feels better when it's 95 degrees outside, and ice cream tastes better. The sky seems clearer, the stars brighter. For a few months, it seems that anything is possible."

"When did you stop growing up?" His voice was steady, calm. He had a talent for asking questions in an unobtrusive way, a subtle nudge to keep the conversation going. Or he could be one-hundred-and-eighty-degrees opposite—aggressive, pushy, demanding. The good cop or the bad one. She wasn't sure which she preferred.

"I don't know. Somewhere along the way I realized summer was also a time of beginnings and endings. The end of school, the beginning of college, the end of college, the beginning of a career.... Phil and I got married in August, and he died in July. Beginnings and endings...." She waited for the usual melancholy to slip over her, for the urge to curl up somewhere and weep, but it didn't come. Oh, there was sadness, certainly, but not the encompassing sorrow she was accustomed to. This sadness was bittersweet, bearable, almost forgettable.

"Do you still love him?"

She sneaked a glance his way, but as if it wasn't enough that mirrored shades hid his eyes, his head was turned to the left, his gaze on a ski boat off to the west. "I'll always love him. I don't believe love dies just because a person does."

"Maybe it doesn't just die, but it can damn well be killed."

Now she openly studied him. He spoke as if from experience—and he probably did. She didn't know how old he was, though allowing for college and seventeen years as a cop, she figured late thirties. Surely he hadn't lived that long without falling in love at least once. "Which one was she? Julie or Amanda?"

Slowly he turned until his gaze connected with hers. "Amanda."

In the past few days it seemed everything reminded her of a song. *Amanda, light up my life....* Amanda, who did her duty by coming for Thanksgiving and never intended to visit again. "Was she mean to your parents? Was that why you warned me not to hurt them?"

"Nah. Mom and Dad didn't like her from the git-go. They were happy when she dumped me a few weeks later. I warned you because they do like you, and I would prefer they didn't know that you have this nasty habit of not being honest. If they thought you were lying to them every time you opened your mouth, they would be disappointed, and I try very hard to not give them reasons to be disappointed."

There was so much in that snippet of conversation that she wanted to respond to that she didn't know where to start. Amanda had dumped him? Why? Had he loved her? Was he

over her, or did it still hurt? His parents liked *her?* How did
he know? Had they told him so? If they liked her enough to
be disappointed because of her, did that mean they had hopes
for her and their son? Had he said anything to dissuade them?
Did *he* have any hopes?

For the first time in years, *she* was having a few. At least,
she thought that was what the quivery, anticipatory, apprehensive feelings in her gut were. She'd been without hope for so
long, though, she couldn't be sure.

It would be foolish to start hoping again, she chastised herself. So what if she'd been safe and happy and comfortable at
Buffalo Lake? So what if she'd let other people into her life,
even on the most superficial basis, for the first time in three
years? So what if some of those people seemed to genuinely
like her? She couldn't stay. Sooner or later, something would
happen. Jace would get tired of all his questions and start
snooping into the stories she'd told him. Some cop would run
her tag and want to know why Cassidy McRae's car was registered to Stacy Beauchamp—if not her, then to Linda Valdez—and if he was particularly nosy, he would want to know
why neither Cassidy nor Stacy nor Linda really existed.

Sooner or later everything would fall apart and she would
have no choice but to run away again, and it would be so
damn hard if she'd let herself hope.

Now the melancholy she'd expected earlier came, settling
over her like a fog that diminished the sun's brightness and
made the hot heavy air even heavier. It made breathing difficult and tempted her to strip off her clothes, dive into the water
and not come up until she was certain she could breathe again.

Instead, she fixed her gaze on Jace and took steady, if shallow, breaths. "Tell me about Amanda."

He shrugged. "She hung out at the same bar a bunch of
cops did. We dated. She moved in. I planned to give her an
engagement ring on Valentine's Day."

So Jace had a romantic streak. Sometimes she'd missed that
with Phil. His idea of a romantic gesture had been having his
secretary order flowers for her on her birthday, anniversary

and Valentine's Day. Red roses. Even though they were her least favorite flower in the world.

"You brought her home to meet your family and neither side was impressed. Then what?"

"I found out she'd suckered me. She didn't love *me*. She loved *cops*. That's why she hung out at that bar and hadn't dated anyone in five years who wasn't a cop. When I..." For an instant his features hardened and took on a cold distance. It passed in degrees, though his jaw was still clenched when he finally went on. "When I got suspended, she started looking for a replacement. I went home one day and she was gone."

It didn't matter that she hadn't loved him, Cassidy thought. The important thing was that *he* had loved *her,* had wanted to marry her. "When I asked you that day if you'd ever come close to getting married and you said no, it wasn't exactly the truth," she said softly.

"No," he agreed, his mouth curving in a cynical smile. "Not exactly."

"You still love her?"

"No."

He could be lying again, to salve his wounded ego, but she believed him. As he'd said earlier, love could damn well be killed, and apparently, Amanda had been lethal.

"I'm sorry."

He gave an easy shrug that made the muscles in his arms ripple. "It was for the best. If we'd gotten married, it wouldn't have lasted. Getting dumped by a girlfriend has to be easier than getting divorced. There was no home to break up, no kids to uproot, no property settlement to fight over."

Leaning forward, she picked up the Royals cap he'd tossed into the bottom of the boat and settled it on her own head. "And it's easier to be philosophical about it six or eight months out, isn't it?"

He grinned. "Damn straight."

Slipping off her shoes, she crossed one ankle over the other and gazed around. She knew from the map that, as lakes went,

Buffalo Lake was rather small, but it didn't look it from the middle. The water seemed to stretch out forever, though she suspected from the concentrated shimmer that *seemed* was the operative word. Some of it, she was sure, was merely an optical illusion, caused by the blinding sun almost directly overhead.

They saw plenty of boats in the distance, everything from canoes to john boats to ski boats, and once a couple of Jet Skis driven by two Indian boys raced past. Both raised their hands in greeting, and one swung the Jet Ski in a wide circle around them with a whoop before tearing off after the other.

"Let me guess," Cassidy said dryly. "More Barnett relatives."

"Actually, Greenfeather relatives. My uncle Ronald's grandsons."

Even when she'd had family, she'd never had a lot of them. She envied him so many relatives that he could hardly leave home without running into one. If she could stay, if she could have a future and have it with him, *she* could have all those relatives, too. *She* could go to family get-togethers of seventy people or more—could even contribute to the *more* part.

No foolish daydreams, she cautioned herself.

Even if daydreams were all she could have.

Before long they reached the boat ramp and the store Jace had told her about—a tiny cinder-block building flaking sky-blue paint. The goods it offered were about evenly divided between ice and cold drinks, fishing equipment, and barbecue chips and cookies. While she waited near the door, Jace bought four pork sandwiches, a family size bag of potato chips and a package of Oreos. Outside once again, they settled at a warped redwood table under a shade tree near the water's edge.

"When I was a kid," she began after they'd each had a chance to make a good start on their meal, "I truly believed Mom did something special to the food we took to the lake with us. She usually fixed tuna-salad sandwiches, chips and brownies, and it always tasted so much better when we were waterlogged and sunburned than it did any other time.''

For a long time he looked at her, his expression intense. Then he reached into his pocket, pulled out a handful of change and slapped it down on the table in front of her.

''What's that for?''

''There's a pay phone around front. Call home.''

She stared at the coins, then abruptly picked up the second half of her sandwich. Her movements were so shaky that pork spilled onto the paper wrapper. ''I can't.''

''Why not?''

''I just can't.''

''Whatever you did, whatever your husband did, it's over and done with. They'll forgive it.''

''It's not that simple.''

''It can't be as difficult as you make it.''

Heat flushed her face. ''*I* haven't made *anything* difficult! It was Phil who—'' Breaking off, she clamped her mouth shut.

''Phil who did what? Who forced you to choose between him and your family?''

She said nothing.

''Phil's dead. Call your mom and dad. They'll be happy to hear from you.''

''That's never been the problem.''

''Then what is?''

She stared at him, grateful for the sunglasses and ball cap that offered her some small protection. As soon as the thought formed, though, he reached across, removed the cap and tossed it on the table, then followed it with her glasses.

''What *is* the problem, Cassidy?'' he repeated. ''If you're sure they would be happy to hear from you, why won't you call? Are you angry with them? Are you punishing them?''

Breaking contact with him, she looked down and saw her sandwich was gone. Of course. She got upset, she ate. She reached for the last sandwich, tore it in two and took a bite. After washing it down with bottled water from the cooler, she

met his gaze with a callousness she was far, far from feeling.
''Not everyone thinks family is as important as you do.''

''Are you telling me you don't miss your parents? You
wouldn't love to talk to them, see them? Because there's no
way in hell I'll believe that.''

''It's true,'' she replied coolly, and he snorted. ''Whether
you believe it doesn't matter. *You* don't matter.''

Two more damned lies. Dear God, someday they were going to collapse and bury her under their weight.

In some perverse way, she looked forward to it. At least
then she would have some peace.

Chapter 10

Pointing the boat at the grass, Jace added enough power to run it partly out of the water, though thanks to the additional weight, not as far as usual. That didn't deter Cassidy, though. The instant it stopped moving, she was on her feet, stepping out onto the ground quickly enough to rock the boat. By the time he cut the engine, she was striding past the cabin, and by the time he hauled the boat the rest of the way out of the water, she was crossing the bridge.

He couldn't think of many better ways to spend the first really hot day of summer than on the water with a pretty woman—except in bed with the same pretty woman—but their conversation over lunch had zapped the enjoyment right out of the day. Instead of the lazy going-nowhere afternoon he'd planned, after lunch they'd headed straight back home. She'd sat stiffly on the bench, her back to him, and said nothing the entire trip. He hadn't spoken, either. After her closing shot—''*You* don't matter''—he hadn't been able to find anything worth saying.

He'd had it with trying to be friendly, with acting neighborly. He didn't need this kind of hassle. From now on he would be the kind of neighbor she wanted—distant. Uninterested. Unattracted.

He couldn't contain the snort that broke free at that last thought. As if it was that easy to turn off sexual attraction. But, damn, getting laid was *not* worth the trouble. There were plenty of women out there who would require a whole lot less effort. He was going to stick to that type and to hell with Cassidy McRae.

He grabbed the cooler and went inside, leaving it on the kitchen counter before stripping down and climbing into the shower. The steady beat of the water cooled him down significantly, though he was pretty sure that the steam filling the bathroom came from him and not from the lukewarm water.

He'd just pulled on a clean pair of cutoffs when a slam echoed across the inlet. He looked out the living-room window in time to see Cassidy step off her deck, her arms cradling an open box from which kitchen stuff stuck out. Without stopping to put on shoes, he charged out the door, across the deck and across the bridge.

She had showered, too, leaving her hair damp and finger-combed, and changed into a sleeveless cotton dress that ended well above her knees. She stopped abruptly when she saw him, hesitated, then, her mouth in a thin line, dropped the box in the open trunk of her car before starting back to the cabin. He followed.

The screen door slamming in his face didn't deter him one bit. He jerked it open, let it slam again behind him, then glanced around. The cabin looked as if it had been ransacked while they were gone. Stacks of clothes still on hangers were spread across the couch, the laptop was zipped into its carrying case, and boxes were scattered haphazardly, holding dishes, books, bath stuff and linens. He could see through the open door that the bed had been stripped, accounting for the pile of sheets on top of it.

Cassidy approached with another box, clearly expecting him

to politely step aside and let her pass. He stood his ground, arms folded over his chest. "Running away?"

Her fingers tightened around the box, but she didn't raise her gaze higher than his chest. "Help or get out of my way."

"Okay." He took hold of the box, containing the boom box, an assortment of CDs and a plastic zippered bag filled with silverware, and set it on the floor before taking hold of *her.* "What the hell are you doing?"

"I'm leaving."

"Running."

Her jaw clenched. "Going home."

"And where is that?"

"I told you—"

He snorted. "I'll wager every penny I might ever have that you've never set foot in Lemon Grove, California, in your life."

She tried to pull free, but he held tighter—not enough to hurt her. Just enough to let her know she wasn't going anywhere. "Where I've been and where I'm going are none of your business," she declared hotly. "Like I said, either help me load the car or get the hell out of my way!"

"You're wrong, sweetheart. I'm making it my business."

"As if you have the right." She wrenched away hard and he let her go. He could have restrained her, but not without causing pain, and while she might enjoy doing that, he didn't.

She retrieved the box he'd set on the floor, pushed past him and carried it outside. Jaw clenched, he turned to watch as she shoved it in the trunk, then ducked out of sight for a moment. When she straightened again, for one instant she looked so damn bleak, but she hid it immediately behind a coldly emotionless look.

He felt a twinge of guilt for thinking she enjoyed inflicting pain. She didn't. God knew, she seemed to have suffered enough of it herself. Maybe there had never been a husband or a murder, and maybe there was no estrangement between her and her family. Maybe every damned word she had ever said to him was a lie…but she was still more alone and lonely than anyone he'd ever known. She was vulnerable and needy, and even though the last thing in the world he wanted was to get involved in somebody else's problems, he couldn't just let her leave like this. He wished he could.

She came back inside, picked up another box and started toward the door. He waited until she was even with him to speak. "Where are you going?"

Still refusing to meet his gaze, still wearing that tautly controlled look that showed nothing, she gave a hint of a shrug. "Away."

Not *home*. He doubted she had a home. Everything she owned was in this shabby rented cabin and the dirty red Honda. Whatever the reason, she stayed on the move and she made up lies about a home that didn't exist. The big question was, Were the lies for him, to satisfy his curiosity?

Or for herself?

"Where?"

She shook her head.

"Do you even know, or do you plan to just get in the car and drive until you come to a likely place? Is that how you wound up here?" Building anger made his voice louder than normal. "You came here on a whim? You screwed around with my life on a whim?"

"I didn't—!" Finally she looked up at him and he saw that she'd been crying. He was as compassionate as the next guy, but years as a cop had given him a certain immunity to tears. He'd seen too many women turn them on and off at will to trust in their sincerity most of the time.

But Cassidy wasn't trying to manipulate him with her tears. She hadn't wanted him to know—that was why she'd refused to meet his gaze—and even now she was doing her best to keep the fresh tears welling in her eyes at bay. *Walk out the door,* he counseled himself. *Wish her well and get the hell out before you do something you can't turn away from.*

Good advice, and it sounded so *doable.* All he had to do was look away, walk away, forget her. But he couldn't manage even the first step.

"Yes, you did," he disagreed, his voice no more than a murmur after practically shouting his accusation at her. "I was just fine here alone, doing nothing, thinking about nothing, and then you showed up, and nothing's been the same since. From the first time I saw you, I wanted—" He broke off to clear the hoarseness from his throat. It didn't work. "I wanted you. I did everything I could think of to get you to spend time with me, to pay attention to me, to get you to want me, and now you plan to leave...damn it, Cassidy, you can't just go."

"I have to," she whispered as a tear spilled over. He stopped its downward slide, catching it with his fingertip, drying the wet path it left on her cheek. Closing her eyes, she rubbed her cheek against his palm so lightly he could have imagined it. Then, as if that moment of weakness was all she could allow herself, she opened her eyes, squared her shoulders and tried for cool and unemotional again. It was a pathetic attempt, though, and one he didn't give a chance as he cupped her face in his hands, tilted her head back and kissed her.

She gave a helpless whimper and raised onto her toes, leaning into the kiss. They couldn't get closer, though, not with the box she still held between them. He took it from her and shoved it blindly in the direction of the couch, then heard a series of thuds as it apparently dumped its contents onto the floor. It didn't sound as if anything broke, though, and it certainly didn't break their kiss. Without the barrier, she closed the distance between them, wrapped her arms around his neck, pressed her body against his and made a soft, satisfied *mmm* sound deep in her throat.

He slid his hands to her bottom, lifting her against his erection, and she made that sound again, a sweet moan from her mouth into his. Only dimly aware of what he was doing, he moved toward the bedroom, coaxing her, kissing her, with him, and she followed without protest. By the time they reached the bed, she had unfastened his cutoffs enough to slide one hand inside and, with one caress, she made his vision go dark and his heart skip a few beats. Now the groan was his, frantic, raw.

He found the zipper on the back of her dress and yanked it down. She shimmied out of it, unhooked her bra—the pretty lacy kind designed for nothing more than driving a man out of his mind—then added her panties to the pile of clothes on the floor. His cutoffs and briefs followed, then they fell to the bed, the pile of sheets lifting her hips at an inviting angle.

Once he'd pushed inside her, stretching her until she'd taken every inch of him, he clasped her hands in his, pinned them to the mattress at either side of her head and stared down at her. She wore a strained look of need, and her maybe-brown eyes had gone soft and hazy. Her lips were parted, her breath coming in soft puffs, and her nipples were hard, her breasts rising with each breath. With her tousled blond hair, pale, golden skin, kiss-swollen lips and taut muscles, she looked the perfect picture of aroused woman.

She looked beautiful.

She was staring back at him, and he wondered if he looked as fierce as he felt. Fiercely turned on. Fiercely in need. Fiercely possessive and protective and all those other things he'd sworn he would never again feel for anybody. In that moment he wanted more than anything to be the solution to all her troubles—to make her less lonely, less vulnerable, less afraid. To keep her safe. To be her home. To give her security and trust and the certain knowledge that he would always be there, would always protect her, would always love her.

Love her.

It was the heat of the moment, he told himself as he closed his eyes and bent to kiss her again. The throes of passion. Men equated sexual feelings with emotional ones, at least until the act was over and they were ready to do it again. That was all it was—a mistake.

As he slowly started moving inside her, the little devil inside *him* grinned cynically. Who was lying now?

She couldn't breathe. Her lungs were trying frantically to drag in great, heaving gulps of air, but the best she could manage was a faint gasp here and there. Her entire body was shuddering, stunned by the intensity of her release, relieved after three years of abstinence, shocked back to life.

Had it always been so good? Had she always felt as if she very well might collapse into unconsciousness? How in the world had she gone so long without?

Because she'd been waiting for Jace.

Her lashes fluttered a few times before she got her eyes open. He lay on his side next to her, one arm flung up to pillow his head, the other resting across her middle. His leg was across her, too, a heavy weight low on her abdomen. He was watching her, a much too serious look on his face that lightened when he saw that she was alert again. He traced one long finger across her breast, first circling her nipple, then flicking the nail across it. A shudder rippled through her and her breath caught in her chest.

When the sensation faded to a bearable level, she smiled drowsily. "You look pleased with yourself."

"So do you."

She pictured her smile, foolish and lazy and oh, so satisfied—just as *she* was. "Mmm," was all she said, but it meant a lot. She was most definitely pleased with him. Her entire body hummed with pleasure, so incredible at its peak that now she felt drained of all stress, empty of tension, lethargic and relaxed and good. Oh, yes, she felt *good*…though she knew it wouldn't last. In a few hours, a few days, a few weeks, she would regret this. It would break her heart when she had to say goodbye—and she *always* had to say goodbye.

But for right now, she felt better, happier, more peaceful, than she had in years. She felt…touched. Special. Damn near treasured. She felt *alive,* after being dead for so very long.

Alive…peaceful…satisfied…exhausted….

The sun was low over the horizon when Jace woke up, hot, thick-headed from his unaccustomed nap, his skin sticky where it pressed against Cassidy's. At some point in the afternoon they'd made a halfhearted effort to straighten the rum-

pled sheets over the mattress—then had turned around and
rumpled them again, he remembered with a grin.

He turned to check the time on the clock, but the nightstand
was empty. Oh, yeah. She'd been running away. *Again.*

It didn't matter what time it was. He had nowhere to go,
and as long as he had a say in it, neither did she. Probably
the only way he would continue to have a say in it was to
keep her locked up and naked—an idea that was entirely too
appealing for a man who wasn't looking to get involved.

He sat up, careful not to disturb her, then turned to watch
her. She slept on her stomach, her head cushioned on one arm,
her face turned away. This close he could see the dark roots
starting to show in her hair. If he hadn't already known she
wasn't a natural blonde, he would have figured it out around
the time those lacy little panties had hit the floor.

Her shoulders were slim, her spine long and delicately
curved. Shapely hips flared out from her narrow waist, and
her legs were long and lean, lacking the muscular definition
his had, but strong all the same. She'd taught yoga, she'd once
told him, which would explain the difference in musculature.

It also explained the agility she'd shown this afternoon.

She slept motionlessly, her breathing steady and slow, as if
she were utterly relaxed. Just looking at her, watching that
faint in-and-out of her lungs, made him start to harden again.
He turned away, grimacing, pulled on his cutoffs and went
into the kitchen to find something to drink.

There was a pitcher of tea in the refrigerator, but the only
glass around was one she had apparently intended to take with
her. It sat on the counter next to her car keys, with a couple
of smudged lip prints on the rim and a puddle of condensation
around it. The ice had melted, diluting the tea to a weak gold-
ish brown.

He looked in the nearest box and found a mix of items from
every room in the house, but no glasses. The second was the
same. She must have packed in a panic, throwing things wherever there was room. Why? What had made her decide in one
moment that she had to be hell and gone from the lake—from

him in the next? Was it because he'd badgered her about calling her parents? Because the last words she'd said to him had been intentionally nasty?

He grimaced at his own ego. "Maybe it had nothing to do with you, idiot," he murmured as he sorted through a third box. Maybe this was just Cassidy's way. Bizarre, yes. Impossible for him to understand, sure. But he could say that about other aspects of her life, as well.

The third box didn't turn up any drinking glasses, either, but he caught sight of a large insulated mug in the one next to it, barely showing underneath the laptop case. He picked up the computer, caught off guard by its weight. Though the laptop looked very much like his own, together with its case, it weighed about double what his did. Of course, she could have reference books or research material stuffed inside the pockets.

As he laid the bag on its side on the table, Cassidy's driver's license fell out of the open flap of the front pocket. He picked it up, glanced at the picture—the standard death-warmed-over look—and started to slide it back inside. Abruptly, he stopped.

Except for a few differences in color—the hair was brown, the eyes listed as blue—the picture was definitely Cassidy, but the license identified her as Stacy Beauchamp of Desert Vista Lane, Tucson, Arizona.

That explained the Arizona tags on the Honda...but not much else. Why was she calling herself Cassidy McRae? She could be hiding from an abusive husband or boyfriend...though his instincts didn't agree. He'd dealt with plenty of abused women, and she didn't fit the mold. She was too strong, too independent.

She could be running from the cops.

She could have escaped from a mental institution.

Or she could just be a very private person who'd wanted to keep that privacy intact. Maybe Stacy Beauchamp was wealthy or famous. He'd never heard the name before, but he didn't pay much attention to anything besides sports on TV and didn't pay *any* attention to the lifestyles—or names—of America's rich and famous. She could be heir to a $10 billion shipping fortune, and the name still wouldn't mean squat to him.

So he would ask her. When she woke up, he would say, *While I was looking for a drinking glass, this driver's license fell out of your computer case. Tell me about it.* Simple enough.

He leaned forward to return the license to the pocket, but when he lifted the flap, another license slid out. For a long time he stared at it before picking it up. It was from Georgia. Elizabeth Hampton, residing on Magnolia Drive in Atlanta.

Swallowing hard, he reached inside the pocket and withdrew all the contents, laying them out on the table. There was a license from Mississippi in the name of Rachel Montgomery. Anna Wallis was from Wisconsin, Katherine McKinley from Utah and Jessica Taylor from Washington.

There were eleven in all, each from a different state, each bearing a different name and each showing Cassidy's faintly smiling face. He assumed she had one in the name she was using now, probably in her purse, which made it an even dozen. Jeez.

And there was more. He knew what the triangular-shaped padded nylon pouch was before he opened it—had one just like it sitting on the top shelf of his closet across the inlet. His held a .45 Heckler & Koch. Cassidy's held a Smith & Wesson 9 millimeter.

She was a single woman who traveled a lot, who was living, for the time being, in a remote cabin with no telephone. He knew a lot of women who carried guns for their own safety. There had been times when his own mother had tucked one into her purse. It was illegal most places, unless the owner had a carry permit, but not unusual, and he'd never known a cop to arrest for it as long as she was honest about it up front. He couldn't count the number of times he'd stopped a woman on a traffic offense when he was in uniform and she'd immediately said, *I have a pistol in my purse,* or briefcase or glove compartment, and he'd let it slide. It was no big deal.

Except that this pistol belonging to Cassidy/Elizabeth/ Rachel/Diane/Linda appeared to be missing its serial number.

Damn, damn, goddamn.

Without touching the weapon, he zipped the gun rug and set it aside, then picked up the last object. It was rectangular, black-and-white stripes, a makeup bag…but it wasn't holding makeup. He thumbed through the bills inside—hundred-dollar bills. He quit counting around fifty, and hadn't reached the middle yet. He zipped it, set it down and took a half dozen steps back.

A dozen bogus driver's licenses, a pistol with its serial number blasted off and at least ten grand in cash. Hadn't he once thought Cassidy was trouble?

He hadn't known the half of it.

So what did he do now? Part of him wanted to confront her, to force her to give him a reasonable, rational explanation for all of it. Part of him knew he should call Reese. The mere possession of those licenses was a felony, to say nothing of the gun. And part of him…part of him wanted to forget what he'd seen, take off his clothes, climb back into bed with her and make love with her one more time.

One last time?

Finally he put the money and the gun back into the computer case. He scooped up the licenses and started toward the door, then detoured back to the kitchen and carefully picked up the glass she'd been drinking from earlier. Hoping she wouldn't wake up until he was back and able to act somewhat normally, he went to his cabin, emptied the glass and set it on the dresser in his bedroom, then sat at the table to copy the information on the driver's licenses. He could get on the Internet and search for the names and addresses to see if any of them actually matched, but that would take time and would most likely be fruitless. No doubt there really were women out there named Stacy Beauchamp, Elizabeth Hampton, Rachel Montgomery, Linda Valdez and the others.

No doubt not one of them was the woman he'd just made love to.

What now? *Forget it,* the devil in him said. *She's a beautiful woman, and she's not gonna be around long, and besides, it's not your problem anyway. You're out of the protecting-and-serving biz.*

But he couldn't forget it, any more than he could forget *her.* He'd never been able to look the other way, and leaving the department hadn't changed that. There was something seriously wrong here, and he had to find out what it was. If she was running for her life, he could protect her. If she was running from the law, he could help her.

Help her…help bring a criminal to justice. He'd done it thousands of time before and had derived great satisfaction from it. Seeing Cassidy locked up awaiting trial and prison *wasn't* going to bring satisfaction.

If she was running from the law. *If* she'd done anything wrong besides obtaining bogus licenses. *If* she was guilty of anything more than a few lies.

Innocent or guilty, criminal or victim, he needed to know. Needed to know her name. Needed to know exactly who he was falling in love with.

Grimly he went into the bedroom and retrieved the cell phone from its charger, turning it on, dialing a number he knew by heart. As he waited for Reese to come on the line, he stared at the water glass on the dresser, stared so long and hard that he was startled when his cousin spoke.

"Hey, Jace, what's up?"

"I've got a favor to ask of you, bubba. I'm gonna take Cassidy into Tulsa for dinner this evening. While we're gone…" He squeezed his eyes shut, hating what he was about to ask, sure that it qualified as betrayal but feeling he had no choice but to ask. "Can you come out to the cabin, pick up the drinking glass that's on the dresser and run it for fingerprints? You'll find mine around the base of it."

"Who else's am I looking for?"

"Damned if I know. I'm gonna leave a list of names next to the glass. They're from driver's licenses. Can you run them, too, and let me know if any of them are legit?"

Reese was silent a long time before he exhaled heavily. "I take it Cassidy's keeping a few secrets."

"Just a few," Jace agreed bitterly. *Like her name. What she does. Where she's from. Why she needs a gun. Where she got more than ten grand in cash. Why she's running.*

"You think she's got a warrant out for her?"

"Possibly." *Probably.* "Or maybe she's just crazy as a mud hen and chooses a new name and personality for every place she goes."

"Crazy people don't generally get bogus IDs to back up their delusions." Reese paused, then muttered a curse. "I'm sorry. I liked her."

"Yeah. Me, too. I was thinking…" *That she might be the one. That God or Fate or whatever had arranged for Amanda to dump him so he would be free when Cassidy came around. That he might love her.*

How could he love her when he didn't even know who she was?

"What time are you planning on leaving?"

Jace glanced at the clock. "We'll be out of here by six-thirty."

"I'll be out soon after."

"Thanks, bubba."

"Yeah. Be careful."

Good advice, Jace thought as he hung up. Too bad it was about four hours too late.

Cassidy was waking up in her favorite way—slowly, feeling rested and easy all the way down to her toes—when she realized that someone was watching her. Panic flared, then disappeared instantly. She hadn't been found and wasn't in danger—at least, not physically. Emotionally was another thing.

He cradled her delicate, slender body against the blazing power of his own body, overwhelming her with his strength, his size, his protection, making her want to stay there forever. If he would say the words, she would stay. Blunt words—"I need you." Pretty words—"You're the light of my life. I won't live without you." Simple words—"I love you." She wasn't picky. Any of them would make her forget her plans to leave. Any of them would convince her to stay.

It was her sweetest wish, her dearest dream—the two of them together forever. Living in their little house. Raising babies. Loving. Laughing. Never knowing fear. All sunshine, no shadows. All joy, no sorrow. Sweet, joyful, satisfying, peaceful, safe and perfect.

Perfect.

Perfection didn't exist, Cassidy thought with more regret than she wanted to feel. Not in her world. Neither did peace nor safety nor forever.

To escape the melancholy path of her thoughts, she opened one eye and peered through a fringe of hair to see Jace crouching at the side of the bed, studying her. She smiled sleepily, even though she was a bit disappointed that he was no longer naked. "Hey."

"Hey. Get up, get dressed and let's go to Tulsa. I'm hungry."

"How about we stay here and I'll cook?"

He made a derisive sound. "Your kitchen is divided up among a dozen boxes in the living room, the dining room and the car trunk. Come on. There's a great Mexican place on 71st. I guarantee, you'll like it."

"You don't even know if I like Mexican."

"Do you?"

"Yes, but—"

"Good." He surged to his feet with energy to spare. He continued to look at her, but this time his gaze didn't make it anywhere near her face. Instead it was settled a few feet lower on her backside.

"Hey!" she exclaimed, realizing that she was completely exposed. She whipped a corner of the sheet around her, then struggled to her feet and wrapped it around her toga-style. "I need a shower."

"Okay, but make it fast."

She padded into the bathroom and took his advice to heart.

Of course, considering that she'd showered, shampooed and shaved her legs just a few hours earlier, there wasn't much to repeat.

She finished in record time and returned to the bedroom in time to catch him hanging an armload of clothes in the closet. He didn't comment on her plan to run away. He just handed her a dress, said, "Wear this," then went back for the rest of the clothes.

The dress he'd chosen was a simple sheath in emerald green. She sorted through the clothes until she found the summer-weight cardigan that went with it, then located clean underwear and returned to the bathroom to dress. By the time she was finished, he had put away all her clothing, as well as most of her books and a good part of the kitchen stuff.

Did he think unpacking meant she would stay? she wondered as she retrieved her keys from the kitchen. He was wrong. Making love to her...*that* was enough to make her stay. At least, for a while. Until some of the emptiness inside her had been filled, until the chill had been banished.

Until it was an absolute certainty that leaving would break her heart.

She was about to say she was ready when her gaze fell on the computer. Every other time they'd gone out, she had left it sitting on the table, but those times the outside pocket had been empty. She couldn't just go off and leave her only protection—gun, ID and money—out like that. If someone broke into this shabby cabin, the laptop would surely be the first thing he took. There was nothing else of any value.

But she couldn't exactly say, *Oh, wait, Jace, I need to hide my gun and my cash—oh, and my fake driver's licenses, too.* Once a cop, always a cop. He would turn her over to Cousin Reese in a heartbeat.

"Are you ready to go?" he asked from the opposite side of the table.

She stared at the laptop a moment longer before meeting his gaze and smiling unsteadily. "Uh, yeah, almost. Would you mind getting those boxes out of the trunk while I—"

nervously she tugged at her ear, and inspiration struck "—while I put on my earrings?"

For a moment he had no response, and she waited for him to point out that she rarely wore earrings, and there was no reason why tonight should be any different. But the moment passed, and all he did was nod and head for the door.

She stayed where she was until the screen door closed, then she darted to the table, ripped open the Velcroed flap and gathered the items inside, making a mental note to replace the rubber band that had held the licenses together until it had broken. Then she rushed into the bedroom and shoved them as far under the mattress as they would go before grabbing a pair of earrings from the open box on the dresser. She stabbed them through the holes in her ears, secured the backs, then forced a leisurely smile as she strolled back into the living room. "I'm ready now," she said when he came through the door, one box balanced on top of the other.

He left the boxes on the table, then held the door for her. After locking up, she stepped off the deck into the hot, heavy evening. "Until today I thought the stories I'd heard about Oklahoma summers were exaggerated."

"Okies? Exaggerate?" He gave her a sidelong look of pretended shock as well as genuine amusement. "We're far enough north to get cold in winter and far enough south to get hot and humid in summer. We generally start hitting a hundred degrees in July, though it came close today."

"How do people without air-conditioning manage?"

"Hey, we're sturdy stock. Pioneers, oil men, cowboys." He gave her another of those sideways looks as he opened the truck door for her. "Indians."

Heat rolled out of the SUV in waves, making her take a step back. Gingerly she climbed in, then tugged at her dress as she settled on the leather seat, trying to stretch the cotton to protect the backs of her legs. As soon as he started the engine, he turned the AC to high and rolled down all four windows, but they'd gone more than a mile before the sauna feeling gave way to semicomfort.

After three miles Cassidy got chilled and pointed the vents away from her. When Jace adjusted the fan speed, she murmured her thanks, then directed her gaze out the window.

A man and a woman who knew each other well enough to make love shouldn't feel so awkward afterward. She couldn't think of anything to say— No, that wasn't true. There was plenty to say…just not things she was brave enough or foolish enough to risk. Things such as, *Thank you for two incredible orgasms.* And *May I have more, please?* Or *You want to pull off the road and pretend we're teenagers again?*

How about, *Ask me your questions once more—who I am, where I'm from, why I'm running—and I'll answer them truthfully in exchange for your protection, your body, your love.*

If you're going to dream, dream big, her mother used to tell her. Obviously it was advice Cassidy had totally embraced. How else could she even suggest that Jace might care enough about her to protect her? Hadn't he made it crystal-clear that he wasn't getting involved in other people's troubles, including—maybe even especially—hers?

And as for loving her…what were the odds of an honest man ever learning to love a dishonest woman? A man to whom trust and right and honor were important loving a woman who discounted all three as meaningless?

She intended her snicker to remain entirely in her head, but some part of it must have escaped because he looked at her curiously. "You okay?"

"Yeah. Uh…yeah." She focused her gaze on their surroundings and realized they were only a half mile or so from the highway. She was beginning to recognize pastures and fences, farm houses and barns and even a particular white horse who liked to graze along the barbed wire.

God, she would miss this place when she left!

A black-and-white SUV with lights on top was approaching from the opposite direction. She half expected Jace to stop if he knew the driver, but all he did was lift one hand from the steering wheel in a wave that was returned by Reese as he drove past.

"No chitchat?"

"He's probably working, and I'm hungry." Suddenly he grinned at her, transforming from merely handsome to handsomely wicked in the space of a heartbeat. "I worked up quite an appetite this afternoon."

A faint blush warmed her cheeks even as she tartly replied, "You already *had* quite an appetite."

"Hey, it had been a long time. Besides, you were a little on the greedy side yourself."

Greedy? Oh, yeah. She'd needed release, intimacy, comfort and memories. Memories to keep her warm—to keep her alive—in the months to come.

"I, uh, I didn't realize until later that...we, uh..." He was looking straight ahead and a hint of a blush colored his bronzed cheeks. After flexing his fingers on the steering wheel, then taking a breath, he said bluntly, "I didn't even think about using a condom. I know it was stupid and reckless and...and stupid, but..."

Cassidy couldn't blame him. After all, the thought hadn't popped into her head until just now. Though he was the one with all the experience. He should have been prepared. But she was the one who was weak, so she should have been equally as prepared.

"I don't think timing is a problem as far as getting pregnant and...other than Phil, you're the only man I've ever..." She ended with a shrug as he stopped at the intersection with the highway. "For what it's worth."

He murmured something, his head turned away to look for oncoming traffic. She didn't ask him to repeat the words. If she'd misunderstood, she didn't want to know, because it had sounded as if he'd said exactly what she'd wanted to hear.

It's worth a lot.

Chapter 11

The restaurant was part of the rapid overgrowth in southeast Tulsa, built to look like a Mexican hacienda. A pretty young hostess showed them to a table in the central dining room, where another pretty young girl brought chips and salsa. Jace didn't look at the menu—he always ordered the same dish—but he watched Cassidy instead. She'd put on a silky-looking jacket a few shades lighter than her dress, then pushed the sleeves partway up her arms, and she was studying the menu as if the dishes were too tempting to choose between.

Blonde or brunette, brown eyes or blue, she really was pretty. Fine features, delicate bones, natural sensuality. He called her city girl, but she had a freshness about her, almost an innocence, that reminded him instead of the country. She could be right at home in a rural small-town environment...if she let herself.

The waitress returned for their order, then they talked about nothing important. He didn't mention her parents. She didn't talk about leaving. He didn't ask about the driver's licenses or the gun or the money, and she didn't volunteer any new truths. As far as he could tell, though, she didn't offer any new lies, either. That counted for something, didn't it?

As their food arrived, so did a new diner, a man alone. The hostess escorted him to a table near the back. Instead he gestured to the empty one nearest theirs. She called for a busboy to clear the table, then seated the customer. As he settled in, Cassidy glanced at him. So did Jace. White male, late thirties, early forties, five-ten, about one hundred and eighty pounds, blond hair, blond mustache.

Jace never would have given him another thought if Cassidy hadn't sent frequent, skittish glances toward the guy. Her growing discomfort was visible, finally reaching the point that he had to ask. "What's wrong?"

Her voice was little more than a whisper. "That man keeps looking at me."

Jace checked, and sure enough, the guy was watching her. "So? You're a beautiful woman."

The look she gave him was as dry as the desert. "Oh, yeah, men stare at me wherever I go."

"Maybe not stare, but look. He's just being a little obvious about it." He paused to consider the wisdom of what he was about to ask, decided silence would be the wisest course, then asked it anyway. "Is someone looking for you?"

He expected her to brush it off—to laugh, maybe, and say, "Of course not. I'm just a romance writer researching and writing a new book. Why would anyone be looking for me? The people who need to know where I am know."

Instead, for one uncomfortable moment, she looked stricken. She took a long, long drink from the wine she'd ordered, then set the glass down with unusually controlled movements before looking at him. "Don't make me lie to you, Jace. Not tonight."

Hell. Damn it all to hell. He wanted details, particularly who and why—wanted to shake her until she told him everything. Wanted to kiss her until she couldn't tell him anything. Wanted...

With another uneasy glance toward the nearby diner, she folded her napkin and laid it on the table. "Can we go now?"

He paid the bill, then walked with her to the door, his hand on the small of her back. There he glanced back and saw the blonde still watching. Resisting the urge to make an obscene gesture, he followed her through the door and swore he could actually feel when the solid wood blocked the weight of the man's gaze.

"You need to stop anywhere while we're in town?" he asked as they crossed the parking lot to his truck.

"Well, actually…"

He unlocked the doors, then opened the passenger door for her, but instead of letting her get in, he pulled her up tight against him and bent his head so his mouth brushed hers. "There's a twenty-four-hour drugstore down the street. If what you want is different from what I need, can you get it there?"

She nodded, then he kissed her. He shouldn't want to, not knowing what he knew. She was guilty of at least twelve felonies, and who knew what else. When Reese got back the results on her fingerprints, most likely he would come knocking with a warrant for her arrest. She was one of the people he'd spent his entire career trying to take off the streets and put behind bars. Kissing her, wanting her, needing her more than he'd ever needed any woman…he shouldn't.

But damned if he didn't.

When they got to the drugstore, she primly volunteered to wait in the truck, confirming that the purchase she'd wanted was the same as his. "You have any preferences?" he asked, the door propped open, one foot already on the ground. "Ribbed? Glow-in-the-dark? Flavored?"

She laughed in spite of her proper demeanor. "They don't come in flavors…do they?"

"They do, though I doubt you can get them *here*."

"Hey, you're the expert. Get what you want."

It took him less than five minutes to make the purchase. He picked up the same conversation thread when he got back in the truck. "What do you mean, expert? You make it sound like I sleep around, and I don't."

"Have you been with another woman besides Amanda and me?"

"Yeah."

"Then you have more experience than I do."

"That still doesn't make me an expert."

"It sure felt like it to me," she said softly. Her smile as she looked away wasn't intended for him, but he saw enough of it. It was the smile of a satisfied, well-pleasured woman, and it made his body tighten and go hard.

Maybe it was wrong, but right at that moment it didn't matter who or what she was in the bigger scheme of things. He had an answer to one of the *whos*—she was the only woman he wanted, the only one he could remember needing this much.

For the moment, that was enough.

It was dark when he pulled onto the grass near the cabin. His headlights illuminated the yard and lake directly in front of them, with the light spilling to the sides showing both cabins. His was dark. Cassidy's porch and kitchen lights were on. Did the fact that she didn't like coming home to a dark house have anything to do with the question she couldn't have answered this evening without lying—*Is someone looking for you?*

Not necessarily. Women who'd never broken any laws, who had never come within five miles of a crime or a criminal, left lights burning when they went out. It was called common sense.

He shut off the engine and met her at the front of the truck. For the first time since she'd awakened to catch him watching her, he felt awkward. Even when he'd stood there near the dining table, playing dumb while she debated the best way to get her secret stash out of the computer case and into hiding, *awkward* hadn't been the word that came to mind. But now, standing in the moonlight, everything quiet around them, no one else for miles, with a light breeze blowing and the temperature dropped past bearable to almost pleasant, with a paper bag containing a box of twelve condoms in his hand, *awkward* sounded just about right.

"Well..." Cassidy tucked a strand of hair behind her ear, appearing as uncertain as he felt. Her smile was none too steady as she gestured with both hands. "Your place or mine?"

He was ninety-nine percent certain Reese hadn't left any evidence of his visit behind, but if he took her inside, he would be all too aware that his cousin had been there. That he'd betrayed her. That he'd betrayed himself in beginning an investigation he'd sworn would never happen. That he had probably set in motion events that would result in her arrest.

Of course, he had plenty of defenses. He hadn't forced her to acquire all those bogus licenses. He hadn't pulled the money from her purse to purchase a gun that had been illegally tampered with. He hadn't twisted her arm and made her lie to him. He damn well hadn't chosen to fall in love with her.

But none of that changed the fact that, thanks to him, her future, as well as his, would probably turn out pretty damn bleak.

"How about yours?" he responded at last. "We've still got some unpacking to do...among other things."

Her laugh was soft and light as she started toward the bridge. For a moment he just stood there and watched, admiring the way her hips swayed with such invitation and the way her dress clung to her curves and exposed so much shapely leg. Then, shaking his head to clear it, he caught up with her at the far end of the bridge, scooped her into his arms and carried her, laughing, the rest of the way.

"What's out there?"

Cassidy lay on her side, Jace's arms around her, her own hands tucked beneath her head for a pillow, and gazed into the dark woods that stretched into the distance behind the cabin. When she'd first moved in, she had fully intended to do some exploring, but she'd never managed.

With a smile, she corrected herself. She'd just gotten preoccupied with discoveries of a different nature.

"Gremlins," Jace replied, his mouth near her ear. "Wood sprites. Creepy, crawly creatures."

"There's no such thing as a gremlin."

"Better not say that too loudly or one of them will slither through your window one night and feast on your bones."

"Don't say *that* or I'll have to start sleeping with the windows closed, and I'll shrivel away to nothing in the heat."

"Or you could just sleep with me."

"Hmm…shriveling away or sleeping with the big strong man next door…." While she pretended to consider it, he gently pinched her nipple at the same time his tongue stroked over her ear. A soft moan escaped her before she found her voice again. "That's an easy choice. I'll take the big strong man protecting me, please."

At the sound of the P-word—protecting—tension streaked through every part of his body she could feel. Taking into account the way they were lying, that was a considerable amount of tension.

"Bad choice of words, huh?" she asked quietly. "I should have said ravishing. Seducing. Exhausting. Pleasing. They would have been more accurate. I'm not looking for protection. I don't—I don't need it. So don't feel your being a cop— having been a cop—has any bearing on why you're in my bed again for the second time in half a day. Besides…" She rolled to face him without giving up his embrace. "It's not as if the gremlin is really going to come and eat me up." Stealing a hopeful look at him, she added, "Is he?"

For a time he simply looked at her, his eyes dark with indecision and hesitation. Then, as if her last words had finally sunk in, he laughed, pulled her into the middle of the bed, then raised over her. "Is that an invitation?"

"Just a question," she replied, coquettishly batting her lashes.

"A hopeful question."

"If we were discussing the same about you, you would be hopeful, too."

"Damn straight." He kissed her throat, the swell of one breast, the underside of the other, her stomach, her hipbone, her—

Her eyes fluttered shut and her back arched, granting him

better access. Hopeful? That, and every other incredible, intense, breath-stealing, quivery emotion in the world.

Damn straight.

She didn't have a clue how much time passed before she started thinking clearly again. It was late, but she had energy to spare. She eased out of bed without waking Jace, dressed—for the fifth time that day!—and went into the living room, pulling the bedroom door closed behind her.

He'd done some unpacking while she had dressed for dinner. Now, standing between the sofa and the dining table, she rested her hands on her hips and surveyed the boxes that remained. The first time she'd run, there had been no time to pack anything. She'd taken off with nothing more than her purse, her laptop and the clothes on her back—and the money Phil had insisted they squirrel away for emergencies. At the time she'd thought he was being paranoid. They were safe. They were protected. What kind of emergency were they likely to face?

But he *had* insisted, so they had lived off his income and every payday, she'd cashed *her* check and put the majority of it in their hiding place in the garage. She had suggested a savings account, but he'd adamantly refused. Cash was the only way to go. It was readily available, impossible to track, and their banker, an old tin popcorn can, hadn't given them any hassle about withdrawals.

Thank God.

Other than the times she'd come close to getting caught, she wasn't so careless about packing, but when they had come back from lunch, she had been so upset. All Jace had wanted was a nice afternoon, and all he'd done was show some concern for her. In return, she'd lied to him—nothing new—and hurt him. That was why she'd decided to leave. Not because she'd hurt him, and done it deliberately, though she regretted it deeply, but because hurting him had hurt her, too. Because she'd cared too much.

Still cared too much. A broken heart was inevitable, she'd realized sometime this afternoon, so she intended to enjoy every moment of getting there. She was going to create memories and maybe even lie to herself for once by pretending that they could be together forever. By pretending there *was* a *forever*.

With a sigh, she began to unpack the nearest box. After a time, she opened all the windows and turned on the ceiling fan, then went to the kitchen to fix a glass of tea. As she drank, she rested one hand on the counter, then pulled it away, wet. Hadn't she left a glass there while she was packing that afternoon? Jace must have washed it and put it away with the rest of the glasses.

A man who wasn't afraid of housework. Now *that* was hard to find.

Before long, everything was pretty much in order, the boxes broken down and stashed in the closet. She considered reading a few pages from the top book on her to-be-read stack, then thought enjoying the cool stillness outside on the deck sounded better. Then the bedsprings squeaked in the next room, and she headed that way.

Lying naked beside Jace was the best idea of all.

Wednesday dawned another bright, hot day. Leaving Cassidy fixing breakfast, Jace went home to shower and change. He combed his hair, brushed his teeth, tossed his dirty clothes into the hamper, and generally dawdled before doing the one thing that had been his real reason for coming home alone. When he couldn't put it off any longer, he got the cell phone.

The screen showed one missed call, coming in at 9:03 a.m. from the Canyon County Sheriff's Department. There was a part of him that wanted to ignore it, the way he ignored most calls. Whatever Reese had found out, he didn't want to know. Not yet.

Still, he pressed the button that would dial back the number. He'd started this. Now he had to have the guts to see it through. Besides, it could be good news. It was too soon for a response from the FBI on the fingerprints, but maybe the licenses had checked out. Maybe they were all legitimate. Maybe she was as crazy as he'd joked, and every time she moved someplace new, she changed her name, and maybe she even did it legally.

Yeah, sure. And maybe *he* was the crazy one here.

It took a minute to get Reese on the line. Once his cousin said hello, Jace couldn't think of anything to say. It wasn't until the second hello that he managed a response. "Hey, bubba."

For a moment everything was silent, as if it was Reese's turn to go blank. Then came the sound of a deep exhalation. "Nothing back yet on the prints, of course, but...I ran the operator's license numbers."

Another heavy pause, meaning the news wasn't good. Jace clenched his jaw to keep from either hurrying Reese along or blurting out that he didn't want to know.

"About half the OLNs are legit—but *just* the numbers. The number on Elizabeth Hampton's license comes back to a man in Hepzibah, Georgia. The number on Katherine McKinley's belongs to a sixteen-year-old girl in Provo, and Rachel Montgomery's number belongs to an elderly man in Jackson. By the way, there really is a Rachel Montgomery in Jackson, but she's seventy-nine and black."

Closing his eyes, Jace raised one hand to rub the ache settling behind them. "What about the half that aren't legit?"

"Not in file. The numbers are as bogus as the licenses. I also looked for a female by the name of Cassidy McRae between the ages of twenty and forty, and got nothing. No warrants, which is good, but no license."

So Cassidy wasn't her real name. Big surprise. When she'd told him, *It's certainly not one I would make up,* he should have known immediately that making it up was *exactly* what she'd done.

"I also got her tag number while I was out there last night and ran that. It comes back to a Linda Valdez, at a nonexistent Phoenix address. By the way, the Linda Valdez license is from New Mexico, not Arizona. There are a bunch of Linda Valdezes in New Mexico, but none of them is her." Reese paused, and another voice sounded in the distance as he talked with whoever had interrupted him. When he came back, he asked, "Do you have any clue what this is about?"

"Not much more than a clue. I think she's hiding from someone."

"Husband? Boyfriend? Cops?"

"I don't know." Someone who made her think a pistol was necessary for her own protection? Someone she'd stolen more than ten grand from? Someone who threatened just her freedom...or her life?

Someone who made the risks she was taking worthwhile. He presumed there was a Cassidy McRae license in her purse, bringing the total of bogus IDs to twelve, which also brought the total of felony counts to twelve. Add another for the possession of an unregistered firearm on which the serial number had been altered, defaced or destroyed. The gun charge alone was punishable by ten years in prison and a ten-thousand-dollar fine. Why was she risking one hell of a prison sentence?

"It'll probably be a couple days before we get a response back on the prints. Do me a favor—don't scare her off. If she *is* wanted, whoever's looking for her will be real pissed if we had her and then she's gone."

"I won't say anything." He wasn't the best actor in the world, but hell, he'd worked undercover enough. He could fool someone, especially someone who wasn't expecting him to lie to or betray her.

"You okay?"

No. "Yeah."

"Look, it may not be nearly as bad as it looks." He didn't add the flip side, but he didn't need to. Jace heard the words anyway. *Or it could be a whole lot worse.*

"Let me know when you find out something, will you? I appreciate it." He disconnected, concentrated on breathing deeply for a moment, then cleared his head—and his expression—and returned to Cassidy's cabin.

She was sitting on the deck in the shade cast by the trees to the east. The other metal chair was drawn up at an angle, and an upturned box formed a table between them. He sat and picked up the plate awaiting him.

"And men gripe about how long women take to get ready," she remarked as she made an egg, bacon and biscuit sandwich on her own plate.

"Hey, you've never heard me complain, have you?"

"Only because I've never given you reason."

"You are quick. Amanda—"

When he remained silent for a time, she asked, "Does it still hurt to talk about her?"

"Hurt...nah. I was just thinking that she was a big part of my life for a hell of a long time, and now...it's like she doesn't even matter enough to talk about."

"That's a good thing, isn't it? Unless you hope to win her back."

He made an obscene sound. "Hey, I learn from my mistakes. Whoever's got her now is welcome to her."

Propping her bare feet on the box now that the food was out of the way, she gazed out across the lake, her expression as distant as the clouds low on the western horizon. "Do you believe that—that loving someone can be a mistake?"

"It's not always worth the cost, is it?" If he'd known the first time he'd met Amanda what the end result would be, he wouldn't have bothered with the relationship, and he doubted she would have, either. She'd thought she was getting a hot-shot detective, not someone who would wind up suspended, in disgrace and off the job.

"Look at you," he went on. "You loved Phil. You left home and gave up your family for him, and in return, he went off and got himself killed. Was it worth it?"

She gave him a level look. "He didn't *get* himself killed. He was murdered. And if I had it all to do over again, I would. He was going to be the father of my children. We were going to grow old together. It wasn't his fault things turned out the way they did. He didn't *plan* to take me away from my home and family or to get killed. He just tried to do what was right, and I loved him for it. Sometimes—" her voice quavered, but she quickly got it under control "—sometimes I resented him for it, but I never stopped loving him or wanting to be with him, no matter what the cost."

Jace shifted uneasily in the chair. He didn't want to hear her talk like that about another man, not even her dead husband. Those were the things he wanted her to think and feel about *him,* not some three-years-gone ghost.

"Are you willing to pay that cost again?" he asked, disliking the challenge in his voice but unable to tone it down. "You stayed celibate for three years. I'll bet I'm the first man you've gone out with or kissed or even spent time with since Phil died. And you're not willing to stick around long enough to see what comes of it, are you? Because you're not willing to care like that again, or to get hurt like that again."

The bleakness that stole into her eyes was enough to make his lungs tighten, to kill his appetite and rouse his need to wrap his arms around her and hold her until everything was all right.

Even though it might never be all right.

She polished off her biscuit sandwich, set the plate on the deck, then folded her hands across her middle. "I admit, I'm not eager to get my heart broken again."

"What makes you so sure that's what would happen?"

"If you knew everything I know, you would be sure, too."

"So tell me."

She looked tempted. He hardly breathed, silently urging her to give in to the temptation, just once more, and trust him with all her secrets. Instead, she let her feet drop to the floor. She picked up her plate, then held out her hand for his. After taking it, she walked to the screen door, where she stopped and glanced back. "I have enough deaths on my conscience as it is."

Then she went inside.

Whose deaths? Phil's? He couldn't believe it. Granted, she was a liar, but he *wouldn't* believe she'd killed her husband. She had *loved* him...unless it was an act. The cold-blooded killer playing the grieving widow. Too often people who tried to cover up killing their spouses didn't get the emotions right. Their tears lacked sincerity and their sorrow seemed manufactured. Their behavior was tinged with guilt or colored with arrogance. But on occasion there was the one who nailed it dead-on, whose grief was so perfect, no one could recognize it for the act it was.

But his cop instincts insisted Cassidy wasn't one of those people. Whatever else she was, she wasn't a killer. She *wasn't*.

Surging from the chair, he went inside and to the kitchen, where she was washing the breakfast dishes. He rinsed the plates she'd already washed, then picked up a towel to dry them. "Tell me one true thing," he demanded.

She gazed out the window for a time before turning a wan smile on him. "It's too early in the day to be having a heavy-duty conversation like this."

True enough, but not quite what he had in mind. "Did you kill your husband?"

The skillet she'd just picked up slid from her hand and landed in the sink with a splash of soapy water as she turned her shocked gaze on him. "*No!* How could you *think*—"

"Then whose deaths are on your conscience?"

Color slowly seeped back into her face as she stared at him. She breathed evenly, shallowly, regaining her self-control in small increments. Finally she answered haltingly. "The...the man who killed Phil...also killed...two other people that—that same night. I had...I had called one of them for help. If I hadn't...they wouldn't be dead."

Jace studied her a long time. It was stupid, but he believed her. There wasn't a shred of evidence to support her story, and more reasons than he could list to discount it, but he believed her. Maybe because he'd been a damn good cop for seventeen years. Maybe because his instincts were the best. Maybe because he loved her and *wanted* to believe her. Whatever the excuse, he did.

"Is that who you're hiding from?"

Stubbornly she turned back to the dishes. "That's none of your business."

"Whoa, hold it right there, sweetheart." He caught hold of her arm and made her face him again. "Didn't we have this conversation yesterday? *Before* we ended up in bed? If it was my business then, it damn sure is now."

"You're not interested in solving other people's problems, remember?"

True. Noninvolvement had been his policy since turning in his resignation, and he'd done a fine job of living by it in the months since then…right up until the day Cassidy had moved in. Did he want to get dragged back into the problem-solving business? Not only no, but *hell* no. He just wanted answers. Information. Explanations.

And would he be satisfied with that? Once she'd told him everything he wanted to know, could he sit back and let her run away again? Could he let her live in fear that whoever was chasing her would catch her? Could he let her risk dying rather than get involved?

Yeah. Sure, he could. Not a problem.

Someone would just have to kill him first.

Apparently he waited too long to answer, because a cool, shuttered look fell across her features. "That's what I thought," she said softly. "Jace, just accept this thing between us for what it is—two adults agreeing to spend time together, to have sex, to have some fun, for as long as they're both around and willing. There's nothing more to it than that. There can't *be* anything more to it than that. Okay?"

He narrowed his gaze and scowled at her. "Lying to me is one thing, Cassidy. But lying to yourself…that's pathetic. There's already more to this than a casual affair, and you damn well know it. If you want to pretend otherwise, fine, but don't expect me to play along. I've *never* been in the game-playing business."

"Oh, Jace…" The words were part plea, part cry, part groan, then she pulled free of his grip, moved closer and wrapped her arms tightly around him. "You're something, Jace Barnett. Damned if I know what, but *something*."

The time was coming when Cassidy would have no choice but to move on, and this time she couldn't let Jace stop her, no matter what. She suspected he knew it, too. Their time in bed together was incredible, but put clothes on them and they couldn't carry on a civil conversation for long. The tension between them was suffocating. It made her head ache and her stomach knot. Still, they both kept trying. Trying to wring every little bit of pleasure they could out of the time given them. Trying to control their frustration and anger and resentment. Trying—at least, on her part—to preserve every small memory she could for future examination.

By Friday evening they were both worn to a frazzle. He'd turned down Neely's invitation to have dinner with her and Reese, and Cassidy had rejected his suggestion of going out for dinner. Instead, they had driven into Buffalo Plains that afternoon, where he had run a few errands before they went grocery shopping. Now, as the sun started to set, she fixed stuffed potatoes, salad and mushrooms sauteed in wine while he marinated, then grilled steaks. They ate on the deck, talking little, each unhappy in their own way.

She'd never felt so alone.

What would she have to do to make things like they were before? To coax a smile or a laugh from him? To bring some sense of normalcy to their time together?

That was easy. Tell him the truth, the whole truth and nothing but the truth, so help her God. Could she do that? If she knew ahead of time what his reaction would be. There were two basic choices: he would want to help or he wouldn't. If he offered help, of course she couldn't accept it. If anything happened to him because of her, she couldn't bear it. It would destroy her.

And if he didn't offer help, if he got that distant, distasteful look as if she was forcing him to do something he'd sworn he would never do again? Well, she could bear that, but it would break her heart. It would prove how little she meant to him, and she *really* needed to believe he cared.

After they finished eating, as dusk settled over the area, he turned his chair to face the lake, propped his feet on the railing, then extended his hand to her. When she took it, he tugged her into his lap, her head resting on his shoulder. "Where do you think you'll be in five years?"

She didn't know where she would be in five *days,* but she didn't tell him that. It would just make him get tense and/or annoyed again, and she'd had enough of that to last a while. *Alive* was another good answer, but she didn't offer that, either. "I don't know. What about you?"

"Here," he answered decisively, then waved one hand carelessly. "Maybe not exactly right here, but somewhere in the county."

"And married."

He frowned as if offended by the idea. "I haven't gotten married in the past five years. What makes you think I will in the next five?"

"Your father's yearning for grandbabies to spoil rotten."

"He told you that?"

"Uh-huh. About three minutes after meeting me." She smiled to hide the hurt at how dearly she would love to provide Ray and Rozena with those grandbabies. "Besides, you've got so many happily married friends and relatives. If there's one thing they can't resist, it's matchmaking."

"True. And there is a real pretty redhead in town by the name of Isabella... She had a thing for Reese until he hooked up with Neely again. As far as I know, she's still available."

He was teasing, Cassidy knew, but that didn't ease the pain one bit. Of course he would get married. She *wanted* him to. She knew all too well how awful it was to live utterly alone, and she wouldn't wish it on anyone. He would fall in love with the right kind of woman—one who loved him for who he was, who would never lie to him, never leave him—and he would live happily-ever-after. She really, *really* wanted that.

So why did the mere thought bring tears to her eyes?

Because *she* wanted to be his happily-ever-after, damn it, and wanted him to be hers!

No matter how impossible it was.

"You're not really a writer, are you?" he asked after a time.

"Not a real one. I've never sold anything. I've never actually written anything before this summer. I've been trying, but..." She shrugged, then settled against the hard, comforting warmth of his body again.

"Can I read what you've written?"

The sound of a boat engine drifted across the lake, drawing her gaze to the water. Far-off running lights showed in the dim light, and she watched until they were out of sight before replying, "Maybe." For all he'd put up with, all he'd done, he deserved answers to his questions, and by not giving them until she'd already disappeared, she could avoid having to know his reaction. Once she was gone, never to be seen again, there would be no danger in his knowing. There would be no risk of finding out that he didn't care.

"Have you ever considered writing?" she asked in an effort to steer herself away from thoughts that would make her even bluer. His response was a derisive snort that vibrated through her and made her give him a primly chastising look. "You were a cop for seventeen years. You must have some amazing stories to tell. And it's not as if you're a stranger to writing. You had to write reports and stuff on the job, didn't you?"

"Have you ever read a police report? They're not exactly stimulating reading." In the snooty, pretentious tone of a reviewer, he said, "'The prose is ponderous, the dialogue contrived, and what little plot there is defies credibility. Sentence structure is poor, the author has a misguided notion that "myself" is a proper substitute for "I," and where in hell did he find all those commas?'"

She smiled, lazily amused. "Then what *are* you going to do?"

"Right now, nothing more than this. In an hour or two, I plan to strip you naked and do things that will curl your hair."

"Mmm. But I mean in the future. Unless you're independently wealthy, eventually you're going to need a paycheck. What will you do to get it?"

"Don't know."

"You don't want to ranch."

"Nope." He nuzzled her hair back from her ear and brushed a kiss across it, making her shiver, but she refused to be distracted.

"And you don't want to be a cop."

"No." Another light kiss, more fluttery sensations dancing through her body.

"You have a college degree. It wouldn't be difficult for you to get certified to teach."

"School?" He snorted. "I couldn't wait to get out of it, and you're suggesting I go back and put other kids through the same torture I went through?"

"It's different when you're on the other side of the desk."

"If it's so great, why aren't you doing it?"

Truth or lie? She'd lied to him before—told him she didn't like kids. She could repeat the tale now, and if he believed her, fine. If he didn't, that was fine, too. Or she could remain silent. She doubted he would consider her not answering much better than lying, but morally it was an improvement.

Instead of straight silence, she opted for a subject change. "I bet you didn't really hate school. You were a jock, weren't you?"

"Football and track."

"And you were handsome. I bet all the girls had a crush on you."

"Enough of them."

"And you probably charmed the teachers and made good grades."

"Usually. All that aside, you couldn't pay enough to get me into a classroom again. When I have to work, I'll probably take that job my dad's been offering. Mending fence, hauling feed, castrating, branding, breaking up ice in winter…"

"With that kind of enthusiasm, you'll last a whole week or so." And then he would go back to being a cop. As Reese had said via Lexy Marshall, being a cop wasn't something you did, it was what you were, and Jace was a cop. For whatever reasons, he liked pretending otherwise at the moment, but he could avoid the truth only so long. Someday he would put the badge and the gun back on, and he would be satisfied once more with his life.

Knowing that brought some small bit of satisfaction into her own heart.

Off to the northwest, lightning flashed across the sky, jagged lines briefly appearing, then disappearing. When Jace had turned on the evening news at six, the weather guy had mentioned a ninety percent chance of thunderstorms that night. Maybe that colored her impression, but the air seemed heavy with a sense of expectancy—hot, unnaturally still, broken only by an occasional breeze that fluttered the leaves and carried a fresh, damp scent with it. Of course, every breeze coming across the lake carried a bit of dampness with it, but this one felt different.

Or maybe she just wanted it to be different. The way she wanted everything in her life to be different.

The silence between them had gone on forever when Jace finally, quietly, spoke. "You're planning to leave soon, aren't you?"

She didn't answer. She didn't have to.

His arms tightened around her. "Promise you won't go without giving me a chance to change your mind."

Though she smiled, it felt as phony as *she* had become. She needed to clear her throat to answer, to ease the tightness there and in her chest, to blink away the moisture suddenly welling in her eyes. "Okay. I promise."

But she lied.

Chapter 12

The storm took its sweet time moving in. The lightning flashed more frequently, followed only occasionally by a rumble of distant thunder. The wind freshened enough to make sitting on the deck comfortable when it blew, bearable when it didn't. Heavy clouds spread across the sky from horizon to horizon, blocking the stars and the moon, turning the night into varying degrees of shadows.

Jace knew Cassidy had lied to him when she'd made the promise—had felt it in the subtle tensing of her muscles, the catch in her breath, the unsteadiness of her voice. She had lied and he had accepted it as truth. Had *pretended* to accept it.

If she wanted to leave, he really couldn't stop her. Short of stealing her keys or keeping her handcuffed to the bed, all he could do was ask. Argue. Plead. Tell her he loved her.

And risk finding out that didn't mean nearly as much to her as it did to him.

Maybe he and his love weren't such a prize. Amanda sure hadn't been willing to settle for just that. Neither had Julie.

Odds were Cassidy wouldn't, either, and damn if he hadn't
had enough rejection to last a lifetime.

And damn if he could face a lifetime without her.

As he considered the bleakness of that prospect, the sound
of an engine filtered into his brain. It came from the south,
making it a vehicle and not some late-evening boater. Where
the road forked, angling to the northeast to go to Cassidy's
cabin or to the northwest to reach his, the engine came toward
his.

A moment later she became aware of it and tensed again.
''Are you expecting company?''

''Not really.''

''What does that mean?''

''When you're not available any other way, people sometimes drop in unexpectedly.''

''Because it's the only way to reach you. Your father said
you had to get over the idea that your cell phone was for *your*
convenience.''

He smiled faintly. He'd used the cell phone more in the past
few days than in the past six months combined, making regular
calls to Reese for updates on the fingerprint request. Every
time he'd gotten the same answer—nothing yet. He wanted
good news, wanted to hear that her fingerprints weren't on
file, that she wasn't wanted by any cops anywhere.

Bad news...well, it would be better than not knowing. At
least then they would have a place to start on making things
right.

As headlights illuminated his truck, the yard and Cassidy's
cabin, Jace lifted her to her feet, stood and walked toward the
far end of the deck. She stayed behind, leaning against the
house in the shadows, nothing more than a shadow herself.
Was she afraid? he wondered. Ready to bolt over the railing
and disappear into the night?

The headlights went dark and the engine quiet as Reese got
out of the Blazer.

''Hey, bubba,'' Jace greeted him. He didn't look over his

shoulder but pitched his voice louder. "It's just Reese, Cassidy."

"*Just* Reese?" his cousin repeated. "Jeez, thanks a lot. And after I drove all the way out here just to see you."

The board in the middle of the deck squeaked when she stepped on it, then she stopped next to him. "Hi, Reese."

"Cassidy. I didn't interrupt anything, did I, with you two sitting out here in the pitch dark?"

"We're just watching the lightning," Jace replied. He kept his voice even and casual, as Reese did, but his gut was knotted. His cousin wouldn't have come all this distance without news...without bad news? Would he have simply called for good news?

"So what brings you all the way out here?" he asked.

"I got tired of talking to your voice mail this evening, so I thought I'd try for the real thing." Reese moved around to the front of the two trucks, then gestured. "Cassidy, can I talk to him alone for a minute?"

"Sure." She grabbed an armload of dishes, maneuvered the screen door open, then went inside. A moment later lights shone through the windows and music came from the stereo.

Jace walked down the steps, then followed Reese to the footbridge. "We've been outside all evening. I haven't checked messages," he said by way of an apology. He opened his mouth to go on, hesitated, took a breath and finally asked, "You got an answer?"

"You look like you don't want to hear this."

Jace shrugged. What he wanted had ceased to matter the afternoon he'd lifted that glass from Cassidy's kitchen.

"The news isn't particularly good or bad. The prints came back not on file."

Jace would have been happy with a rush of relief, but it didn't come. There was just a faint easing of tension. Regardless of her real name, she'd never been arrested and fingerprinted. That didn't mean she wasn't wanted—didn't mean she hadn't committed some crime. It just meant so far her fingerprints hadn't been connected to any crime.

It really didn't mean much at all.

"Now what?" Reese asked.

Jace rested his hand on the silvered rail cap and stared into the smooth water of the inlet. "I don't know."

"Do I arrest her?"

"For what?"

Without looking, Jace knew Reese's expression was incredulous. "Hell, I don't know. That little stash of bogus driver's licenses, maybe? How about registering her car under a fake name with a fake address? That's enough to earn her a cell at the Canyon County Courthouse."

"We don't know the car registration is fraudulent."

"Oh, come on, Jace…does she *look* like a Linda Valdez to you?"

"Watch it, bubba. That remark could be construed as racist. Linda's a common name, and Valdez could be her married name."

"Okay, so you think, to the exclusion of all the other names she's used, Linda Valdez just might happen to be her real name. Why the fake address?"

"Are you sure—"

"It's an empty field. It's been an empty field for ten years. Before that, it was a warehouse."

Reese didn't repeat his earlier question, but it hung between them. *Now what?*

His options were limited. He could turn a blind eye to the felonies he knew about, ignore any he hadn't yet uncovered and ask Reese to do the same…except that while he might manage, he had no right to ask Reese to. He was the sheriff of this county, sworn to uphold the law. There was some room for discretion, but not enough for Cassidy to wiggle through. Asking Reese to show that much discretion would change their friendship forever.

He could stand back and do nothing while Reese arrested Cassidy and took her to jail.

Or he could try one more time to get the truth from her, then go from there.

It wasn't much of a choice.

"Let me talk to her," he said at last. "Are you working this weekend?"

"I'm on Saturday. Brady's got it Sunday."

"I'll bring her by your office tomorrow."

"Okay." Reese started to walk away, then turned back. "Whatever she tells you…don't let her leave."

The warning he left unsaid was clear. Don't become an accomplice because you're sleeping with her. Don't compromise yourself because you love her. Don't forget you're a cop. It's not what you do; it's who you are.

Once a cop, always a cop.

And Cassidy might pay the price for that.

Silently they walked back toward the cabin. At the foot of the steps, Reese clapped Jace on the back, but said nothing as he went to his truck. Jace stopped on the deck and watched him leave, then took a fortifying breath and went into the cabin.

Music still played, something low and bluesy and sexy—something belonging to Cassidy. Only the bulb over the sink was on, though dim light flickered through the open bedroom door. The ceiling fan in the living room turned, and more faintly came the whir of the box fan in the bedroom window.

He was supposed to talk to her, he reminded himself. Ask hard questions. Force hard answers. *Make* her trust him with the truth. But if he walked through that door and found her anywhere near his bed, talking would be the *last* thing on his mind. And since there was nowhere in the bedroom that wasn't near his bed…

Taking the first step was tough. The second came easier and brought with it the faint fragrance of something sweet. The fourth stride took him right to the door, where he stopped and just looked. The flickering light and fragrance came from the same source—candles on the nightstands and dresser. They smelled like a dessert served in an expensive restaurant, something rich and extravagant and, like the music, they were hers, too.

She was near the bed, all right, standing beside it, wearing an old tank top of his that threatened to become indecent with one good breath. She didn't appear to be breathing, though. Just standing. Watching. Waiting.

The sight was instant-arousal material, with the white ribbed-cotton brushing her breasts, skimming over her belly and falling just past her hips. The shirt hung low on her, revealing the rounded sides of both breasts, the thin fabric clinging to her nipples. If she moved, one breast or both would be exposed. If either narrow strap slipped an inch farther, she would be naked. Standing there, lit only by candlelight, her blond/brown hair tousled, her brown/blue eyes shadowy, her long, long legs exposed, she was the most incredible sight he'd ever seen.

Her smile was faint and shy. "What did Reese want?"

"Who?" he asked blankly, then blinked. "Oh...Reese. He...I don't recall."

The smile grew stronger, less shy, more womanly, as she raised both arms to encompass the room. "I hope you don't mind..."

The tank top slipped over her left breast, then caught, covering her nipple but nothing else. The blood rushed from his brain, making his body fiery hot, making his arousal throb painfully. "M-m-mind...?"

"Inviting myself in. Making myself at home." She lowered her arms, then turned to fold back the top sheet on the bed before sitting on the mattress. She was all light against the navy blue of the sheet, long and willowy, revealing and concealing, tormenting. He couldn't think, couldn't speak, couldn't move—could only stand there staring and wanting so badly he would beg, plead, forgive anything, forget everything.

As he stared, she lay back on the bed. The tank top rose to the tops of her thighs, the fabric fluttering invitingly thanks to the fan. He kicked off his shoes, pulled his T-shirt over his head, then undid each warm metal button on his cutoffs before sliding them and his briefs down his hips. He sat on the bed, the mattress dipping beneath his weight, and rested one hand on her knee. "You look…" No surprise—words failed him. They were all there in his head—beautiful, incredible, hot, sexy, amazing, enticing—but he couldn't give them voice, so instead he showed her.

He removed the tank top one excruciating inch at a time, kissing her, stroking, rubbing, suckling, licking. The air in the room grew heavier, hotter, damper and slicked their skin with sweat. All sound faded away until there was only Cassidy's whimpers, his own groans, their ragged breathing, all underscored by rumbling thunder moving slowly toward them. He settled between her thighs and made her gasp, cry out and go as taut as a bow string, then she knelt between his legs and chased every coherent thought from his mind with her long, lazy kisses and tormenting caresses. Finally he rolled a condom into place, raised himself over her and slowly, as lightning brightened the room and thunder shook the walls, slowly sank inside her.

The storm struck full-force, the wind whipping through the trees, the fan drawing the cool, clean smell of rain into the room. The rain beat against the roof as he thrust, long and hard and deep, inside her. Thunder vibrated through the cabin as her groans vibrated through him, as her body clenched tighter and tighter around his.

He came, and was dimly aware of her own orgasm, and then he came again, fierce shudders knotting his muscles, making him go rigid, forcing his breath out in short desperate gasps. Unable to support his weight any longer, he collapsed against her, feeling her own convulsive shivers, hearing her own greedy gasps.

They lay like that for minutes, maybe hours, until the sweat had dried, their breathing regained some sense of normalcy, their hearts were no longer pounding. He summoned the energy to move off of her, lay beside her and rested his arm heavily across her, then met her gaze in the lightning-illuminated room. "Tell me one true thing."

* * *

He hadn't curled her hair, but it had taken Cassidy a good long while to uncurl her toes. She lay on her back, barely breathing, not sure she could move to save her life, and gazed at the ceiling. Outside the thunderstorm was still raging. Inside…she felt safe. Protected. And scared by Jace's request.

She had lied to him from the day she'd met him…but never when he'd asked for *one true thing*. She could give him something as simple as the line from a song that had popped into her head—"I just died in your arms tonight"—and satisfy his request.

Instead, off-key, she sang a line from another song. "'Jenny, Jenny, tell me true….'"

He gave her a dry look. "You just make that up?"

"No. My father used to sing it to me. There's more, but I don't remember it."

"Were you in the habit of lying to him, too?"

"Never. Except for the typical teenage girl stuff—you know, 'Of course there won't be any boys at Cathy's party' or 'I don't know how that dent got in the front fender.'" She watched the shadows cast by the flickering candles, breathed deeply of their hazelnut-cappuccino fragrance, then eased out from under Jace's arm and sat up. "When I came here, I claimed to be a storyteller. Would you like me to tell you a story?"

He rolled onto his back, stuffed both pillows under his head and nodded. He looked so undeniably *male* lying there, not the least bit uncomfortable with his nakedness. Lacking his comfort level, she searched for and found the T-shirt he'd discarded earlier and pulled it on. The sleeves reached her elbows, the hem falling well past her hips. It smelled of laundry soap and sunshine and him.

"Once upon a time, there was a man by the name of Richard Arthur Addison, called Rich by his friends. He was the oldest child and only son in a family that included four daughters. In high school he was voted the 'boy most likely to succeed,' and in college he was the big man on campus." She smiled faintly. "Have I missed any clichés?"

Jace must be wondering who Rich was and what he had to do with her, but he didn't ask and he didn't show it. He just watched her, his expression serious, his manner patient.

"Rich met a girl named Jennifer, and they married at the end of her junior year. He got a job working for a company that was in construction and land development, among other things. When she finished college, they bought a pretty little house in an old neighborhood not far from where she grew up. Every day he went to his job and she went to hers, teaching at the same elementary school she'd attended, and every night they worked on their fixer-upper and planned for the babies they intended to have."

A particularly loud clap of thunder made the entire cabin, even the bed, vibrate. Rich, big, strong man that he was, would have been swearing and pacing now, she thought with a fond smile, but Jace didn't appear to have noticed it.

"One day Rich was reviewing the accounts at the big land development-slash-construction company and he came across some…discrepancies. He asked a few questions, didn't like the answers and continued to snoop around, and before long he'd uncovered evidence of extensive wrongdoing, much of it involving government contracts. With Jennifer's support and encouragement, he took the information to the FBI, and eventually he testified against his bosses in court. Because these bosses were very powerful, very ruthless men, he and Jennifer were placed in the U.S. Marshal's Witness Security Program. They were given new names, new backgrounds and relocated to Portland, Oregon."

She fell silent for a moment, remembering the blankness with which she'd greeted the naming of their new home. The marshals might as well have told them they were resettling on Mars. She'd never been west of the Mississippi River, except for that one childhood trip to San Diego. She didn't know anything about the Pacific Northwest, except that it was wet and lots of computer types lived there and it was far, far away from home.

"So Rich and Jennifer Addison became Philip and Rebecca

Martin. They adapted to their new life, though it was difficult. They had another fixer-upper house, and jobs, and a few friends. They missed their families, though, and had pretty much given up on the idea of having all those babies they'd wanted. Still, they were alive and they were together and they were safe.''

Until that awful summer night. In almost three years she'd never spoken of that night. She'd dreamed about it, thought about it, cried about it...but who could she have told? Who could she have trusted?

"One evening Jennifer—rather, Rebecca—went home after work and found Rich—Phil—there with a guest. Bill Edmonds was a deputy marshal. He was their contact, their problem-solver. Phil called him their baby-sitter. I went in—Rebecca went...'' Swallowing hard, she drew her knees to her chest, tugged the T-shirt as low as it would go, and wrapped her arms around her legs. "I went through the garage and into the kitchen, and I heard them arguing in the living room. Phil—Rich was angry, but there was something else in his voice, something I'd never heard before. Fear. The man had testified in court against people who thought nothing of killing other people, and he'd never shown fear, but that night...

"Edmonds said he was sorry, said the money Rich's bosses had offered was too good to pass up. I walked to the living-room door and saw him point a gun at Rich. Rich yelled at me to get out, and...Edmonds...shot him. His next shot was at me, but I threw the bags I was carrying and ran. I've been running ever since.''

She stared at her clasped hands, afraid to look at Jace, afraid to see that he didn't believe her. There was no reason why he should, given her track record, but she desperately wanted him to show that much faith in her. If he didn't, she had no one to blame but herself...oh, but she hoped!

The silence drew out, broken only by sounds that had nothing to do with them...the whir of the fan motor, the thunder, the pounding rain. Finally the springs creaked as he shifted into a sitting position. "What happened next?" His tone was emotionless, the cool, detached voice of a cop who wanted information but had no emotional investment. It made her throat tighten, but she managed to sound just as cool and detached when she answered.

"From the time we settled in Portland, Rich had insisted we keep as much cash on hand as we could—for emergencies. We stored it in an old, beat-up popcorn tin in the garage, right next to the door, where it would be easily accessible. I grabbed the can on my way to the car, and I took off. I was hysterical. I drove for thirty minutes, maybe an hour, then finally I went to a pay phone. I called another marshal who had worked with us and told him everything. He wanted me to meet him, but I refused. He said he would talk to his boss and they would see that Edmonds was arrested and that I was safe. But...when I checked into a shabby little motel a hundred miles away, I heard on the news that both the marshal I'd called and his supervisor had been shot to death in the parking lot outside their office. I got right back in my car and disappeared."

Again Jace remained silent a long time before asking in that same unemotional voice, "You never tried again to get this guy Edmonds arrested?"

"No."

"And he's the one you're hiding from."

She nodded, then, not knowing if he was looking at her since she *wasn't* looking at him, said, "Yes."

"You think he's looking for you?"

"I've seen him twice. The first time he almost caught me. The second time was a year ago. That time I saw him, but he didn't see me. I ran like hell."

After a third, long, stiff silence, he muttered a curse. "This is so typical. A traffic violation turns into a felony stop. A domestic dispute becomes assault with a deadly weapon, and a simple affair becomes...hell."

Ice spread through Cassidy, starting in her chest and working its way out. She was grateful for it, though it made her suddenly, unbearably, cold, because if she was frozen inside, it would temper the pain. "You asked," she said, barely able to move her lips.

"And you couldn't have lied or clammed up, like you did every other time? No, for once you have to answer, and now I'm supposed to…what?"

She forced her fingers apart, slid her feet to the floor and stood. Unlike him, she hadn't undressed in a hurry. Her shirt, shorts and underwear were neatly folded on the chair near the bathroom door, together with her sandals. She didn't bother getting dressed, but picked up the pile and held it to her chest as she faced him. "You're not supposed to do a damn thing. You've made it amazingly clear that you're not in the help-giving business anymore. My life is my problem, not yours. I just wanted—"

She'd just wanted him to know. Wanted to show him she trusted him. Wanted him to wrap his arms around her and to assure her everything would be all right. Wanted him to—

Oh, hell, she *did* want him to do something—to fix it. To take care of Edmonds and to solve all her problems because that would mean he cared. She wanted him to make her safe so she could quit running and spend the rest of her life here with him. She wanted him to love her…and prove it.

Oh, God.

Tears burning her eyes, she turned and walked out. He called her name and the bedsprings squeaked again, but she was already outside and stepping off the deck into the water-logged grass by the time he got his cutoffs on and followed.

"Damn it, Cassidy, stop!" he shouted, then made her do so by grabbing her arm and swinging her around. "You can't just dump something like this on me and expect me to—"

"*Dump* it on you?" She jerked free. "You've been asking questions and demanding answers since the day we met, and now that you've got them, you accuse me of *dumping* it on you?"

"That was a bad choice of words, okay? I didn't mean—" He held out both hands in a placating gesture, but she backed away. "I appreciate your telling me. It's just an awful lot to take in at once. Come back in the house—"

She shook her head.

"Look…" He took a breath, then wiped the rain from his face, for all the good it did. It plastered his hair to his head and ran down his face, washing over the reluctance obvious there but not washing it away. "Come back inside and…we'll figure out what to do. I know some people who can help you."

She didn't want *people* to help—she wanted *him* to. She wanted to be that important to him, wanted him to care that much about what happened to her. But the best he was willing to offer—the best he *could* offer?—was to put her in touch with strangers who were paid to help people in trouble.

"Don't put yourself out," she said politely. "It's not your problem. I've taken care of myself for the past three years, and I'm sure I can do it for the next thirty." With a taut smile, she walked away from him for the second time in minutes.

"Cassidy…Jenny! *Damn it!*"

She let herself in her cabin, closed and locked the door, then went into the bathroom to dry off and change clothes. After spreading all the wet clothes around to dry, she calmly fixed herself a glass of tea, turned the boom box on for company, set a roll of packing tape on the table and removed the stack of broken-down boxes from the closet. There was no way she could sleep right now, and no way she could stop moving without falling apart, so instead she would do something productive.

As soon as the storm passed on its way, she was leaving.

And this time, *nothing* would stop her.

He'd known she was trouble practically from the start. He'd told himself to stay away from her, but had he listened? Of course not. That would have been too freakin' smart. God help him if he ever got smart where a woman was concerned.

Jace undressed, dried off, then pulled on a pair of boxers. His hair standing on end, he hauled out the laptop, hooked up the cell phone and got online. As usual, he ignored the e-mail.

went straight to a search engine and typed in Richard Arthur Addison. "Sounds like a rich kid," he grumbled as he began scanning the hits. A couple were from Penn State, where he'd attended college. The rest were clips from news articles about the trial.

So far, Cassidy's story—Jennifer's story— Whoever the hell she was, her story was holding water.

Then he scowled. He didn't need corroborating proof to know she'd told him the truth. He'd seen it in her eyes, heard it in her voice, felt it in his gut. It was all true. I'm-never-gonna-get-involved-again had stepped right square into a triple homicide with a cop for a bad guy who wouldn't rest until the only witness was dead.

He was ashamed to admit that there was a part of him that wanted to tell her to pack up and hit the road again—that wanted the temptation she represented out of his life.

But what kind of life would he have without her in it? What kind of life could he have if something happened to her and he could have prevented it?

He was going to help her, to keep her safe, even if it meant living with her in the Canyon County Jail. Even if she chose to leave him once it was all over, if it turned out that what he'd thought was affection had really just been a ploy to get his protection, he was going to handle this as if it were the most important case of his life.

Because it was.

He read through everything he'd found on Richard Addison and Philip Martin, as well as the unsolved murders of two U.S. marshals in Portland. Depending on the newspaper, the archived articles weren't always available in their entirety— some required a subscription to access the complete article— but he found enough to verify everything Cassidy—Jennifer had said.

If I were making up a name, don't you think I would choose something other than Cassidy? she'd said before. And another time, *Why would I fib about something so basic as my name?* But she *had* made it up, out of thin air, like all the other names, and she *had* fibbed about it. The knowledge made his teeth hurt.

It was nearly 6:00 a.m. when he signed off. At some point while he'd read, the storm had passed on, though the rain continued. He hadn't even noticed the relative quiet.

He stood up and stretched, then looked at the bed. He was tired as hell but doubted he could sleep, not with the sheets and the pillows and the very room smelling of Cassidy and him and sex. Instead, he got dressed, fixed himself a cup of coffee and went to the living-room window to stare out over the lake. Without knowing the time, a person would be hard put to guess. Black clouds hung low in the sky, heavy with moisture, and off to the northwest, forks of lightning indicated another storm cell making its way in. Lousy weather to be out. Not bad at all for staying home.

Slowly he let his gaze shift to the other cabin. The lights were on, but the blinds were closed. Was she writing? Reading? Crying? She'd been crying when they'd stood out in the rain, but he'd tried hard not to notice as she'd oh, so politely told him to screw himself. Okay, so she'd said, *Don't put yourself out. It's not your problem.* But she'd *meant* "Go screw yourself."

And he'd given her every possible reason to mean it. Hell, she didn't even know all the reasons he'd given her—didn't have a clue that he'd snooped through her computer case, that he'd found the cash and thought she'd stolen it, that he'd turned the driver's license numbers and her fingerprints over to Reese to try to narrow down the list of suspects.

And for all that, they hadn't learned a thing.

Absently he rubbed at an itch between his shoulder blades. Of course Cassidy McRae didn't show up in the system because she didn't exist, but Jennifer Addison *did* exist—or, at least, used to—and she *was* in the system. It was standard procedure. Everyone taken into the Witness Security Program was fingerprinted, but that didn't mean a cop got a match when he ran their prints. Instead, those prints were flagged and a heads-up went to the Marshals Service, while the cop got back a *not in file* response, just as Reese had.

So before Reese had heard a word, the Marshals Service had known one of their missing witnesses had been found, and they would have passed that information along to the local office that had overseen the Addisons' new life as the Martins.

And if Bill Edmonds was still working out of that office, still doing WitSec, he would be among the first to know that Jennifer Addison was in Canyon County, Oklahoma.

The coffee mug slipped from Jace's hand to the floor, breaking into a half dozen pieces and spilling hot coffee everywhere. Ignoring it, he went into the bedroom, shoved his feet into running shoes, grabbed his gun and holster from the top shelf of the closet and a waterproof jacket. By the time he reached the front door, the gun was tucked in the small of his back and he was wearing the jacket.

His hair and jeans were soaked before he'd gone ten feet. The rain blew in horizontal bands, changing direction as the wind did the same. His shoes splashed through puddles as he crossed to the bridge, where the inlet had reached the top of its banks. In another month, everyone would be praying for a rain like this, but this morning it was just a nuisance. It was going to be hell to drive through into town, with every mile of dirt road between here and there turned into a muddy bog.

He took the steps two at a time, banged on the door and yelled, "Cassidy! Open up! I need to talk to you!"

It was so still inside for so long that he thought she was going to refuse, but finally the lock clicked an instant before the door opened six inches. She stared through the space, pale, eyes bloodshot, face utterly expressionless.

"Let me in."

Though she would obviously rather not, she didn't waste time arguing. She walked away from the door, as if she didn't care whether he came in or left to never return.

He stepped inside, swiped the rain back from his face, then looked at the boxes stacked next to the dining table. This time there were no open flaps, no items sticking out. This time she'd taken the time to do the job right, with each box taped shut and neatly labeled.

He looked at her again. "Last night you promised not to leave without giving me a chance to change your mind. I guess you lied again. Big surprise, huh?"

She said nothing. She looked wounded, fragile, as if a gust of wind might carry her away, and he wanted nothing more than to scoop her up in his arms and to hold her tight for...forever. First, though, he would have to make up to her for last night, and before he could do that, he had to take her someplace safe.

"You have a slicker?"

"Why?"

"We're going to Buffalo Plains."

"For what?"

"To see Reese." He glanced around, saw her computer on the floor next to the boxes and headed that way.

"Why?" she asked suspiciously. "I haven't done anything wrong."

Nothing *wrong?* Phony licenses, an illegal weapon, fraudulently registering her car...her list of felonies kept growing. But instead of pointing that out—after all, she'd committed those crimes for the best of reasons—he just shook his head, moved the computer to the table and jerked open the front flap.

"Hey! You can't— That's mine—" She clamped her mouth shut as he pulled out the licenses, now rubber-banded together, and the cash, discarded both on the tabletop and reached in again for the gun rug. He tossed the rug aside, too, and pocketed the pistol, then turned to find her staring at him accusingly.

"You searched through my things."

Guilt warmed his face and made him shift uncomfortably. "It wasn't... I was moving the computer case and one of the licenses fell out and—"

"When?"

"The other day. When we..."

''Had sex,'' she supplied flatly, and his gaze narrowed.

''Made love,'' he corrected.

She folded her arms over her chest. ''So...you've known *something* was wrong all this week.''

His laugh was rueful and short-lived. ''Sweetheart, I've known something was wrong from the day we met.''

''You're having your cousin arrest me—that's your idea of helping?''

''No, I'm having him lock you up for your own good.'' He crossed to the closet just outside the bedroom and found it empty, saw that the bedroom was empty, too, then turned back to the living room. There on the sofa were her purse and a hooded rain jacket. Grabbing the jacket, he went to her and thrust it out.

She refused to uncross her arms. ''I won't be locked up like—like some kind of criminal.''

''Honey, you *are* a criminal. All those licenses, that gun, the registration on that car—that comes to about fourteen felonies and a hell of a lot of jail time.'' Gently he pried one arm free, then slid the corresponding sleeve over it before prying the other arm away.

She jerked it back to her chest. ''I'm not going to jail. If Reese wants to arrest me, let him come out here with handcuffs and pick me up.''

''Damn it, Cassidy! They know you're here!'' He breathed deeply, calmed and lowered his voice. ''I gave Reese a glass with your fingerprints, and he ran them through NCIC. They showed up as 'not in file'—that's standard with people who have been relocated. It's also standard for the bureau to notify the Marshals Service that inquiries are being made about you by the Canyon County, Oklahoma, Sheriff's Department. They *know* you're here—not exactly where, but the general location.''

Fear widened her eyes and turned her expression stark, but it didn't steal the belligerent tone from her voice. ''You searched my things and stole my drinking glass, and you still feel self-righteous enough to condemn me? *I* haven't hurt anyone. All I've done is try to stay alive. *You* might have killed me.''

Using handfuls of fabric, he yanked her hard against him and bent his head until his mouth practically brushed hers. ''The only way you're gonna die is if I'm already dead, sweetheart. Now you can be as pissed with me as you want later, but right now you're putting this jacket on and we're going to the sheriff's department, understand?''

After a long moment she nodded. He kissed her, then stepped back and held out the jacket's sleeve. She slid her arm through, then zipped it to her chin. Wasting no more time, he hustled her outside and across the inlet to his truck. They would have plenty of time to talk on the way into Buffalo Plains, though he suspected anything he might say would go across better if he was holding her close, forcing her to listen and to believe.

As they settled into the seats, he removed his pistol from the holster and laid it on the console between them. Cassidy looked at it and her features took on a sickly cast, as if the full impact of what was happening had finally sunk in.

''I haven't touched that gun in six months,'' he remarked as he backed around the cabin, then set off down the road. ''But don't worry. I'm an expert shot. Have been since I was ten.''

She didn't respond.

''You know how to use your gun?''

A faint nod.

''Here.'' He maneuvered it out of his pocket and handed it over. ''You bought it—illegally, I'm sure—so you can carry it.''

Accepting the gun with a sniff, she slid it into her own pocket. ''It's hard to buy a handgun legally when you don't exist.''

''What did you do? Go to a gun show?''

''Yes. I'd heard stories on the news about how sales at those shows aren't as regulated as they should be. I found a sympathetic guy, told him my ex-husband was trying to kill me, showed him some cash, and he came up with this.''

''And how'd you get the licenses?'' At the moment he didn't particularly care, but if it kept her talking and at least a little distracted, then he would gladly listen to every minute detail twice.

''Same guy. Since he'd been so helpful with the gun, I went for broke. He set me up with a friend of his who's a mild-mannered computer geek by day and a documents forger by night. Thirty-six hundred dollars later, I had an even dozen identities.'' She glanced sidelong at him. ''Normally he charged four hundred per license, but since I was doing business in volume, he gave me a discount.''

''Let me give you some advice—when all this is over and the Feds start questioning you about those IDs, just tell them the bare bones. Forget what city that gun show was in, forget these guys' names if you knew them, and just give the vaguest of descriptions.''

Now she was doing more than glancing. He could feel the steady weight of her gaze on him. ''You're telling me to lie?''

''No. I'm telling you that these guys would do serious prison time if they got caught. You don't want that.''

''Don't *you* want it? They're criminals.''

''No, I don't want it.'' He reached for her hand. She resisted, but he succeeded in raising her palm to his mouth for a kiss. ''They helped you. I don't want to see them punished for it.''

The tension eased from her fingers and the attempt to pull away disappeared, too. He laid her hand on his thigh, then covered it with his own for a moment before returning his attention to the narrow lane. Visibility was limited to the extent of his headlights. The morning was a heavy, murky gray, and the rain came down faster than the windshield wipers could clear it away. The windows were fogging inside in spite of the defroster running at high speed, and the road was inches deep with mud. They should make better time when they reached the dirt road—it was wider, harder packed and had some gravel—but at less than ten miles per hour, it was taking forever to get there.

"How much of what I told you were you able to verify?"

He slowed to steer around a fallen branch that had landed partly in the road, then glanced at her. "Are you so sure—"

"Yes."

"I wasn't verifying. I just wanted to know more."

"Did you find it?"

"Enough." His fingers flexed around the steering wheel. "Cass—Jen—" When he'd begun to suspect that Cassidy wasn't her real name, he'd tried other names for her and found a few that fit, but Jenny didn't. It was a name for an innocent young girl, carefree and full of hope. Cassidy was a strong name, for a strong woman. "I know my response last night was less than either of us had hoped for. I didn't mean...it was just so..." His sigh seemed loud even over the defroster and the rain. "I knew something was wrong, but I didn't expect *that*. I wasn't prepared and I didn't—"

He broke off abruptly as another vehicle came around the curve ahead. He braked, glanced at Cassidy, who wore a look of fear, then reached for his pistol, sliding it onto the seat between his thighs. The car, an average-size, average-price, average sedan that would have been easily identifiable as a rental even if not for the rental car agency sticker on the front bumper, stopped at a point twenty feet away, blocking the road.

It was too rainy, too gloomy, to see inside the car, but Jace didn't need to see to know it was trouble. He didn't know anyone who drove a car like that, didn't know anyone who would come out to the cabins at seven on a Saturday morning, didn't know anyone who would venture out there in this weather for anything short of an emergency. Quickly he considered their options, but they were depressingly few. He could try to maneuver around the car, but even from a distance he could tell there wasn't enough clearance between the vehicle and the trees on either side. He could back up until he found room enough to turn around—and go where? The road dead-ended at their cabins. The SUV was built for off-road driving, but the timber was too thick here. Rough terrain, he could handle. Dozing down trees? Uh-uh.

After a time the driver's door opened, then a man climbed out and stood there, bare-headed, something clutched in his right hand. Beside Jace, Cassidy shrank back and whimpered. *"Oh, God."*

"Is that Edmonds?" he asked grimly.

Her only response was another sound, one of pure terror.

Edmonds stepped away from the car and started toward them, bringing up the weapon he held to sight on them. An H&K MP5A4. A .9 millimeter submachine gun. Trouble with a capital *T.*

Jace waited until only about ten feet separated them, then jerked the truck into reverse and hit the gas. The tires spun, spraying mud into the air, before they caught. Though he twisted in the seat to see where they were going, he steered by faith and prayer because the damn windows were still fogged over, giving him only a dim impression of shadows for trees and a faint lightness for road.

Faith didn't get them far, though—only to the fallen branch he'd already forgotten about. The SUV jerked to a stop, then the engine ground as he tried to go forward again. The damn thing was hung up.

"Come on!" he commanded, jumping from the truck, but Cassidy didn't move. Leaning back inside, he unfastened her seat belt, then hauled her across the seat and out the door. Hearing Edmonds's car approaching, he grabbed her hand and headed for the thickest growth of blackjack oak, sumac and honey locusts. The tangle made going more difficult, but kept them out of the open.

Back on the road a car door slammed, then a voice called, "You might as well come on out, Jennifer. If you do, I won't have to kill your friend, too. Come on, sweetheart. You're already responsible for Jack Keaton's and Marcus Hightower's deaths. You don't want to add your boyfriend to the list, do you?"

Jace felt Cassidy's steps slowing and he tugged hard at her hand, jerking her off balance. "Don't listen to the bastard!" he whispered fiercely.

She tugged back. "He's not interested in you. It's me he wants."

"And you think he'll let me walk away after he kills you? Don't be a fool, Cassidy!" Even through the steady splash, he could hear the crashing of footsteps as Edmonds started after them. As he wiped the rain from his face, he tried to figure out exactly where they were and where to go from here. The nearest neighbor was a couple miles west, the cabins a half mile north, and nothing else in any direction but woods and lake. There were no hiding places, no heavily traveled roads to run to for help. But there was one place....

"This way," he whispered, then headed northeast, dragging her along behind him. They slid down steep hills, splashed through runoff and slipped and slid their way back up on the other side. The pace he set was just one step below all-out panic, and it didn't take long to wear Cassidy down.

They were climbing yet another sandstone-littered hill when her feet slid out from beneath her and she landed with a grunt, stopped from falling farther only by his hold on her. As he hauled her to her feet, he realized for the first time that, along with shorts that offered no protection from the undergrowth, she was wearing sandals that provided zero support. Her legs were covered with scrapes, and she was lucky she hadn't already twisted or broken an ankle.

He swore at himself for not noticing it back at the cabin, for not suggesting she change into jeans and sturdier shoes. But he had been expecting a cautious drive into town, not a mad dash through the woods.

When she regained her feet, she sank onto the boulder next to him. "I need...not in shape..." She drew in a huge, wheezing breath, shuddering as she exhaled, then took another deep gulp. "Oh, God...I should exercise...this is tough..."

He took a few deep breaths, too, leaning over, elbows resting on his thighs. "We'll start jogging tomorrow." He watched her wheeze again, then managed a grin. "Or maybe Monday."

Her breathing still shallow and ragged, she looked at him a long moment. Wondering if he really believed they would be alive tomorrow? Or maybe considering his assumption that if they *were* alive, she would still be with him? As if he was going to let her go.

She was opening her mouth to say something, or maybe to drag in more air, when pieces of the boulder where she sat splintered, striking her thigh with enough force to pierce the skin. She yelped and looked down, not realizing at first what had happened. Jace knew, though. As he caught a glimpse of Edmonds on the next ridge south, he grabbed her hand and raced for the downside of their own ridge.

She couldn't go on, Cassidy thought. She was one step away from total exhaustion as well as total panic. Her lungs were burning, her leg bleeding and throbbing. Her feet hurt, she had never been so scared in her life and she'd been strong as long as she could. She had to stop, to rest, to catch a breath that didn't hurt, to examine the cuts on her thigh. She had to stop...but that meant Jace would stop, too, and then Edmonds would kill them both. Jace had been right earlier. Edmonds wasn't going to let him live after he killed her. Heavens, he wanted her dead because she'd seen him kill Rich. He wouldn't let another witness escape unharmed.

She forced the pain out of her mind and concentrated on putting one foot ahead of the other. She ignored the branches that slapped at her face and the brambles that tore her flesh. She paid no attention to the rain that made a miserable run doubly so, that made them slip and slide, that sent her tumbling more times than she could count. Left foot, right foot. One step, then another.

We'll start jogging tomorrow, Jace had said. As if of course they would be alive tomorrow. As if of course they would be together. As if they had a future together. *To start jogging* implied an ongoing thing. It wasn't something you started and finished in one day, or one week, or even one month. He'd been jogging all his life. Maybe he would do it the rest of his life. Maybe he wanted to do it with *her* for the rest of his life.

She didn't know how much time had passed, how much distance they'd covered. Less than she wanted to believe. Of course, she would like to think they'd crossed the Kansas state line some time ago, while Edmonds remained somewhere around Buffalo Lake. She tried to listen for him, but heard only the rain, the thud of her heart trying to pound out of her chest, the harsh rasps that were all her oxygen-starved lungs could manage.

"Last time I heard you breathing like that...you were enjoying it a lot more," Jace said, finally getting winded himself.

She would have made a face at him if she'd had the energy. Instead she settled for a grunt.

Under better circumstances, she would have enjoyed a leisurely stroll through the woods. Lazily climbing up and down the gentle hills. Sitting for a while on a sun-warmed outcropping of rock to enjoy the stillness, to study the clouds overhead, to sniff the sweet fragrance of the wildflowers peeking through here and there. Talking, or maybe saying nothing at all. Making love.

Oh, yeah, she had enjoyed the heavy breathing *much* more when it came from making love.

She wanted to ask where they were going and if he had a plan. She wanted to tell him how sorry she was for getting him into this mess and that she would love him until she died...which might not be very long. She wanted to thank him and—

The strap on her sandal gave way, sending her headlong the ground. This time she fell with such force that Jace was able to lessen the impact. Instead, he went down with her. What little precious air she had went out with a rush, and she lay there stunned, her mouth working but no sound coming out, no breath going in. Every part of her body ached—her head from oxygen deprivation, her arm and shoulder from Jace's constant dragging, her throat, her chest, her lungs. She had a dozen stitches in her sides, her thigh still burned and bled, her arms and legs stung from their myriad scratches, and bruises were forming from all the bumps and slips she'd taken.

Now, to top it all off, her ankle hurt like a son of a bitch.

Jace rolled over, apparently as dazed from the impact as she was. He gave his head a shake, then got to his feet and, for the umpteenth time, hauled her to her feet. The instant she tried to bear weight on her right foot, she landed on the ground again, on her butt this time. He dropped to his knees, examining her rapidly swelling ankle, then grimly looked away. "Can you move it at all?"

She tried, but the pain made her vision go dark. Gritting her teeth, she shook her head. "You have to leave me."

The look he gave her was heavy with irritation. "I'm not leaving you." Then he looked around again and the scowl slowly gave way to a faint grin. "But I *will* use you for bait." He got her to her feet again, then turned his back to her and bent his knees. "Hop on."

"You can't carry me—"

He caught hold of the hand she rested on his shoulder for balance, pulled it around to his chest, then reached back for her other hand. "I need you on the other side of that," he said, nodding toward an open grassy area. "Since you can't walk, the only way to get you there is piggyback. Come on."

Reluctantly she locked her hands around his neck, then gave a little hop. He caught her, one arm bracing each thigh, then started, not for the grassy area, but down the hill where it dropped off steeply. Thrown off balance by her weight, he had to move more cautiously, and he was breathing heavily by the time they reached the bottom. A shallow stream cascaded over rocks and sand on its way to the lake, passing through the hill courtesy of a concrete tunnel. It was tall enough for Jace to stand upright in, wide enough for three men to stand abreast. The stone was damp and gave off a chill, and had an ancient look. It gave her the creeps.

"When my granddad was young, they did some logging out here," he said, his voice quiet and breathless. "The road kept

washing away with the rains, so they built this culvert, then
built up the road over it. The logging ended decades ago and
the road's pretty much grown over, but this old tunnel will be
here forever.''

"Thank God," she whispered, resting her head against his
back.

"I'm gonna put you out there—" he nodded to the clearing
up ahead "—and leave a trail too obvious for Edmonds to
miss, then I'll be waiting for him." He walked out of the
tunnel, sloshed through the water where the creek widened,
then onto the grass. With a grunt that sounded seriously relieved, he lowered her to the ground next to another of the
ubiquitous boulders, then straightened, stretching his back.

When she started to sit on the rock, he shook his head. "On
the ground. I want you to be bait, not a sitting duck."

Sitting had never felt so good. Never mind that it was on
the ground, that she was huddled next to a rock not quite big
enough to hide her from the man intent on killing her, or that
runoff was washing over and around her. Forget that she was
cold, exhausted, hungry—what a time to think of that!—and
hurting. What did it matter that she would be too scared to
think straight if she wasn't already too fatigued to think
straight? She wasn't running, climbing or falling, wasn't demanding anything of her body except that it relax. She didn't
even have to hold her head up, because the rock she leaned
against would do it for her.

Jace crouched beside her, cupped her face in his hands and
locked gazes with her. "What color are your eyes?"

"Blue."

The corner of his mouth quirked in a smile. "Did I eve
tell you I've always been a sucker for blue-eyed blondes?''

She managed the tiny beginning of a smile, too. "My hair
really brown."

"I like blue-eyed brunettes even better." His thumb stroked
lightly across the swelling where her cheek had come into
contact with a tree root on her last fall. "Take the safety off
on your gun and have it ready. If you get a can't-miss chance

to shoot Edmonds, do it, but don't waste time trying to wound him. Go for the kill.''

She nodded.

''I love you.'' Finally he gave her the kiss she'd anticipated from the moment he'd taken her face in his hands. By necessity, it wasn't the most intense kiss he'd given her, but it very well might have been the sweetest.

Then he left her alone.

She removed the pistol from her pocket, thumbed the safety off, then hid it inside her jacket, her fingers wrapped tightly around the textured grips. It took one hell of a man to go from ordering her to shoot to kill one instant to saying *I love you* in the next—and one hell of a man to risk his life to save hers. *Please, God,* she prayed. *Don't let him lose his in the process.*

Jace climbed to the top of the hill on this side of the tunnel, taking care to flatten the weeds as much as possible. At the top, he dug his foot into the soft earth, leaving a long slide of mud showing, then continued the trail twenty yards back the way they'd come. Satisfied, he ducked into the woods on the far side of the clearing and started back down the slope.

He intended to be in position just inside the tunnel when Edmonds spotted Cassidy and went after her. Jace had checked while he was leaving tracks, and though the rock concealed most of her, there was flash of hot pink visible above it—the hood of her jacket hanging down her back. Even if Edmonds could get a decent shot from up above, and Jace didn't think he could, the bastard would be forced to climb down the hill to verify that it was her and not just the jacket left as a decoy.

And Jace would be waiting.

He was halfway down the hill when he saw a long muddy scrape—probably one of the hundred places where Cassidy had slipped, he thought, cursing himself again for not making sure she had on decent shoes. He stepped over the fresh mud, took two steps, then froze.

He'd carried Cassidy down this hill on his back, and he hadn't slipped.

Edmonds had come this way.

Heedless of the rocks and mud, he jumped from one unstable footing to another, landing with a splash in the creek at the bottom of the slope. Quietly he moved into the tunnel. It was long enough and tall enough to create some pretty good echoes, so he took care not to splash or stumble over the loose rocks on the tunnel floor. Ten feet from the open end, he stopped, took a couple deep breaths, then eased forward along the cold stone wall.

A voice drifted on the rain, the same one that had yelled to Jennifer to come on out—God, had that been only minutes ago? Edmonds didn't sound threatening—more chastising, actually, like a parent or teacher admonishing a child.

"—know how much time and money I've spent looking for you?" he was asking mildly. "Every bit of free time, thousands of dollars."

"Which you got for murdering my husband," Cassidy said belligerently.

"Which I got for taking care of a problem."

"A *problem?* My God, you're a cop! You don't take care of problems by murdering people!"

"I did what I had to do."

Jace took the final step, flattened against the wall, that brought them into sight. Cassidy still huddled next to the rock. There was no sign of her gun, but he knew she had it ready, out of sight, just in case he failed her.

God help him, he *couldn't* fail.

Edmonds stood ten feet in front of her, his back to Jace. He was bigger, heavier and better armed—but no more desperate. He wanted Cassidy dead. Jace *needed* her alive.

He stepped out of the tunnel, placing his foot carefully the creek, checking for solid footing before he shifted weight. He was seriously tempted to take aim and blow guy away before Edmonds even knew he was there. After all, the bastard was a dirty cop. He'd killed an innocent man and two other cops. He was carrying a fully automatic submachine gun that could fire at a rate of eight hundred rounds per minute, which meant he could empty that fifteen-round magazine into Cassidy in little more than a second.

But shooting a suspect in the back...Jace wasn't sure he could do it.

But what was the other option? Draw Edmonds's attention to him? Give him a chance to drop the weapon and surrender? Hope that the realization that they weren't alone, that there would be a witness to his crime, would deter him from shooting Cassidy?

Rich yelled at me to get out, she'd told him in the middle of the night, *and...Edmonds...shot him.* The son of a bitch had known there was a witness that night three years ago, and he'd shot Rich anyway, right in front of his wife, and then shot at her. What would stop him from killing her now, then shooting at *him?*

Jace took another cautious step, out of the creek and onto solid ground. He saw a flicker of awareness cross Cassidy's face, though she didn't risk so much as a glance in his direction. One more step put him three yards behind Edmonds. *Don't waste time trying to wound him,* he'd advised Cassidy, but he didn't take his own advice. He had a bigger caliber gun than she did, with a hell of a lot more knock-down power, and he had a specific target in mind.

He extended his right arm, the .45 steady, cutting the distance between him and Edmonds by a third. He sighted in, then squeezed the trigger slowly. The explosive report seemed to echo around them, making Cassidy jump and gasp, but he didn't flinch at the sound. Edmonds's scream was another matter.

The MP5 went flying, landing in a puddle of water fifteen feet away, as the impact of the bullet spun Edmonds around, then dropped him to the ground. Blood and bits of tissue and bone had sprayed over the ground. Not much left of what had, seconds before, been a man's elbow. "You bastard!" he screamed, curling onto his left side and cradling his damaged arm to his chest. "You've ruined my arm!"

Still holding the pistol, Jace bent and raised Edmonds's

jacket, jerked a pair of handcuffs from his belt, slapped one around his good wrist, then dragged him a few feet to secure the dangling end around a sturdy sapling. Next he located Edmonds's key ring, including the handcuff key, and slid it into his pocket. Ignoring Edmonds's curses, he returned his pistol to the holster, crouched in front of Cassidy and reached inside her jacket, carefully loosening the .9 millimeter from her death grip, then putting it in his pocket, too. Once more, he cupped her face in his hands. "You okay?"

Looking as if she might cry at any moment, she nodded.

For a long time he studied her. She looked pretty beat up— bruised, bloodied, muddied…and more beautiful than he'd ever seen. He could have lost her forever this morning, and then how would he have survived? How could he ever live without her?

He could. He was a strong man and could do damn near anything.

But he didn't want to.

Gently he brushed her hair from her face, wiped a rain-drop—or teardrop—from her cheek, then quietly, pleadingly, demanded, "Tell me one true thing."

Bit by bit the fear and the tears left her eyes. Her lip stopped quavering and the faint promise of a smile curved her mouth slightly. "I love you." She kissed him then, long and deep and hungry, clinging to him, holding him tight. When she broke it off and looked up, the promise was made good with a dazzling smile lighting her face. "Now you tell me some-thing, please."

"I love you."

She laid one hand against his cheek. "That's sweet. But had something else in mind." She waited for his nod to ʒ ahead before dryly asking her question.

"How exactly do you define the difference between bait and a sitting duck?"

Epilogue

*F*ormer Deputy U.S. Marshal William Edmonds survived getting shot in the woods outside Buffalo Plains, though he lost the use of his right arm. At trial, he was convicted of the murders of Richard Addison and fellow marshals Jack Keaton and Marcus Hightower, as well as the attempted murders of Jennifer Addison and Jace Barnett, along with a number of other charges, including conspiracy. His sentence ensured he'd never be eligible for parole.

Jace Barnett has gone back to being a cop again. The job had taken a lot from him, but it had also given in return. The skills he'd acquired in seventeen years as a police officer allowed him to save Jennifer's life as well as his own. He currently works as chief criminal deputy for the Canyon County Sheriff's Department, but doesn't live for the job anymore. He's got a life now and makes the most of it.

Jennifer Addison is teaching fourth grade again. She writes on the side, makes frequent trips back home to Pennsylvania, goes fishing on Saturdays and most especially enjoys making

*love with her husband in the middle of Buffalo Lake on the
hottest days of summer—*

"You can't say that."

"Can't say what?" She scanned the paragraphs on the computer screen. "Oh." Paging up, she positioned the cursor and changed the opening line of the last paragraph. *Jennifer Addison, who now goes by the name of Cassidy Barnett, is teaching fourth...*

"Not that," Jace said with a snort, then pointed. *"That."*

"'Most especially enjoys making love with her husband in the middle of Buffalo Lake on the hottest days of summer'?" She gazed up at him innocently. "What's wrong with that? It's true, isn't it?"

"Of course it's true, but that isn't the point."

"But you made me promise to always tell the truth. Remember? It was part of our wedding vows." Sliding from the chair, she wrapped her arms around his neck and brushed her lips across his jaw. "I promised to love, honor and cherish and always tell the truth. And you promised to—"

"Do things so wicked they would curl your hair." He covered her mouth with his, sliding his tongue inside, leaving her naturally brown hair untouched but curling her toes and making her blood hot and body tremble.

When he finally ended the kiss, she was too dazed to think, too weak to stand on her own. She leaned against him, breathing deeply of his oh, so familiar scent, thinking maybe the last pages of the book could wait until later. There was something so sweet about being at the lake, just the two of them, settled for a week in Junior Davison's old cabin—*their* cabin for the past year, though she doubted folks would ever stop identifying it as Junior's. This was where it had all started—and, in the woods outside, where it had all ended.

But that wasn't true. One part of her life had ended that rainy day. Another—the best part—had just begun. Love, marriage, babies when they were ready....

Summer. Beginnings and endings.

"It looks like you're almost finished with the book," Jace remarked as he nuzzled her ear.

"Uh-huh."

"Then what?"

"I don't know."

"Are you going to try to sell it?"

"I don't know." She'd learned a lot about writing in the past year—not enough to know if her telling of the story of Rich's life and death and her own years on the run was any good, but enough to know she liked doing it. She liked putting words on paper and making a story come alive. She especially liked happy endings.

"If you do, you have to take out that part about the lake first. Your mom and dad would see it."

"They know we're married," she reminded him with a laugh.

"*My* mom and dad would see it."

"*They* know we were having sex *before* we got married."

"We'd never be able to make love out on the lake again because everyone in Canyon County would be watching us every time we got near the boat."

"Well, since you put it that way…" Twisting in his arms, she bent to highlight, then delete the line in question, and then she kissed him. She didn't succeed in making his hair curl, either, but there were some definite changes in his body.

Taking his hand in hers, she started toward the bedroom, cool and quiet in the sunny afternoon. "I was thinking about starting another book, about a strong, brave, handsome hero and the woman who loves him. They'll have problems, of course, but they'll work through them and live happily-ever-after."

"Sounds like our kind of story," he said as he pulled his T-shirt over his head and tossed it aside.

She removed her own shirt, folded it and laid it on the chair near the window. His cutoffs dropped to the floor next to the T-shirt. Her shorts were folded and placed on top of her own shirt. His boxers landed half under the bed. She folded her lacy bra and panties, took one long, appreciative look at her husband stretched out on the bed and dropped them to the floor.

"Our kind of story?" she echoed as she joined him. "Darlin', it *is* our story. Happily-ever-after."

And that was the one, truest thing of all.

*   *   *   *   *

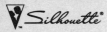

INTIMATE MOMENTS™

Coming in April 2004
from

MELISSA JAMES

Dangerous Illusion
(Silhouette Intimate Moments #1288)

Secret agent Brendan McCall
is assigned his most difficult
mission: he must find and
protect a woman who may
or may not be the runaway
wife of a dangerous
international villain—and
the woman he once loved
and lost. Brendan can save
Beth Silver's life...but will
he succeed at winning
her heart?

*Available April 2004
at your favorite
retail outlet.*

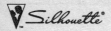

If you enjoyed what you just read,
then we've got an offer you can't resist!

Take 2 bestselling love stories FREE!
Plus get a FREE surprise gift!

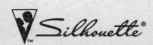

COMING NEXT MONTH